# All Lies Hidden

Also by Marc Turner

**The Chronicles of the Exile**

*When the Heavens Fall*
*Dragon Hunters*
*Red Tide*

# All Lies Hidden

A NOVEL

## Marc Turner

ignition books
San Diego

**All Lies Hidden: A Novel**

Ignition Books®

Names: Turner, Marc, author.
Title: All lies hidden : a novel / Marc Turner.
Description: San Diego : Ignition Books, [2023]
Identifiers: LCCN 2023014913 (print) | LCCN 2023014914 (ebook) | ISBN 9781937868970 (paperback) | ISBN 9781937868987 (epub) | ISBN 9781937868994 (kindle edition)
Subjects: LCGFT: Detective and mystery fiction. | Novels.
Classification: LCC PR6120.U775 A79 2023 (print) | LCC PR6120.U775 (ebook) | DDC 823/.92--dc23/eng/20230331
LC record available at https://lccn.loc.gov/2023014913
LC ebook record available at https://lccn.loc.gov/2023014914

Cover design by TJCD via 99designs.com (TonyJohnsonCreativeDesign.co.uk).

Cover images by Syda_Productions (closed eyes); londondeposit (open eyes); and Frank-Peters (London panorama), via depositphotos.com. Composition and typesetting by Euan Monaghan, throughthepages.co.uk.

Ignition Books are published by Endpapers Press, a division of Author Coach, LLC. Ignition Books is a registered trademark of Author Coach, LLC.

To Mum. Finally.

# PART ONE

# The Accident

# 1

Monday, 23 October
Afternoon

**FOR A DEAD MAN, ERIC** Devlin looks surprisingly healthy. He sits across the table from me in the interview room at Wandsworth police station. The end of his nose is peeling, and through his thinning hair, his scalp emits a glow that would set off a Geiger counter. In his early sixties, he is a prize-winning interior designer with an unrivalled eye for form and colour. It's true, he told me himself. As he meets my gaze, he tries his best to look relaxed, but his act is given the lie by the drumming of his fingers on the table.

A week ago, Devlin went missing following a break-in at his house in Putney. A pool of blood in the kitchen suggested a violent confrontation, and for six days no one has seen or heard from him, leading some people—his wife Emma included—to assume he was dead. During that time Emma has refused to speak to us, saying her grief was too great. Then yesterday her husband walked into a police station in Tuscany claiming he was suffering from amnesia.

My partner Detective Inspector Paul Ranger and I have worked on Devlin's case, and this is the first chance we have had to speak to him since he returned to the UK. Naturally, we are keen to clear up what happened on the night he disappeared, together with why he took out a life insurance policy shortly before his "death". And how he came to finish up in a picturesque village in Italy where he happens to own a holiday house.

This should be good.

Beside me, Ranger rolls up his shirt sleeves, ready for battle. A head taller than me, he has the slouch of a man who is used to stooping when he goes through doors. With his overlong side-burns he looks like he has stepped off the set of Life on Mars. I am glad we are on the same side. Ranger lacks only for a mask and cape to appear in his own Marvel comic. A true superhero, but I try not to hold that against him. Someone with as many failings as I have is wise to forgive them in others.

A uniformed officer with a goatee enters the interview room carrying three cups of coffee. I thank him, and he responds with a wary nod. I have never met the man before, but he appears to know me. My role as a psychic in Wandsworth CID is not publicised within the force, but nor is it something that could be kept secret for the two and a half years since I joined London's Metropolitan Police Service. Most uniforms regard me with suspicion, perhaps fearing I will use my abilities to snoop on their memories. But they have nothing to fear. I have learned not to trespass on the thoughts of others. And even if I were to inadvertently read one of my colleagues' minds, I would never share their secrets.

Unless they were particularly embarrassing, of course.

Ranger gets the interview with Devlin underway. For the benefit of the audio tape, he states the date, the time, and the names of everyone present, introducing me simply as a consultant. He then gives Devlin the usual caution before proceeding to highlight Devlin's right to take legal advice. Devlin, though, doesn't want a solicitor. Apparently he has nothing to hide, and he clearly believes that by not lawyering up he will make himself look innocent in our eyes. It is a futile hope.

Ranger starts the interview before Devlin can come to his senses.

"So, Mr Devlin," he says. "Are you feeling okay? Is there anything we can get you to go with the coffee?"

"I'm fine," Devlin replies.

"Glad to hear it. I know this last week has been difficult for you. Though I must be frank and say we have some concerns regarding the circumstances of your disappearance. This is your chance to give us your side of the story. To get it down straight, right from the off. And obviously any information you can provide about the person who attacked you could help us catch him."

"Or catch *her*," I say, feeding Ranger his next line.

"Absolutely. Because the attacker could be a woman. Your wife, for example, who I'm afraid we have yet to rule out as a suspect."

Devlin puts on an exaggerated frown. "My wife had nothing to do with this. The last week has been as much an ordeal for her as it was for me."

Ranger nods gravely. "Such an ordeal, in fact, that she waited a full two days before contacting your life insurers to claim on your policy. A policy, I might add, that was taken out less than a month before you went missing."

"I don't know what you're suggesting," Devlin says stiffly. "Besides, my wife couldn't have been responsible. The person who attacked me was a man."

"Ah, so you do remember what happened. I thought you were suffering from amnesia."

"I am. I mean, I can remember only fragments. Most of it is a blur."

I take up the baton from Ranger. "Can you describe your attacker, Mr Devlin?"

As I speak, I tune into Devlin's thoughts as if they were a radio frequency. The memories of those around me are not present in my head unless I concentrate on them.

Devlin pretends to think back, but his mind remains blank. Usually when I ask someone to describe a person they know, even someone close to them, they have to picture that person in their thoughts. The fact that Devlin has not done so means there is a good chance his attacker doesn't exist.

"He was big—much bigger than me," Devlin says. "But I didn't see his face because he wore a balaclava."

"A balaclava," I repeat. "Can I ask why you let him into your house, then?"

Devlin stares at me.

"We found blood in your kitchen," I explain. "So I'm assuming that's where you were attacked. But if you had answered the door to a man in a balaclava, the struggle would have taken place in the hall."

"I didn't answer the door to him. He must have broken in."

If Devlin's story gets any taller, we will have to move to a room with a higher ceiling. "Strange. We didn't find any signs of forced entry."

No response.

I leave a pause for uncomfortable thoughts, then add, "What do you remember of the attack?"

Devlin sighs as if he has answered this question a hundred times before. "It was just after eight o'clock," he replies. "Emma had gone for a walk and I was in the kitchen making a coffee when I heard footsteps behind me." Devlin looks more comfortable now that he is onto the script he must have prepared beforehand. "I turned and saw a man coming at me with a knife."

"What sort of knife?" I ask. "A flick knife? A kitchen knife?"

It is an innocent question, and instinctively Devlin thinks back. When his memory comes, I find myself in his kitchen. The knife in front of me is a steak knife with a black plastic handle. But of more interest is the fact that Devlin has visualised the weapon in his own hand, rather than in the hand of an attacker.

"I think it was a kitchen knife," he says. "I don't really remember."

"That's alright. We haven't found the weapon yet, but we have a few ideas for where to look. I'm sure it will turn up soon."

I have laid a trap for Devlin, and he obligingly walks straight into it. Since I have told him I am confident of finding the knife, he cannot resist recalling how he disposed of the weapon in order to reassure himself I am wrong. I get a vision of him putting it in a black bin bag before dropping it in a public litterbin. A week on, that knife will now be collecting flies at some nameless landfill site. We may never find it.

But that doesn't mean Devlin's memory is useless. Far from it.

"You were telling us about the attack," Ranger says.

"Right. So the guy goes to stab me, but I grab his wrist. We fight for the knife. Then he hits me on the head and I black out." Devlin pretends to consider. "Maybe that's why I developed amnesia."

"What did he hit you with?"

"Er. The handle of the knife?"

The intonation in Devlin's voice makes this a question rather than a statement. He is trying to work out what we already know and if his version of events tallies with the evidence. A cynic might almost think he is making up his story as he goes along.

Ranger says, "It's just that the doctor who examined you earlier didn't find a bump on your head. Or any other defensive wounds, except for the cut on your arm. I'm guessing that's the source of the blood we found in your kitchen?"

Devlin nods.

"I have to say that confused our scene of crime officers—the blood. They tell me there was barely enough to fill a thimble, but someone had spread it across the floor to make it look like there was more."

"Maybe the attacker wanted you to *think* I was dead," Devlin says in his best patronise-the-policeman voice. "Did you consider that?"

"We did. But in our experience people try to hide their crimes, not tie bells and whistles to them to make them stand out."

Devlin says nothing.

"And that's not the only unusual thing we found." From a folder on the table, Ranger pulls out a photo of Devlin's kitchen from the night of the disappearance. "I've seen a lot of home invasions in my time. A lot of crime scenes. And I can't remember a single one as clean as yours." Ranger pushes the photo across to Devlin. "This is where you say you wrestled the attacker for the knife. But there is no sign of a struggle. One of the stools at the breakfast bar has been knocked over, yes, but otherwise the picture could have been taken from Country Homes magazine."

More silence from Devlin.

"Let's turn the clock forward a few hours," I say. "What's the first thing you remember after waking up from the attack? Do you recall where you were? Or how you got there?"

I get a glimpse of Devlin lying in a dark, confined space that jolts and shudders around him. He blinks sweat from his eyes and draws in a lungful of heavy air. He is in the boot of a car, I realise. Beside him is a lit torch, a bottle of Evian water, a battery-powered fan. For a second I wonder if he might actually be telling the truth about his abduction. But there is another, more plausible, explanation for what I am witnessing.

Devlin says, "I remember nothing until I woke up yesterday and found myself in San Rocco."

"San Rocco? Is that your village in Tuscany?"

He nods.

"Was anyone with you when you came round?"

"No."

"You're sure your wife wasn't there?"

"No, I said," Devlin snaps.

"The reason I ask is, she drove to Italy a few days after you disappeared. I was wondering if the two of you bumped into each other while you were out there." I glance at his peeling nose. "On the sun terrace, perhaps, while you were topping up your tan."

Devlin is out of his chair like someone has lit a fire under him.

"Sit down," Ranger tells him.

"I don't have to listen to this!"

"Please."

Devlin glares at me before retaking his seat.

Ranger proceeds to question him at length about his Italian farmhouse and the problems Devlin has experienced since buying it two years ago. An increasingly exasperated Devlin explains that yes, the renovations have proved more costly than he anticipated, but no, an empty bank account and three mortgages on his Putney home do not signify he is desperate for funds. And yes, Devlin does remember being seen by an inquisitive neighbour yesterday morning in San Rocco, but no, that definitely did not prompt him to go to the police station because he knew the game was up. Through it all, I monitor his memories. When he talks about his farmhouse, I see a small, stone-walled room with exposed beams and rotting wooden doors. An outbuilding, I would guess. In one corner is a rusty plough and a mound of firewood; in another, a fold up bed, a gas camping stove, and enough tins of Campbell's soup to feed a third-world nation.

Ranger concludes his questioning and clucks his tongue. "A curious case," he says, before looking at me. "Cu-ri-ous. Do you know what puzzles me most?"

Aside from how Devlin thought he could get away with this? I shake my head.

"It's the motive of our mysterious attacker." Ranger turns back to Devlin. "Clearly the man who broke into your house wasn't a thief because he didn't steal anything. But if kidnap was his goal, why didn't he try to ransom you to your wife?"

"Do you have an explanation?" I ask Devlin. "Can you think of anyone who would want to stage your death, smuggle you out of the country, then transport you to your dream home in Italy?" I hold my pen at the ready. "Because if so, I was wondering if he took bookings."

Devlin rises again. "That's it," he says. "I'm leaving."

I let him get as far as the door before I say, "One more thing before you go. I wanted to run a different version of events past you. Just to get your opinion, you understand. In this version, you and your wife staged your murder so you could claim on your life insurance policy. You cut your own arm before wrapping the steak knife in a black bin bag and disposing of it. Then, to avoid UK passport controls, your wife sneaked you across the Channel in the boot of your car with your torch and your battery-powered fan. And finally you moved into one of your farm's outbuildings with a stove and a supply of Campbell's soup, intending to lie low until the dust settled." I pause. "This is all purely hypothetical, but you have to admit it fits neatly with the facts."

Devlin stands slack-jawed. It is the details that work against him. Much of what I saw in his memories I could have deduced with educated guesses. But not the specifics. Not the fan, the steak knife, and the Campbell's soup. What is Devlin to think? He can't know I am a psychic, so the only reasonable conclusion is that someone has ratted on him. Someone with inside knowledge of his scheme. His wife, in other words.

And by coincidence we invited Mrs Devlin to the station along with her husband today, then kept them apart for an hour before Eric's interview. Plenty of time, he will think, for her to have caved in to questioning and admitted everything.

Devlin swears under his breath. "She couldn't keep her mouth shut, could she?" he mutters.

"So, Mr Devlin," Ranger says brightly. "Is there anything about your story you'd like to change?"

# 2

Monday, 23 October
Evening

I CLOSE THE DOOR TO the restaurant, and the buzz of the crowds falls away. Shaziers is an ocean of walnut and black marble, and the lights are dimmed low so people can't look closely at their portion sizes. As I enter, two City types are harassing Zofia, the young maître d', so I flash my ID and put them back in their box. Zofia whispers a thank you, then takes my coat and tries to convince me I am looking radiant tonight. In spite of the evidence to the contrary.

I have travelled to the City to meet my daughter, but courtesy of a broken-down train on the Central line I am nearly an hour late. Cate sits alone at a table at the back, and I feel a rush of emotion. Her blouse is buttoned all the way up to her neck, and her hair is tied in a ponytail. She is only twenty-two, but tonight she looks older than I do—or older than I like to think I do, should that be?

As I cross the restaurant, I get a flashback to Devlin in the boot of his car. I suppress a shudder. I hate enclosed spaces, and I suspect the recollection of Devlin imprisoned in the breathless heat will never leave me. When I read his mind, I experienced the memory as if it were my own rather than as an overlapping second sight. In a way it *is* my memory now, for when I use my ability, I am not on the outside of people's minds looking in. I see things through their eyes and feel the same sensations they do.

I first learned I was psychic at school in Islington. I was taking my GCSE biology exam—if blundering aimlessly from one question to another counts in that respect. At the end of the paper was an especially testing problem on nervous tissue. I remember staring at the exam hall's ceiling for inspiration before realising I could . . . hear the thoughts of the boy in front of me. He was summoning up a memory of his study notes, and he must have been stuck on the same question I was, for the diagram he pictured was of a motor neurone. Just like that, the answer to my problem lay in front of me, and I used my newfound ability to take advantage.

After I had finished freaking out, that is.

Later, I told no one what had happened because they wouldn't have believed me. I had trouble believing myself. I searched on the net for information on psychics, and that only scared me further, since the results threw up a circus troupe of oddballs offering to contact dead relatives, interpret dreams, or sell me next week's winning lottery numbers. The exception was a professor of psychology testing claims of paranormal ability, but I never had the courage to contact him. I wasn't yet ready to reveal myself to the world. Instead, I did some testing of my own, reading people's minds before checking the accuracy with a few discreet questions.

I didn't always use my "gift" for cheating at exams. I also used it for more worthwhile pursuits such as finding out who was sleeping with whom at school and discovering what *really* happened to the missing vodka bottle at Vanessa Mason's house party. Then it all started to go wrong. I spent so much time in Vanessa's head that one day I went to her school locker and couldn't understand why my key didn't work in it. I was convinced the locker was mine, because for a second I was convinced that *I* was Vanessa. We are made of our memories, and by taking in some of Vanessa's I had begun to lose my sense of self.

For a long time afterwards, I didn't dare use my abilities. Reading people's minds had been a game, an amusement. But the incident with Vanessa brought home what else it could be. I realised I knew nothing about my gift or what it could lead to. I had never speculated on why I possessed it or where it had come from. So I tried hard to forget it existed. And for years I used it only in the most critical circumstances to learn the truth about those closest to me. Afterwards, I would always regret doing so, not just for the disloyalty it represented, but also because of the things I learned at those times.

That all changed when my son died five years ago on an ill-fated holiday in the Lake District. The memories come pressing in upon me now: running beside the swollen stream that Ben fell into; prowling the banks as the sun set; screaming Ben's name until my voice was a mere scratch.

Those memories were ultimately the reason why I joined the Met: so I had an excuse to read other people's minds and thus bury my memories beneath theirs. Does that make me selfish? Perhaps. A lot of coppers—Ranger included—join the force out of a desire to help others, whereas I did it solely to help myself.

Cate rises as I approach, and I hug her.

"Sorry I'm late," I say.

"You know you've reached a new low when even your mother stands you up."

I sit down across from her. On the table is a glass of gin and tonic that Cate has bought for me. God, I need this drink. But Cate is watching, so I exercise restraint and drain the glass in two gulps rather than one.

Cate says, "I took the liberty of ordering the lamb for you." She pauses. "But when you didn't show up, it started going cold. So I ate it. It was nice."

My stomach grumbles. "Good to know."

"Still, there's always dessert. I got you that gelato you like." Another pause. "But when you *still* didn't show up, I ate that too."

I laugh. "Let me guess, it went cold as well?"

"Something like that."

A waiter passes, and I order two more gin and tonics. And one for Cate as well. We are surrounded by the clink of cutlery and the murmur of conversation. While we wait for our drinks, I study my daughter. She looks like one of those size zero models. I might worry she isn't eating enough, but judging by what happened to my food tonight, that is plainly not the case.

"Are things okay with Jack?" I ask.

"*Jake*," she corrects me. "And no, we split up."

She shrugs as if it is no matter, but I can see how much she is hurting. So it was Jake who ended the relationship? I have never met him before and thankfully I never will now. I know little about him except that he is a trainee solicitor at a different law firm to Cate's. Or was that her previous boyfriend, Steven? Cate has as much success with relationships as I do. Sometimes I fear it is *because* of my failure at relationships—in particular with her father Scott—that Cate is the way she is. We try so hard to set an example for our children, but more often it is our failings rather than our triumphs that they learn from.

"How is work?" I ask.

"Fine."

Cate talks to me about leveraged leases and equipment trust certificates, but it is obvious she finds aircraft finance no more interesting than I do. As she speaks, her gaze becomes so distant she might be looking from this world into the next. I want to gather up all her sadness and send it in a parcel to Jack, or Judah, or whatever the hell he is called.

Cate asks about me. There aren't many times that I am willing to share details of my work with her, because the life of a detective isn't a ready source of comedic possibility. Today is different, though. I tell her about Devlin's interview, and about how he reacted afterwards when he discovered his wife hadn't ratted on him. Soon Cate and I are laughing so hard we draw looks from the people at other tables. It is times like this that I wonder why I don't meet up with my daughter more often. Both of us are guilty of fitting family and friends around our jobs. Cate works more weekends than she gets free, whereas I am struggling to remember what a weekend is.

The gin and tonics arrive. I take a long drink, and Cate's smile fades. She opens her mouth to say something, then appears to change her mind. Sensing what is coming, I try to think of a way to head it off. But before I can do so, Cate says, "You've forgotten, haven't you?"

"No," I reply, sharper than I intended. Today is the anniversary of Ben's death. I wish I could forget. But the memories we want to remember least are always the ones most clearly stamped in our minds.

"I went to visit him this morning," Cate says. She means she went to Highgate Cemetery. "There was a bunch of flowers there without a card. I thought they might be yours."

I can hear the hope in her voice, but I have to shake my head. Most likely they were Scott's. Scott has always been one for flowers. Back in the day, he used to give me a new bunch before the old ones had died. Almost as if he had a guilty conscience to appease.

The couple at the next table departs. Zofia brings them their coats and escorts them out.

Cate turns her glass in her hands. "I've been seeing a therapist," she says suddenly, then shoots me a look as if daring me to disapprove.

I do not respond.

"She's called Pru. She said if I was missing Ben, I should try talking to him. So I did that this morning. I told him how sorry I was for everything, and that I was having dinner with you tonight. I think it was supposed to make me feel better, but instead I just felt stupid." Cate's voice is flat. "Do you know what the worst thing was? It never felt like he was listening."

I take her hands, but she does not appear to notice.

"The first time I met Pru," she says, "she asked me to tell her about Ben. I couldn't think of anything to say. When I try to remember him, all I see is that day in the Lake District. He's in the stream, drifting away from me, and each time I reach for him, my hand gets a little nearer to grabbing his. I'm so close to saving him."

I am not surprised. Memories are slippery things. Most people rewrite theirs to cast their lives in a fairer light. But for others, like Cate, guilt twists them into darker forms.

"It wasn't your fault," I tell her.

"If I had reacted sooner—"

"It wasn't your fault," I say again.

If anyone was to blame, it was me. Cate may have been the one with Ben when he fell in the stream, but I was the one who sent them outside. I had spent the morning with Ben hunting dinosaurs around our holiday cottage, and I needed some time to let my imagination recharge. But letting a three-year-old play beside a stream swollen with floodwater? I should have foreseen what would follow.

Cate says, "Will there ever be a time when we can move on? When we can remember Ben as he really was?"

"Yes," I reply. Or at least there will be for Cate. Because unlike me, Cate has the guts to confront her loss rather than hide from it. She hasn't let his death define her as I have.

Cate watches me expectantly. I am conscious that it is my turn to say something. I want to be strong for her, but I have nothing to give. After the tragedy, Scott and I tried to talk our way through it, yet in the end it proved our undoing. Ben's absence became a hollow at the centre of our relationship that brought it tumbling down. Now Scott and I speak only when we have to.

I finish my gin and tonic, while Cate's goes untouched. Our conversation turns to the latest episode of Stranger Things, and the Pilates class Cate is thinking of joining. But we are just going through the motions. For a while we sit in silence. I do not want to end the evening on a low note, so I grope for something else to say.

At that moment, my phone buzzes to tell me I have a text.

When I see who it is from, I inwardly groan. Detective Chief Inspector Mertin, my boss. It is now after 8pm, but apparently he needs to speak to me urgently.

# 3

I STAND OUTSIDE DCI MERTIN'S room, feeling like a naughty girl called to the headmaster's office. Through the partition wall, I hear two male voices. Their words are indistinct, but the friendly tone is unmistakable. It will not be the same when I go in. Mertin has worked his way up through the ranks and is desperate to remain one of the lads. Around women, though, he is as awkward as a toddler's first steps—so much so that Ranger keeps pleading with me to flirt with the DCI just to see if the man short-circuits.

Mertin and I have never seen eye to eye. He was promoted to chief inspector three months ago, and he has already shown that he intends to take his new responsibilities *very* seriously. I am a problem he inherited. At the time Ben died, my father was Chief Superintendent of the City of London Police. When I revealed my psychic abilities to my parents three years ago, my mother was suitably horrified, but my father saw the possibilities immediately. He arranged an interview for me with his lifelong friend and colleague, Lee Abraham, the Deputy Assistant Commissioner of Crime Operations at the Met.

When the day came for me to meet Abraham, I could sense his scepticism from halfway across London. But it quickly faded when I sat down with him and told him about his holiday in Rome the previous summer, including a trip with his wife to the Galleria Colonna and an unfortunate run-in with an ice-cream vendor in the Piazza Navona.

That interview was the first of many. I was passed up the chain of command. Once the legitimacy of my gift had been established Beyond Reasonable Doubt, the police wanted to test its reliability. I am not a walking lie detector, nor can I go sifting for information through a person's mind as if they were a library catalogue. For me to experience someone's memories, they must first relive them. But how strong does a memory have to be? And can I be tricked by half-truths or outright lies?

To find out, I was introduced to a series of senior officers and asked to find out things about them—trivialities such as which make of car they drove, or where they had gone for dinner last night. Then I had to question them to extract the answers, while they did everything they could to thwart me, from conjuring up false memories to refusing to say anything at all. I learned not to take what I saw in their minds at face value. I learned to look for where memories rubbed against one another, because inconsistencies pointed towards deception.

But most of all I learned how little control even strong-willed people have over their thoughts. The harder my subjects tried not to think of a thing, the faster it wormed its way into their heads.

Then came the boring part. I had no wish to become an actual policewoman, and the powers that be thought it best to keep my role informal. But I still had to learn about professional standards, and the rules of evidence, and blah, blah, blah. While this was going on, a task force considered the practicalities of having a psychic at the Met. Was reading someone's mind a breach of their human rights? What would the legal status of my findings be? They could not constitute evidence, of course, because it would always be my word against that of the memories' owner. But would my testimony carry sufficient weight to obtain a search warrant? And if my abilities led me to a body or a murder weapon, would the evidence be admissible in court?

On my desk there is a folder three inches thick containing the answers to these questions and many others. I should probably read it sometime.

Finally it was time for proper work. Initially, all I did was interview "friendly" witnesses. That is a much easier task than interrogating suspects because I can encourage people to think back, then record what they see.

Yawn.

It soon became apparent I was wasting my time. If a witness could remember something, I saw the same thing they did. And if they couldn't remember—if they were suppressing their memories for some reason—they needed the help of a shrink, not a psychic. I started badgering my superiors for juicier work, and finally they relented. I remember how excited I felt that day. I am a fan of American TV crime dramas like NCIS and Law & Order. Now I would get a chance to star in my own.

In one of my first cases, I worked with none other than DCI Mertin—or DI Mertin as he then was. Following a nighttime scuffle outside a jewellery shop, a homeless man had fallen down and struck his skull on the pavement. He died of his injuries. The jeweller claimed the homeless man had attacked him, and Mertin accepted the story with unseemly haste. Then I read the jeweller's mind and discovered that the homeless man had been sleeping in the jeweller's doorway—and that the jeweller had been the one to initiate the struggle when he tried to move the homeless man on. Even with my findings, though, Mertin made no effort to investigate further.

Things went from bad to worse between us. In my next case, a woman had murdered her business partner and dumped his body in a wheelie bin, but Mertin could find only circumstantial evidence linking her to the crime. Not his fault; the killer had covered her tracks well. But in my first interview with the woman, I triggered a memory of where she had hidden the murder weapon, and the case was blown wide open. Mertin never forgave me for that. He thought he was a laughingstock. Three months of painstaking work, and I outdid his efforts in as many minutes. The fact that a killer was brought to justice did not enter his mind.

The door to Mertin's office opens. DC Owen Vickers comes out and shoots me a sympathetic look. With him is the DCI. Mertin frowns when he smells the gin on my breath. It doesn't matter that it is now after nine o'clock; the DCI is never off-duty. He gestures me inside his office, then shuts the door.

The room stinks of bleach and shoe polish, but it cannot mask a whiff of self-righteousness from its owner. Together with the obligatory framed certificates and family photos are a row of squash trophies on a bookcase to my left. The DCI sits at his desk. Behind him, the room's blinds remain open, and I see lights in the windows of the buildings opposite. In front of Mertin is Devlin's case file. Mertin adjusts the folder so that the bottom aligns precisely with the edge of the desk. I take the chair across from him.

Mertin skips the pleasantries and moves straight to Defcon 3. "I had Devlin's solicitor on the phone earlier," he tells me. "She's not happy with how you questioned her client."

"Hardly surprising since I got Devlin to confess."

"That's not the point. This is the third complaint—the third *grievance*—made against you in the last month."

"Ooh. Do I get a badge?"

Mertin always brings out the worst in me. I am like a mirror to those I meet. Give me a smile and you will get one back. But raise your fists to me and I will come out swinging.

The DCI scowls. "You think this is funny? You think I don't have better things to do than field calls from the people you piss off?"

I do not respond. No doubt Mertin is expecting me to wring my hands and beg forgiveness, but I take these complaints as compliments. If I am pissing off criminals' lawyers, that is a sign I am doing my job properly.

"Tell me what you saw in Devlin's memories," Mertin says after a while. "I want it *all*."

That stress on the "all" makes it sound like I have deliberately left out something from my written report of the interview. I keep a rein on my temper and talk him through what I witnessed. From the way he concentrates on my words, it is clear he is looking for some flaw in my interpretation of events. But there is no other way of joining up the dots, unless Mertin truly believes Devlin is accustomed to disposing of bloody knives or travelling around in the boot of his car.

When I finish, the DCI's expression is so grave you would think I had admitted to kidnapping Devlin myself. "Did DI Ranger know you intended to confront Devlin with the information you saw in his memories?"

"How could he? He didn't know what I was going to see."

"But you could have agreed a general approach beforehand. Or you could have stopped the interview to get Ranger's approval of what you were planning."

I say nothing. Mertin knows as well as I do that Ranger would have agreed if I had asked him. He has done so previously, but I am not about to point that out to the DCI if it means I get Ranger into trouble.

"You showed your hand too soon," Mertin continues. "You should have waited until we had found the knife or the outbuilding at his farmhouse. What's Devlin going to think when he learns we've got neither?"

"You're worried he might guess I'm a psychic?"

"If he speaks to the press, it could damage—it could *undermine*—the credibility of our case."

"After the lies he's told, I suspect anything he says will be taken with a healthy dose of salt."

"And what about Devlin's solicitor?" Mertin jabs a finger at me. "You can be sure she'll want to know where you got your information. She is already claiming her client's confession is inadmissible."

"On what grounds?"

The DCI ignores the question. "Even if she is wrong, what happens when you cross paths with the solicitor again? Or when she starts telling her colleagues about the woman at Wandsworth CID who knows about evidence before it is found?" His voice is steadily becoming more animated. "You are jeopardising the success of future cases. It is a wonder—no, a *miracle*—that no one on the team has gone to the papers about you yet, but when they do, I am the one who'll have to pick up the pieces. You should be hiding your abilities, not shouting them from the rooftops. The more people who know what you can do, the less use you will be to the force."

As if he cares about that. His only real interest is in picking fault with me. Before I can tell him that, though, the phone on his desk rings.

Mertin snatches the receiver and shouts down it. "Yes?" He listens for half a minute, then glances at me. "I see."

He replaces the receiver, lets his hand linger on it for a moment. When he looks at me again, his gaze is heavy with foreboding. I wonder what I have done wrong this time.

"I am sorry to be the one to break this to you," Mertin says. He is telling the truth, too—I sense he is far sorrier about that than he is about the news he is about to give me. My skin prickles, and I brace myself.

Then he breaks my world.

"There's been an accident," he says. "Your daughter is in hospital. You'd better get down to St Christopher's."

# 4

I SIT AT CATE'S BEDSIDE, holding her hand. I am in the Intensive Care Unit at St Christopher's hospital in Chelsea. Cate's bed is one of eight in the room, though only three of the others are occupied. My daughter is unrecognisable as the woman I met in the restaurant six hours ago; a part of me refuses to accept it is her. Tubes snake up her nose and down her mouth, and there is another tube sticking out of her neck. Her face is one large bruise, her left eye swollen shut, the top of her head wrapped in gauze.

Her legs are supported by an orthopaedic frame made of bars and straps. The surgeons have already operated to repair the broken bones she suffered when she was hit by a car while crossing the road. They have also drilled into her skull to ease the pressure caused by a bleed in her brain. The nurses claim she is doing well, but the tubes and wires tell a different story. Attached to the wall behind her is a monitor crammed with numbers and wavering lines. I stare at those lines, searching for significance in every bump and wiggle.

My daughter has always been in the wars. The first time she rode her bike without stabilisers, she crashed into a tree and knocked out her two front teeth. Then, as a gymnast at twelve, she missed her dismount on the uneven bars and broke her leg in three places. It became a running joke in our family: if there was a way for Cate to hurt herself, she would find it. One time, after a school hockey match, Scott carried her from the car to the front door in his arms, pretending she was injured. The two of them thought it was hilarious, but I had to squint a little harder to see the funny side.

Needless to say, Scott never did it again.

Ben's death changed Cate as it changed everything. Before, she had never shunned risk, but afterwards she positively courted it. Skydiving, bungee jumping, paragliding. The greater the danger it posed, the greater the thrill it held. She seemed to enjoy scaring herself stupid, in spite of the fact that she scared me in the process. Or because of it, who knows.

It dawns on me that it is not yet midnight, meaning today is still the day that Ben drowned five years ago. I could lose both my children on the same day. The thought is . . . monstrous.

I clutch Cate's hand as if through that contact alone I could stop her slipping away. I think back to our conversation in the restaurant, trying to remember the last words I spoke to her. But all I can remember are the words I did *not* say. That I love her. That she means everything to me. So much of what we think of those close to us goes unsaid. We believe there will be time for words later, but in truth the world around us is as delicate as crystal, and as prone to cut when it shatters.

I feel like I am coming apart at the seams. A memory rises unbidden of sitting in a grey room at Keswick police station and listening to the constable tell me that Ben had drowned. The words bounce around inside my head. I have tried to put distance between myself and my recollections of that time, but it feels like a trapdoor has opened up beneath me, and I am back in the same place I was when Ben died. That's the problem with trying to hide from grief: it will always track you down eventually.

Someone clears their throat behind me. I turn to see a female surgeon in green scrubs. Her hair is tied up in a bun, and she wears thick-rimmed glasses that must have come from the doctor shelf in the opticians. She approaches and offers her hand. I stand and shake it, even though that means I have to release Cate's hand first. The surgeon introduces herself as Robyn Neyland, and she has a badge on her scrubs to prove it.

"Can I have a word?" she asks, as if I might have something else to do.

Neyland is brimming with sympathy, yet somehow she manages to sound condescending. I try to withhold judgement. This woman has saved my daughter's life, after all. She asks me how I am coping, and I wonder what she expects me to say. Then she tells me about Cate's injuries. Broken legs, cracked ribs, cracked skull, the list goes on. A numbness spreads through me. Neyland says she and her colleagues have repaired what they could of the damage, but Cate's head injuries are a cause for concern. She throws in terms such as dura mater and extradural haematoma. I am not interested in a medical lesson, though. I just want to know if Cate will get better.

"How bad is she?" I ask when the surgeon pauses for breath.

"We don't know yet," Neyland replies. "The next twenty-four hours will be critical. We'll monitor your daughter's condition through the night, then we'll have a better indication in the morning."

It seems like she is covering her arse. She must have treated a hundred patients like Cate before, so she should have *some* idea about my daughter's prospects. When I press for an opinion, though, Neyland won't be drawn. I realise I'm interrogating her like she is a suspect back at the station, and I apologise.

Just then Cate's monitor starts beeping. Instantly, my heart rate speeds up to keep time. I can see from Neyland's expression that it is serious. Nurses converge on Cate's bed. Neyland calls instructions, but she has changed to doctor-speak, so I recognise only one word in three. The beeping monitor screams its warning.

"What's happening?" I ask no one in particular.

No one in particular answers. Instead, a nurse grabs my arm and leads me away. She says something I don't catch, her voice firm yet composed. I don't know how she manages to stay so calm.

Yes, I do. It's because it isn't her daughter dying in that bed.

Neyland and a different nurse push Cate's bed towards double doors on the far side of the room. I trail behind, pleading for information. Still no one responds. We pass the bed of another patient—an old man doing a crossword. With him is a woman wearing a pink dress and Doc Martins. As her gaze meets mine, I see pity in her eyes. But more than that, I see relief. Relief that she is not me.

Neyland pushes Cate's bed through the double doors, and a nurse transforms into a security guard to block my way. I stare through a window in one of the doors. Beyond is a corridor with strip lights in the ceiling. Their glow reflects off the white-painted walls and lino floor, making the passage so bright that for an absurd moment it seems as if Cate is being wheeled off to an appointment with her maker.

It is nonsense, of course. If God exists, he has long since abandoned the people in this place.

# 5

Tuesday, 24 October
Early Hours

TWO HOURS LATER, I AM back at Cate's bedside. I understand from
Neyland that Cate's spleen ruptured, so they had to remove it.
Now my daughter lies broken in her bed, her arms pressed to
her sides as if she has been arranged for a funeral bier. I asked
Neyland when Cate would wake up, and she fobbed me off with
some half-baked evasion. She has a politician's skill for avoiding
questions, but I did not press the point because I was afraid of the
answers I would get.

Cate is in a coma—that is what I fear. *Coma*. Just to think the
word makes my breath catch. With nothing more to go on, I
am left to draw on the half-truths and sweeping generalisations
gleaned from a lifetime of watching medical dramas. A coma
means Cate has suffered serious brain injuries. It means she may
never wake up. But it doesn't have to be that way. Only last month,
I heard about a man who was robbed in Earl's Court. A single
punch from his attacker put him in a coma, but he woke up several days later. Cate will survive too, I tell myself. She has to.

As I listen to the whisper of the nurses at the nurses' station, I
have never felt so alone. My parents emigrated to New Zealand
two years ago, and whilst I could phone them now, there is no
comfort they can give me from the other end of the world. It is

time for me to text Scott and tell him what has happened. At this hour he will likely be asleep, meaning he won't get the news until morning. I write and delete the text a dozen times, before finally giving him the facts in all their ugly grandeur. He deserves to know the truth from me, not least because he hasn't always had it in the past.

The lights in the ICU are dimmed to help the patients sleep. Two beds along, the curtains are drawn for privacy, and beyond them I can hear a man weeping. I wish I could cry too. I don't usually waste time on tears, but right now it feels like not crying devalues my grief. Earlier, a nurse tried to persuade me to go home, but I refused. I don't want to leave Cate for fear she will slip away in my absence. Yet eventually the infernal beeping of her monitor drives me from the ICU.

I pace the hospital corridors. St Christopher's is empty, and the echoes of my steps trail me along the passages. I see a chapel with its door invitingly open, but I do not enter. I haven't visited a church in more than ten years, so it seems hypocritical to start now. The night drags on. I try to think of something other than Cate, yet the image of her is superglued to the inside of my mind. I should go back to the ICU. I *would* go back if I could remember the way . . .

Then I am roused from my reverie by the bang and clatter of a door ahead. Through it appears Scott. There is a skip in his step like he has to stop himself breaking into a run. It is nine months since I last saw him. There are lines to his face I do not remember, and he has conceded defeat to his encroaching baldness by shaving his head. He falters when he sees me, before coming on at a pace that makes me think he is going to walk right over me.

He stops a step away. He smells so strongly of perfume, some woman must have poured half a bottle on him to mark her territory. But I am years past caring about that. In his expression is some of the same fear and misery that I feel.

A pause, then he wraps his arms around me.

And my tears finally come.

# 6

Tuesday, 24 October
Morning

SCOTT AND I HAVE BARELY exchanged a word in the past hour. Last night, we agreed to take turns watching over Cate, yet when my turn came, Scott didn't wake me. I am both grateful and annoyed at his act of charity—annoyed, because I refuse to play the needy-woman role in support of his macho-man act. Already I am embarrassed at my show of weakness yesterday. I cannot let it happen again for Cate's sake.

Cate's condition has not changed. She lies unmoving on her bed. Daylight has made her facial injuries look worse. Her skin is disc-oloured, her chin grazed and bloodied, and there is more blood at the corners of her closed eyes. It hurts just to look at her, though the nurses tell me they have given her morphine for the pain. I wish there was something they could give me for mine. Twice the doctors have wheeled Cate away for scans, but they haven't told me what they are looking for, still less if they have found it.

Finally, Neyland arrives to speak to Scott and me. She gestures for us to move a short distance from Cate's bed. Some hairs have come loose from her bun, and she looks as worn-down as I feel. I thank her for all she has done. She summons up a tired smile, then launches into what seems like a pre-written speech. Cate's condi-tion is critical, she says, but stable. No complications have arisen regarding her splenectomy, though Cate will be more susceptible to infection for the rest of her life.

Then Neyland moves the conversation onto Cate's head injury. I was hoping for a clearer diagnosis than I received last night, but no luck. The surgeon talks for a full two minutes, yet manages to say nothing.

"When will Cate wake up?" I cut in eventually.

"We don't know," Neyland replies.

*We?* Why is it that when people have good news to convey, they say *I*, but when it is bad news, they resort to *we?*

"Is she in a . . . coma?" I can hardly bring myself to say the word.

The surgeon clasps her hands together. "It is too early to know. Your daughter has suffered swelling to her brain, and her injuries could cause a wide range of disturbances of consciousness."

She sounds like she is reciting from a textbook. "What does that mean?" I ask, trying to keep the irritation from my voice.

"It means we won't know your daughter's prognosis until we can better evaluate her level of awareness." Neyland sighs. "If it helps, think of a person's consciousness as existing on a scale. At one end is coma; at the other, full consciousness. In between those extremes, people are able to sense and respond in differing degrees to things around them. Cate's EEG shows normal brain activity, but that only tells us so much. To fully understand her condition we need to carry out further tests, then observe her over a longer period."

"So we just wait?"

"Yes," Neyland says. "I'm afraid there is no specific treatment for head injuries like Cate's. But do not lose heart. Many patients in your daughter's condition recover to live independent lives."

Scott talks for the first time. "Can she hear us? Does she understand what we're saying?"

"It's possible," Neyland replies, and I realise why she signalled for us to move away from Cate's bed before speaking. "Even people in deep comas have reported being conscious of what is going on around them. If Cate can sense you, she will take reassurance from your presence. Talk to her. Read her books or play her music. Anything you can do to show your love and support."

I want to ask more, but Neyland beats a hasty retreat. She has other patients to treat, other families to console, and I cannot begrudge them their moment of comfort.

When the surgeon is gone, Scott says to me, "You do know she's on our side, don't you?"

"Of course I do," I respond. Though Neyland will be more on Cate's and the hospital's sides.

"It might be an idea to keep her there."

I bite back a retort. You would have thought Cate's injuries would have made Scott and I set aside our differences, but it appears we are incapable of spending even a short time together without striking sparks. It has been that way since Ben's death. Truth be told, the fault lines in our relationship developed long before that.

Both Scott and I were twenty-one when we met at an event at King's College London. We spoke for only fifteen minutes that night, but I made a lasting impression by accidentally breaking a glass over Scott's head. He needed ten stitches in his scalp as a result. The next day, I hunted him down on the pretext of apologising. In reality, I wanted to see him again, and the feeling was apparently mutual. We spent the morning in Starbucks exchanging tall tales and playing footsie under the table. And as quickly as that, the two of us fell head over cliché in love.

Three months later I was pregnant with Cate. Before they died, Scott's parents were the uptight sort who cared about nothing more than what the neighbours thought. So being grandparents to an illegitimate child was out of the question. They pressured Scott into marrying me, and I was happy to go along. We tied the knot on a winter's day in York—Scott's hometown—with frost gleaming on the cobbles and the Minster's bells ringing in the distance. By this stage my due date was just a week away, and I had to waddle down the aisle looking like Little Miss Greedy.

There was one small problem: Scott and I had nothing in common. He liked rock, I liked hip hop. He liked rugby, I liked anything that wasn't sport. At university, that hadn't mattered because we were always surrounded by friends. The morning we spent talking in Starbucks was probably the longest we were ever alone together. And what did we really learn about each other in that time? People never live up to the promise of their first meeting. The things they share are only the things they want the other to know. The ugly parts come out last, because those are the parts we hide from others while we still care what they think.

Once Cate was born, Scott and I had only each other for company, and there is no greater test of a relationship than silence. I grew to realise that I had loved "us" more than I had loved Scott. I don't know if he ever loved me.

Scott's voice brings me back to my immediate surroundings. "Is there anything that needs doing?" he asks. "People to inform? Things to collect?"

He is itching to be about something. Scott is someone who acts first and thinks after. Exhibit A: our marriage. But today I feel as restless as he does. I make a mental list of chores. I should call Cate's work to tell them what has happened, and I have already put off for too long informing my parents. Plus Scott or I should go to Cate's flat in Brixton and collect her toiletries, a book, some nightwear.

Thinking about clothes reminds me that I have slept in mine. I am beginning to stink, and my mouth feels like the inside of a Hoover bag.

"Is there anywhere around here I can get a shower?" I wonder aloud.

"Yes," Scott replies. "It's called your flat." He gives a faint smile to take the edge off his words. "Go home. You can call in on Cate's place on your way back and pick up what you need." He sees me hesitate. "Go on. I'll make sure Cate doesn't sneak off while you're away."

He is trying to be funny to relieve the tension, but it is too soon for jokes. And I know from experience that his humour can cut.

I grab my bag, promising to be back within a couple of hours.

I hope Cate is still alive when I return.

# 7

I AM IN A TAXI on my way back to the hospital from my flat in Camden, staring out of the window. One moment I am passing Regent's Park, the next Hyde Park, and I have no memory of how I got from one to the other. I experienced something similar after Ben died—except then it was months rather than minutes that I lost. It was at that time that my marriage to Scott broke down and every meaningful friendship that I had withered. Grief can end your life as surely as a car crash can.

My phone rings. I assume it is Scott, so I pick up without checking the display.

"Samantha? Is that you?"

It is my father calling from Auckland. Evidently Scott has texted my parents with news of Cate's accident. As Dad fires off a barrage of questions, he sounds like he is hyperventilating. What is the latest on Cate? When will there be more information?

Finally, Mum takes the phone from him, and it is like a door has been closed on a storm. In a calm voice, she tells me that my aunt and uncle pass on their best wishes, before turning the conversation to more mundane matters like the gale that recently blew off part of their roof and the puppy next door that is keeping them awake at night. As I listen, I watch Chelsea pass by outside my window, and for five minutes I can think about something other than what awaits me at the hospital.

Mum warns me that the works to their roof are ongoing, and that handling insurers and workmen will mean they won't be able to fly to the UK for a few days. I tell her they do not have to come at all. But, as usual with my parents, I am left with a lingering sense that they could try a little harder if they wanted to. There is no denying they have always been there for me, but perhaps only insofar as it did not inconvenience them.

When Mum ends the conversation, I catch sight of the taxi driver's eyes in the rear-view mirror. He must have overheard me talking, so he knows about Cate's accident. Before, he could not stop staring at me. Now, he won't meet my gaze.

# 8

MY TIME AT THE HOSPITAL with Scott is turning into one long uncomfortable silence, yet when either of us tries to initiate a conversation it feels so contrived the silence seems comfortable by comparison. I take to pacing the corridors again—so much so that I wish I had worn my flats. Before, I never understood the aversion people have to hospitals, but I am swiftly coming around. There is such a weight of misery about St Christopher's, it seems to hold the ceiling up.

When I return to Cate's room, I find Scott humming along to whatever music is playing in his head. He tells me Neyland is doing the rounds. While we wait to speak to her, Scott reads the *Times* to Cate while I watch the lines on her monitor jerk. I haven't eaten since yesterday, but the thought of food is enough to make me queasy. Or perhaps that is the coffee I've been drinking. I have gulped down so much of the stuff, my hands have a tremble to them.

Maybe it is time for something stronger.

I see two uniformed police officers—a woman and a man—enter the ICU. I don't recognise either of them, but there is no reason why I should. They cross to the nurses' station and are pointed in my direction.

"I'll speak to them," Scott says, moving away.

I hold Cate's hand. It is probably my imagination, but I swear her grip tightens in response. I watch Scott speak to the police. The woman constable's face is pinched and wind-blasted, while the man has ears that could double as landing flaps. Maybe this is just a courtesy call after Cate's accident, but something in the new-comers' expressions spells trouble. The woman does all the talking. Her voice is too soft for me to hear. As Scott listens, he crosses his arms, his posture stiff. I realise I am squeezing Cate's hand.

Finally, the police depart, and Scott returns to me to deliver the news. I leave Cate's side to meet him halfway.

"What is it?" I ask.

"It's about the driver who hit Cate," Scott says. "He didn't stop after the accident. The police are treating it as a hit-and-run."

# PART TWO

---

# Ripples

# 1

Wednesday, 25 October
Morning

RANGER HAS COME TO SEE me in the ICU. The inspector looks maudlin today, and his show of emotion brings my own grief bubbling to the surface. He hands me a bunch of flowers, then steps away from Cate's bed as if he fears what she has is contagious. He is nervous around injuries. Strange, because police work is not for the squeamish. You get to see all kinds of ugly. My mother once told me that working for the Met has made me cynical. Or *more* cynical, to be precise. But when every second person you meet is a criminal, it is difficult not to come away with a tainted view of humanity.

Ranger asks how Cate is doing, and I sidestep the question with a deftness that would make Neyland proud. Last night, I foolishly researched Cate's condition on the net. Among other things, I read articles about vegetative states and minimally conscious states. Now I wish I could un-read them. Because whilst Cate was injured only thirty-six hours ago, I know the clock is already ticking. People who recover consciousness sooner are likely to have suffered less severe brain injuries. They are also likely to make better recoveries—though even if Cate were to wake up now, there would be no guarantee of her regaining full health. Revival is usually a gradual process that can stall at any time.

Ranger consoles me with the sensitivity of someone who is used to dealing with victims' families. Then he tells me he needs to talk to me, so I leave Cate listening to Adele on her phone and lead the way out of the ICU. We go to one of the waiting rooms, but This Morning is showing on the TV there, and I don't want to shout over the debate about a woman marrying her dog. Ranger and I settle for the corridor.

He launches straight in: "I heard about the hit-and-run on Cate," he says. "I made some calls to see what I could find out. I assume you want to know?"

I nod.

"Ali Harman in Serious Collisions has the case. She's a prickly sort, but she agreed to keep me in the loop." Ranger pulls out a notebook and flips through it. "The accident happened just before ten on Fletcher Street. You know it?"

I nod again. It is less than five minutes' walk from Cate's flat, meaning she was almost home when she got hit. I don't know why that should matter, but it does.

"Harman has organised a house-to-house, but so far the best description we've got of the car is 'dark'. The guy who called for the ambulance was fifty yards along the street when the accident happened. By the time he got to Cate, the car was just a set of lights in the distance."

My hands are balled into fists. How does someone do that? How do they knock down a stranger then drive away? I have heard all the excuses before. People say, "I panicked" or "I wasn't thinking", but it is a lie. They *were* thinking, it's just that they were thinking about themselves rather than about the person they left for dead in the road.

"Were there any other cars around?" I ask.

"No," Ranger replies, then pauses as a woman goes by herding four children. "They've put up the usual signs asking for witnesses," Ranger continues. "There's also a pub around the corner that Harman is going to call on in case anyone there saw something. She'll check CCTV as well, but the nearest cameras are on the main road, and we don't know if the driver came that way. Harman needs a description of the car before she can take that further." He glances past me in the direction of the ICU. "Maybe Cate will give her one soon."

"I'm sure she will," I lie. "And thank you for doing this." I know Harman won't appreciate having Ranger look over her shoulder while she works.

My partner closes his notebook and stares at his shoes. From the TV in the waiting room, I hear gasps and giggles.

"Was there something else?" I ask.

"Just one thing. Mertin called me in for a word before I came over. He wants to know how Cate is getting on."

"You mean, he wants to know when I'll be back at work."

Ranger shifts his weight from one foot to the other, but he is not the person who should be embarrassed. "A new case came in this morning," he explains. "The media have got their teeth into it already, and Mertin is feeling the squeeze." He meets my gaze at last. "I'll tell him to go screw himself."

I give a half-smile. "I wouldn't use those precise words."

I was thinking of something stronger myself.

# 2

Wednesday, 25 October
Morning

IN THE ICU, I SET down the book I have been reading to Cate for the past hour, then explain to her that I need a rest. In the next bed, an old man with a handlebar moustache, John, gives me a sympathetic look. I am getting to know the other people in the ward. John had a quadruple heart bypass yesterday, but he is already chatting up the nurses. When his daughter Ruth comes to visit, he is lucky if she stays five minutes. I find myself filling in for her, listening to tales of John's time in the coastguard and of the three wives he has outlived.

Next along, Chrissy, is a crash victim like Cate. She was knocked off her bike but escaped with only broken bones. I try to feel happy for her. Vicky's young daughter is in to see her today, bringing with her a teddy bear as large as she is. I realise I will miss the occasional bustle and chatter of the ICU. This afternoon, Cate will be moved to a private room to continue her recovery, which means I will soon be alone except for the beeping of Cate's monitor.

On the tube this morning, I read a newspaper piece about the family of yet another man injured in a road accident. He is diagnosed as being in a permanent vegetative state without any signs of awareness. His wife described witnessing her husband's plight as beyond torture. I am beginning to understand her sentiment. It is hard seeing Cate with all those tubes in her, but the hardest part is not knowing if she will ever recover. If she doesn't, I know my life will end with hers.

At twelve noon exactly, Scott arrives to take over from me. Perhaps I shouldn't be surprised that he is making time for Cate, but he has never shown an interest in her before. In the whole of her time at secondary school, he went to just two parents' evenings. And when she was awarded the history prize in year eleven, I had to attend the prize-giving alone because Scott was off wining and dining clients of his project management consultancy firm.

Later that night, when Cate was asleep, I argued with Scott about it. He said I didn't appreciate him—that someone had to earn money so we could put food on the table. He actually said that. Afterwards, I learned that on the night in question, he had taken his clients to a champagne bar before moving on to a lap dancing club in Soho.

The sacrifices he made for us.

Sometimes I think he resents Cate for the life he "lost" after she was born. He once told me about all the things he had wanted to do after university—things that were made impossible by him having a wife and daughter—from kayaking along the Zambezi, to scuba diving on the Great Barrier Reef. The way he said it, you'd have thought Cate was responsible for the loss of his dreams.

And that I had never had any dreams of my own.

I fill Scott in on Cate's progress. It doesn't take long. Then, when I collect my handbag, I think I see in his eyes a hint of disappointment that I am leaving. My mistake, probably. It wouldn't be the first time I have imagined something that wasn't there.

# 3

Wednesday, 25 October
Afternoon

AT HOME, TWO PHONE MESSAGES are waiting for me from my parents, the first asking for news about Cate, the second asking why I haven't replied to the first. There are also three "Thinking Of You" cards from concerned friends that I put straight in recycling. What else am I supposed to do with them? Give them pride of place on the mantelpiece where they can remind me of Cate's condition?

I kick off my shoes and feel the chill of the laminate wood floor through my soles. When I left for St Christopher's this morning, I turned off the heating, and my flat is now cold enough to make ice cubes. Thinking of ice cubes reminds me of the bottle of Gordon's in the cupboard. It never strays far from my thoughts. For a time after Ben's death I flirted with alcoholism, but I couldn't commit to a lasting relationship. I go to the kitchen and mix myself a gin and tonic. Perhaps it is a little early to start drinking, but if you can't indulge yourself when your daughter is comatose, when can you?

I've got four hours before I must be back at the hospital. I need to rest, relax, switch off, so I slump in an armchair and turn on the TV. Amazingly, This Morning still hasn't resolved the ethics of marrying a dog, nor the more important question of why anyone should care. When I turn off the TV again, the silence that follows is deep enough to lose myself in. I finish my gin and tonic and turn on the radio, but the first song I hear is a ballad that leaves me wanting to open my wrists.

On the table beside the TV is a framed picture of Cate. It was taken a few months ago in a bar called Jimmy's. One of the advantages of having a daughter when you are young is that by the time she grows up, you are still young enough yourself to go on a girl's night out with her. I forget what worthy cause we were celebrating—the fact that it was Friday, probably. After watching a hideous romcom at the cinema, we moved on to Jimmy's to wash away the memory.

I remember introducing Cate to gin and tonics that night. It is one of my proudest moments as a parent. Later, three guys on a stag do came to our table and tried to chat us up using lines that could have been taken from that romcom.

Thank goodness the bar was within sprinting distance.

I examine Cate's face in the photo. For me, that evening was filled with laughter and dubious jokes, yet when I look at my daughter, I see a shadow across her features. Something lurks behind her eyes.

This isn't helping. I have to get out of the flat. My gaze falls on the phone, and before I can change my mind I grab the receiver and dial Ranger's number.

"That new case you mentioned at the hospital," I say when he picks up. "What is it about?"

Ranger hesitates before replying. "A missing girl, seventeen years old. She disappeared a couple of days ago."

That makes my decision a lot easier.

# 4

MY ARRIVAL AT WANDSWORTH POLICE station turns every head. DC Underhill blushes as he offers me his commiserations, whilst DS Napier gives me a pat on the shoulder. Others shoot me curious looks, evidently surprised to see me back so soon after Cate's accident. I tell myself I am here because a girl has disappeared—a girl not much younger than my own daughter. But I know that that is only half the truth. I am using work to shield me from my problems because that is what I have always done.

Ranger waits for me outside the interview room, carrying a case file. He fills me in on the case. Inside is the missing girl's father, Patrick Thornton. His daughter Lily vanished on Monday night, yet he never reported it to the police. Instead, it was one of Lily's friends at South Thames College who raised the alarm yesterday afternoon following a dozen unreturned calls. Interestingly, Thornton was the last one to see Lily alive when he picked her up from town on the night she disappeared. Shortly after he brought her home to Earlsfield, his Audi was stolen from his driveway—or so he claims. That's right, his car vanished on the same night Lily went missing. What are the chances?

Mertin is working on the assumption that Lily hasn't run away—our team wouldn't be involved if this were a simple missing persons case. Since she was last seen, she hasn't used her phone or her credit card, nor has she contacted her friends. More importantly—and mysteriously—we received an anonymous tip-off last night from a public payphone by a man claiming to have witnessed Lily's murder. The caller didn't identify himself, or say how or where the crime took place. But Mertin is treating the information as credible in view of Lily's disappearance.

Ranger takes me through Thornton's story of what he was doing on Monday night, but I am only half listening. I will go over the details with Thornton myself. Ranger finishes by reminding me that we must tread softly here. Thus far, Thornton has done nothing to aid our investigation, even declining to make a public appeal for help in finding Lily. But there is no evidence that he has done anything wrong, nor is there any history of abuse in the family. Indeed, the only one with a criminal record is Lily herself— four months ago she was done for drink-driving just hours after passing her driving test. However unlikely it seems, Thornton may yet prove to be no more than a grieving father.

"Let's get in there," I say.

The walls of the interview room are painted vomit yellow, and the only furniture is a scratched wooden table and four chairs. Across from me sit Thornton and his solicitor. Thornton is wearing a crumpled shirt and chinos. His eyes are red rimmed. I try to withhold judgement, but he couldn't look guiltier if he dressed in orange and held a board with a prisoner number on it. And the fact that he has lawyered up tells its own story. I meet his gaze. Along with the dread and distress, I am surprised to see determination there. He has come prepared for a fight, and the realisation makes the heat rise within me.

I will break him.

On his ring finger is a gold wedding band. In a whisper, I ask Ranger where Mrs Thornton is. In Brazil, he tells me, visiting family.

Thornton's lawyer, Stephanie Gale, sits beside her client in a trouser suit and a white bow tie. Her hair has been cut

toilet-brush short in an apparent effort to conceal her feminin-
ity. She looks down her nose at me and Ranger—and since she is
only five foot nothing, that means she has to lean so far back in
her chair I fear she will topple over. Her reputation as a brawler
precedes her. To Gale, every encounter with the police is a con-
test to be won or lost, but I know this is no game. Lily is missing,
likely dead at the hands of her father. And even if Thornton isn't
responsible for her disappearance, someone else is. There will be
no winners here.

Ranger makes the introductions. Conscious of Mertin's warning about people finding out about me, I watch Gale for a reaction
to my name. She barely spares me a glance. When I first joined the
Met, it was suggested I should observe interviews remotely so that
suspects and their legal reps wouldn't see me. But I cannot read
minds at a distance. Plus, if I am present during questioning, I am
able to shape a discussion based on the memories I perceive.

Ranger gets the interview underway. He strikes an affable tone
as if we are all friends here. Ranger just wants to find Lily safe, he
says, and that is a proposition her father cannot dispute—at least
not openly. Ranger swiftly brings the discussion around to when
Thornton picked up his daughter in his car on the night she vanished. This was the last time anyone saw Lily, so it may hold the
key to her disappearance.

"I'd like to follow up on something you said in our last conversation," Ranger tells Thornton. "Lily called you just before ten
o'clock, is that correct?"

Thornton nods.

"On her mobile?"

Another nod. It is already clear Thornton is intent not on helping us, but on saying as little as possible.

"The thing is," Ranger says, "we've obtained a record of her calls
and texts from her phone company. The last call she made was at
6.43pm on Monday to a friend of hers, Helen Kross. There are no
calls around the time that you said."

"Then she must have used a payphone."

"That's what I assumed, too. But I also checked your home phone records, and it seems you received no calls that night. Not one. So how did Lily get in touch with you to ask for a lift?"

Thornton is a long time in answering. "I remember now," he says slowly. "Before Lily went out, we agreed I would pick her up at ten o'clock. That's why she didn't phone me beforehand."

"Was that usual, Mr Thornton?" I ask. "You driving into town to collect your daughter?"

"No. Normally she would catch the train. But she'd been shopping that night. Lots of heavy bags."

"Shopping," I repeat. "At ten o'clock on a Monday night?"

Thornton nods.

"Where did you pick her up from?"

"I've already told your colleague—"

"And now you're going to tell me," I cut in. "Please."

Thornton glances over my shoulder as if the answer is written on the wall behind me. I resist the temptation to look around. "The city."

"Where precisely?"

"I don't remember."

"Think, Mr Thornton. This was less than forty-eight hours ago."

"I don't remember."

He is lying, and I can guess why. If he gives us a location we can check local CCTV, and when we do not see his car there, we will know his story is false. But I don't press the issue. For now, my job isn't to expose the holes in Thornton's tale, it is to find out if Lily is alive—and if so, where she is.

It is time for a new approach. Thus far, Thornton has fed me only lies, so he hasn't needed to draw on any memories. Now I will ask him questions to awaken those memories in his mind.

"What was Lily wearing when you picked her up?"

Thornton thinks back, and I get my first glimpse of Lily. On her chin is an old scar, and she has a dark complexion that must be a gift from her Brazilian mother. In Thornton's mind, Lily's clothes are a blur, but when do men ever pay attention to what a woman is wearing? Unless it is revealing, of course. Thornton and Lily are standing beside his car. So he *did* pick her up? It appears that at least that part of his story is true. There are no shopping bags at Lily's feet, but they could be in the boot.

Of more interest is the fact that the poor girl is sobbing. I draw a shuddering breath.

The memory fades to black.

In answer to my question about what Lily was wearing, Thornton says, "I don't remember."

"How did she seem when you met her? Was she withdrawn? Upset?"

"No," he lies.

Finally, his lawyer intercedes. "You are wasting our time," she says. "What does it matter that my client picked up Lily and drove her home? In case you've forgotten, she disappeared *after* she went out again. That is the time you should be concentrating on."

I am reluctant to move on so soon. Odds are, something occurred in Thornton's car that triggered whatever followed. Plus the fact that the Audi is missing suggests it contains evidence Thornton doesn't want us to find. But Gale's words prove an unexpected boon, for they prompt in her client a series of fractured memories. I close my eyes so I can witness them more clearly. Thornton is in his car, gripping the steering wheel with hands turned white. I hear the low rumble of tyres on the road, see the sparkle of traffic lights smeared by rain on the windscreen. Then I realise it isn't raining at all. Instead, Thornton's vision is blurred by a film of tears. Tears of guilt, perhaps?

"Where did you go when you went out again?" I ask, opening my eyes.

The memories end abruptly. "I took Lily to Earlsfield station," Thornton replies. "She was heading back into town."

"What time was this?"

"Just before eleven." He must realise how absurd this sounds, letting his seventeen-year-old daughter go out so late. But he needs to pretend she left the house if he is to shift suspicion for her disappearance onto someone else. "She wanted to see a film," he says.

"Which one?"

"I don't know."

"What cinema did she go to? Was she meeting anyone?"

"I don't know!" he says again. Thornton has the nerve to raise his voice, as if I am the one in the wrong here. His anger sparks my own, but before I can retort, Gale speaks.

"I don't care for your tone," she tells me. "Need I remind you that it is my client's daughter who has gone missing? He is a lot more anxious to find her than you are."

"Of course he is," I reply. "That's why he didn't report her missing for two days."

It is a cheap shot, but I cannot help myself. Gale bristles with indignation, and Ranger has to step in to smooth feathers. I do not hear his placatory words because my attention is back on Thornton. My exchange with Gale has provoked another memory in him. He is driving his car again. It is dark save for a glimmer of moonlight on water to his right. The seat beside Thornton is empty, meaning Lily did not make this journey with him.

There is something wrong with what I am seeing. Something important. It takes me a second to chase the thought down. *The darkness.* Not just to the sides of the car, but in front too. Thornton has turned off his headlights. He is driving slowly, but the car is definitely moving. And the weight of the blackness suggests he is no longer in London. Even in the dead of night, there would be lights on in the capital.

In Thornton's memory, he looks from side to side. He is searching for something. When he looks right, I focus on the glimmer I saw earlier. It comes from a body of water. A river? No, the surface is too still. Also, if this were the Thames there would be lights on the opposite side. It is a lake, I realise.

Where the hell are we?

An idea surfaces in my mind, and I feel a flutter in the pit of my stomach.

"How tall is your daughter?" I ask Thornton.

"Tall?" Thornton repeats, not seeing the relevance.

I use the question as a bridge to the one I really want to put to him. "How big was she? Was she heavy?"

My fear is that Thornton has killed his daughter, then driven somewhere remote to dispose of the body. I had hoped—or rather feared—that my talk of Lily's weight would trigger in Thornton a memory of him carrying her corpse from his car. But his mind remains stubbornly blank. I have used up my first strike.

"I don't understand," he says.

Gale's frown is growing deeper by the second. I have to move quickly before she calls an end to this, but where do I go from here? I can't ask Thornton where he was driving with his lights turned off, because doing so would alert him to my psychic abilities. I need a question about his false story that will keep the real memories coming.

"When you went out with Lily in your car," I say, "did you have trouble finding your way?"

Thornton stares at me. The question makes no sense. He told me that he took Lily to Earlsfield station, so he was hardly going to get lost driving there.

I try again. "But you got to your destination eventually, right?"

Finally, my words have the desired effect. They prompt a new memory in Thornton. This time he is outside his car and at the top of a muddy slope. Tattered banners of cloud float across the sky. Ahead stretches the lake, smooth as glass. I study the banks for landmarks, but there is nothing apart from trees and more mud.

The image blurs, and suddenly Thornton is behind his car.

He starts to push.

At first, the Audi does not move. Thornton's shoes slip and slide in the muck as he struggles to gain purchase. Then he turns so his back is to the car, sets his legs, and pushes again. He must have taken the hand brake off because the vehicle inches forwards.

Then abruptly it picks up speed. Thornton loses his balance and sits down in the mud. He turns in time to see the car hit the water.

With a splash, the surface of the lake shatters into spray. For a second the car sways drunkenly on the water, before sinking in a rush of bubbles.

I blink and am back in the interview room. Blood pounds behind my eyes. Thornton returns my gaze impassively, unaware that he has given himself away. The man has killed his own daughter and used the car to dispose of her body. That's why he was driving with his lights out—because he didn't want anyone to see where he was going.

The bastard. I want to reach across the desk and throttle him.

Instead I push myself upright and lurch towards the door.

# 5

Wednesday, 25 October
Afternoon

MY TAXI LIMPS THROUGH THE West End traffic. I am late getting to
St Christopher's to relieve Scott, and after my encounter with
Thornton, I feel more fractious now than I did when I left the hos-
pital this morning.

Ranger is looking for Thornton's car. Normally, Automatic
Number Plate Recognition would make this a simple task. There
are thousands of ANPR cameras scattered about the UK. They
take images of every vehicle that passes through the camera site
before digitising them, thus allowing a record of the number plate
to be stored. There is no way Thornton could have left London
and driven to a lake without triggering a multitude of camera
hits. And yet a search of the national database has come up blank,
meaning Thornton must have taped over his car's number plates
or removed them entirely.

Without ANPR, finding the lake will be a daunting task. Lily
disappeared around 11pm on Monday, and the next time Thornton
appears on our scope is at 1.30pm on Tuesday when he phoned
his work to say he was sick. That gave him over fourteen hours to
dispose of his car and return to Earlsfield. If he drove through the
night on Monday, he could have reached the north of England or
even Scotland in that time. There are countless lakes within range,

and we have little to go on to help narrow down the search. Our saving grace is that, in Thornton's memories, he seemed to be looking for a particular place. That suggests it was known to him, so Ranger is checking his previous addresses and favourite holiday spots in case they throw up anything interesting.

Plus Thornton had to get back to London somehow after ditching his car—by train probably. Maybe he has left a trail there we can follow. Odds are, he has made *some* mistake we can take advantage of because he clearly wasn't thinking straight when he pushed his car into a lake. If you want to hide a vehicle, the best place to do so is in plain sight, such as at an airport car park where one abandoned vehicle won't be noticed among hundreds of others.

Still, there is no question that I messed up Thornton's interview by walking out when I did—as DCI Mertin was quick to emphasise when I reported my findings afterwards. If I had asked Thornton more questions, I might have teased out a clue concerning the location of the lake, or about how he got home afterwards. I might also have learned more concerning what happened to Lily on Monday because we still don't know what prompted Thornton to murder her. Hell, we don't even know for sure that she is dead, though if there is another explanation for her father pushing his car into a lake, I cannot see it.

As my taxi stops in front of St Christopher's, the driver wishes me luck.

Earlier, Scott texted me to say Cate has been moved to the HDU—High Dependency Unit. The corridor leading to it is so long it feels like the ward must be located in a different city. When I finally reach my destination, I am buzzed inside. After the bustle of the ICU, the HDU is eerily silent. In the distance, I hear the wail of an ambulance siren. I pass a waiting room painted in faded pastel colours. It is empty, just as the corridors are.

Around the next corner, I find the reception area. Two nurses are talking about the latest NHS pay freeze. They look mildly put out when I interrupt to ask where Cate is. It is only afterwards that

I notice a whiteboard on the wall behind me with a list of rooms and patient names written on it.

The door to Cate's room is closed. Inside, the blinds have been drawn and the lights turned out as if she were merely napping rather than trapped in a deeper, darker sleep. Straightaway, I notice the absence of the hiss of Cate's ventilator. My daughter is now able to breathe for herself. It is a positive sign but—as Scott explained to me in a text earlier—an inconclusive one as regards Cate's ultimate recovery . . .

My steps falter.

Because Cate's eyes are open.

For some reason, my first reaction is panic; I can hear it in my voice as I call for the nurses. I have been praying for this to happen since Cate's accident, so why do I now feel frightened? Is it the shock of the moment? Or do I fear the change in my daughter will be short-lived?

I rush to her bedside. She does not turn to look at me, so I move my head in front of hers. Such is the bruising to her face, her eyes are little more than slits. The white of the left one is stained red. Cate blinks slowly, and the giddy rush of relief I feel is like someone has injected gin into my veins.

I clasp her corpse-cold hand. It conjures up a memory of the time after Ben died when I used to kneel by her bed and hold her hand as she slept. For months she was plagued by nightmares, and I could do nothing to help. Once, she stirred to find me staring down at her as I am doing now. It freaked her out so much she made me promise never to do it again.

So I started watching from her doorway instead.

Behind me, I hear someone enter the room—a nurse, probably. But I do not turn around. I am grinning like an idiot.

"Cate," I say. "It's me." As if she might have forgotten who her mother is.

And yet there is no trace of recognition in her eyes. She looks at me like I am a stranger. In fact, now I think of it, she isn't looking *at* me, but rather *through* me. I move my face from side to side to see if her gaze follows, but it doesn't. Then other details about my daughter begin to register: the fact that she is not gripping my hand as I am gripping hers; that she remains as stiff and straight on her bed as a soldier on parade.

"Cate," I say. "Can you hear me?"

But it is clear she cannot. I wonder if I am nothing to her but a dream. A shadow. I want to grab her shoulders and shake her out of her torpor.

"Cate!"

I sense her slipping back into unconsciousness. She gives another slow blink, then her eyes close and do not reopen. The darkness in the room seems to deepen. It feels like a hole has opened up inside me and my hope is draining out of it.

I release Cate's hand and it drops limply to the bed.

# 6

NEYLAND ARRIVES HALF AN HOUR LATER. She looks a different woman from the one I am used to seeing. Her hair is in a plait, her face is aglow, and her voice is unusually animated as she tells me that Cate opening her eyes is a good sign. I know she is right, but I also know it is only one step on a long road to recovery. And I cannot help thinking of all the other steps she must take.

When I seek reassurance from Neyland in this respect, she declines to give it. Throughout this process, she seems determined to stop me from rising too high or sinking too low. But I have always lived life at the extremes. There was a time when I thought that was a virtue—that life in the middle ground was just different flavours of vanilla. Ben's death taught me otherwise.

Strange how I divide my life now into everything that came before his loss and everything that came after.

When I surface from my thoughts, I discover Neyland has left the room. For all I know she has been gone for hours because outside the sky is black. I watch Cate's chest labour up and down. Around me, the HDU is silent.

My phone vibrates to signal an incoming call. The number shows as withheld, but I answer nevertheless and hear an unfamiliar voice.

"Is that Samantha Greenwood?" asks a man with a broad Scottish accent.

"Who is this?" I say.

"I'm Dominic from Simpson, Ellis & Moore."

It is Cate's secretary. I left a message for him this morning about Cate's accident. I can hear the clicking of his keyboard's keys in the background. He is typing while he talks.

"You asked me to call you back," he adds. "Has there been any change in Cate's condition?"

"No," I reply. I can't bring myself to tell him about her eyes opening because that would lead to more questions. I want this man off the phone.

"Well, I've passed the news around the office," Dominic says, "and we're all very sorry to hear what happened." His voice has all the emotion of a prerecorded message. Press one to leave your condolences, press two if you don't give a shit. "If there is anything we can do, you know you have but to ask."

"Thank you. I'll try to keep you updated, but you'll understand I have no idea when Cate will return to work." I realise I said "when" she will return, not "if". Perhaps I have more faith in her recovery than I knew.

The clicking of Dominic's keyboard stops. I can hear him breathing at the other end of the line.

"Is there a problem?" I ask.

"No," Dominic replies. "It's just that you mentioned Cate returning to work."

"And?" I snap. They can't have given her job to someone else already.

"Cate doesn't work for Simpsons any more. She left the firm a month ago."

# 7

Thursday, 26 October
Morning

"IT'S GOOD TO HAVE YOU back with us," Neyland says to Cate from beside her bed.

Cate's eyes are open, but otherwise she has shown no signs of awareness. I stand next to Neyland, looking down at my daughter and smiling in what I hope is a reassuring manner. I tell myself I see a spark of . . . something in Cate's eyes. But is it really there? Or am I seeing what I want to see?

"I don't know how much you remember," Neyland continues, "but you were in a road accident. You have sustained a traumatic brain injury that is interfering with your brain's ability to communicate with the rest of your body. But don't worry. You're receiving the best possible care, and many patients in your condition go on to make a full recovery."

If Cate is able to hear these words, she will know how empty they are. Neyland's voice is soothing, but there is a lack of authority in her delivery. She should have let me speak to Cate instead. I am a much better liar. But then I have probably had more practice at it than she has.

"Can you blink for me, Cate?" the surgeon asks.

I want to say, "Of course she can blink!" Blinking is the only thing she has been able to do since she came around yesterday.

But it occurs to me Cate's blinking could be an involuntary reflex. Neyland must be trying to find out if she can do it voluntarily.

Cate's eyelids do not move.

"It's not a problem if you can't yet," Neyland says. "Your brain needs to get used to doing its job again. Patients often take time to regain control of their bodies. What about moving a finger? Can you move one finger for me?"

It seems a pointless request. If Cate can't move her eyelids, what chance does she have of moving her hands?

Her fingers remain still.

"That's great," Neyland says, as if Cate not moving was what she wanted all along.

The muscles of my face ache from holding my smile in place. I try to envisage what it must be like for Cate to be imprisoned in her own body: to be able to see and hear—or so I hope—yet unable to communicate. Imagine the frustration she must feel. The worry that this is all she has to look forward to. The newspaper article I read yesterday—the one about the man in the permanent vegetative state—had another quote from his wife that stayed with me. She claimed his injuries meant his situation was much worse than if he were dead. Better for Cate too if that car had killed her. Better she had never woken up.

Neyland departs, leaving me alone with my daughter. It is more important now than ever that she hears my voice, so I sit beside her and talk about everything and nothing. As I speak, I remember my conversation with Cate's secretary. Dominic said she left her job a month ago. Yet she only joined Simpsons in July. So what happened? Was she fired, or did she resign?

Neither option makes sense. Cate has always been more conscientious than is good for her. When she finished law school this summer, some friends invited her to go backpacking around Europe with them, but she chose to start work at Simpsons. I used to wonder if her motivation came from a desire to win Scott's attention. Now I think it is just in her makeup. I work hard because I want to; Cate works hard because she feels she should. I cannot imagine her getting fired.

But then I think of her sitting across from me in the restaurant on Monday, wearing her pinstripe skirt and her blouse buttoned up to the neck. Why was she wearing those clothes if she had lost her job? And why did she tell me about the work she was doing at Simpsons? Not to hide the fact she was unemployed, surely.

She must have joined another firm of solicitors. But moved jobs and forgot to tell me? Does that make any more sense than the alternative?

Another truth dawns on me. Cate left Simpsons a month ago. If I had called her at work in that time, I would have known she had moved on. So obviously I cannot have done so. But I *have* called her on her mobile, haven't I? Or at home? I cast my mind back and realise that Cate was the one who arranged our dinner on Monday, just as she arranged our night out at Jimmy's.

When did I last call my daughter?

There is a knock on the open door, and I turn to see Ranger watching me. I tell Cate I will be back soon, then lead Ranger to the pastel waiting room. When I sit down in one of the plastic chairs, it shifts beneath my weight.

Ranger asks about Cate. I tell him about the false alarm yesterday, and his only response is a nod. He does not need to say anything because I can see his regret in his look. After seven months working together, I have grown adept at reading his expressions. When I first joined Wandsworth CID, Ranger was wary around me. He has a policeman's love of order, whereas I cannot see a corner without wondering how to cut it. On the plus side, Ranger is not averse to a good gossip, and he shares my sense of humour— or lack of it, some might say. Now, I would go so far as to call him a friend. I would like to think the feeling is mutual.

And yet there is much I do not know about him. I know he is in his early forties, and has a cat called Roary, and supports some team called the Gunners. I know he cannot handle his curries and buys a gym pass every year without ever using it. But I have avoided asking him personal questions in case he asks them of me in return. There are many things about myself I would not want him to learn.

"I spoke to Harman again this morning," Ranger says. "I'm afraid she has got nowhere with the investigation into Cate's accident. There are no new witnesses. No CCTV. She is still waiting to hear from forensics on Cate's clothes, but the most they are going to find is glass slivers and flecks of paint. Not enough in themselves to ID the car that hit Cate."

"So what happens next?" I ask.

"We keep working. Or at least Harman does. It's less than three days since the accident, so there's still time for a witness to come forward." Ranger strokes his sideburns. "But I'll be honest. Harman needs to catch a break."

And while she waits, the driver that hit her will be disposing of the evidence. The collision with Cate will have dented his car's bumper and maybe cracked its windscreen. But when the driver goes to get them fixed, he can pretend he hit a dog. Everyone knows someone who will do the repairs with no questions asked.

An image of Cate's driver forms in my mind. I picture him as a man in his fifties or sixties with a face flabby from good living. The sort who drives a BMW or a Merc. He's at home in his lounge, drinking designer whisky to calm his nerves and flinching at every ring of the phone. There is guilt and apprehension in his expression, but also defiance, as if he has rationalised the accident as Cate's fault. When he meets my gaze, I imagine a smirk at the corner of his mouth. He is mocking my powerlessness. He is taunting me to come and find him. With each minute I fail to do so, the evidence trail grows colder.

My teeth are clenched so tightly I have to relax my jaw. Ranger watches me silently. It is clear he has more news to tell me. It must be about Thornton, and Ranger is waiting for me to signal whether I want to hear it.

I don't.

I thank him for coming, and he departs with a promise to return tomorrow.

Back in Cate's room, I know immediately that something has changed. It takes me a second to work out what, though. Cate remains in the same position as I left her, and there is no more focus to her gaze now than there was before. And yet there is something in her look that holds me. I didn't realise before how expressive a person's eyes could be. There is a weight of emotion in Cate's that stops the breath in my throat.

I hold her hand. Her thumb brushes against my fingers. Most likely the contact was caused by my movement rather than hers, yet I sense Cate straining to move now with a force that makes me go tense. I want to ask her if she can hear me. But she won't be able to respond, and her helplessness will only add to her frustration. So I shush her and say, "It's okay, I know", even though I have no concept of what she is going through.

Cate blinks once, twice, three times. Is she trying to communicate with me? Then I see the moisture gather in her eyes.

She is crying.

I reach a decision.

# 8

I AM GOING TO READ my daughter's mind. I will ask her to think back to the night of the accident and picture what happened.

This isn't the first time I have considered doing so. But before now I have been struggling against the fear that Cate is in a vegetative state. That—to use that terrible expression—the lights are on, but nobody is home. The emotion I saw in Cate's eyes, though, tells me my daughter is still in there. She is conscious. And if she is capable of feeling grief and despair, surely she is sufficiently self-aware to understand my voice, and to conjure up memories when I ask her to.

Ranger said we needed a breakthrough in this case. Maybe Cate is the only one who can provide it. If she can picture in her mind the car that hit her, I can pass on the make and model to DS Harman. And if Cate noticed the driver, I might be able to work with an artist to produce a portrait.

On the other hand, she might remember nothing. Maybe her memories were lost when she suffered her head trauma. Or maybe she was looking the other way when the car struck.

I have to try, though, don't I? For all I know, Cate might close her eyes in a minute and never open them again. This could be the last chance I have to catch the person who did this to her. My last chance for justice.

Justice? I mean vengeance, of course.

Still, the thought of what I am about to do makes me nervous. I have never read Cate's mind before. Naturally, there have been times when I was tempted to do so—like when she came back from hockey practice once with a black eye and scratches. Or when she stayed out late on her sixteenth birthday and was a little too coy about where she had been. But there are some lines even I will not cross, and spying on my daughter is one of them.

It has not been that way with Scott. Three years after we got married, there was an important deal at his consultancy firm that demanded he work late for a month. Our relationship was already under strain, and now I had to contend with weeks of unanswered calls and midnight dinners with mysterious coworkers. For a while, I resisted the urge to check on what he was up to. Scott knew of my abilities, and I had promised never to use them on him. But each day the temptation grew. And eventually I cracked. One morning, when he was telling me about a meeting from the day before that ended in fisticuffs, I had a peek at his memories to confirm they told the same story.

Most people in my position would have done what I did. Which self-respecting spouse hasn't checked a partner's call log or pockets at some stage? The principle is the same. If everyone had my abilities, how many would honestly be able to withstand the temptation of using them?

I said honestly.

Needless to say, it was a mistake. I learned nothing incriminating from Scott's memories. But having succumbed to the devil on my shoulder once, it was harder to resist doing so a second time when Scott gave me cause to doubt him again.

And again.

I close the door to Cate's room, then sit in the chair beside her bed. I tell her I love her, and that she is going to be okay. I tell her what we will do together when she recovers, from seeing the Northern Lights, to skydiving over Palm Jumeirah—though by the time she wakes up fully, I hope she has forgotten the skydiving bit. I know she wants to do these things, yet has never found the time. They are on her bucket list, but why should it take a brush with death to make us live a little?

Next, I tell Cate I need her help. I need her to replay in her mind what happened on the night of the accident—to picture the car and the driver as clearly as she can, because any detail could prove crucial to catching this bastard. I squeeze her hand and tell her that I will be with her. That I *am* with her. But if she doesn't feel able to do this, that is alright.

Finally, I close my eyes and tune into her thoughts.

At first all I see is darkness. Perhaps Cate has not understood what I said, or perhaps she does not wish to cooperate. But then the black melts away to reveal the shapes of houses, parked cars, and a treelined road. It is Fletcher Street where she had her accident. My pulse quickens. Cate has obviously registered my instructions and is thus conscious. There will be time later to celebrate that, but for now my attention is fixed on the image before me.

The scene has a dreamlike quality, blurred and wavering. Houses flicker in my peripheral vision. Ahead, the pavement is empty of people. As Cate walks, I hear the growl of an engine along the road behind. The car that hit her, perhaps? It sounds like the driver is doing more than forty, but I am not sure I trust this part of Cate's memory. Since she knows that the car struck her, she may have assumed it was speeding and subconsciously added the sound of a revving engine to agree with this. Memories are not perfect. And I have long stopped equating them with the truth.

The picture "sticks" for a second, as if Cate is afraid to go further. Then in her mind she moves to cross Fletcher Street. I notice there are no parked cars along this stretch of road. A lot of accidents happen when pedestrians step out from between stationary vehicles, but that is not the case here. There must be another reason why the driver didn't see her.

The car comes at Cate from her left. The first warning she has of trouble is the glare of headlights. Immediately Cate looks that way, and I glimpse the car a dozen metres away. There is little I can make out of the vehicle past its headlights. Without thinking, I squint to improve my vision. But this is not reality, this is Cate's memory, and there is nothing I can do to influence what I see.

I wait for the screech of brakes, but I hear nothing. As the car closes to five metres, the image slows. Such is Cate's shock, she stands frozen. Her gaze is concentrated on the car's windscreen, and I get a look at its driver. It is a woman of about my age. I can see her face clearly over the steering wheel. Wavy blonde hair hangs loose to her shoulders. She has dark angry eyes, pencilled-in eyebrows, and a nose with too much of the nostrils showing, as if an invisible finger is pushing back the tip.

But it is her mouth that really catches my notice. For her teeth are bared, her lips drawn back in a cutthroat smile.

*Bang*, and the car hits Cate.

The image goes black.

My heart thumps in my chest, and I hear Cate's monitor beeping faster. Voices sound in the corridor. When I open my eyes, shreds of Cate's memory cling to my vision. I bring the driver's face to mind. Those eyes. That smile. I have to believe I have misinterpreted some detail, yet when I see the woman's expression again, the meaning behind it is plain.

My hands tremble. For I know now the accident was not an accident in truth. The woman I saw wanted to knock down Cate.

Someone tried to murder my daughter.

# PART THREE

## Drowning

# 1

Thursday, 26 October
Morning

"WHAT'S GOING ON?" SCOTT ASKS from the doorway.

It is a few minutes after I read Cate's mind. Her heart rate has returned to normal, her monitor has stopped complaining, but a nurse still fusses by her bedside. I signal to Scott, then lead him along the corridor to an empty room. He follows me inside and shuts the door.

"Someone tried to kill her," I say.

"Kill who?"

"Cate!"

Scott looks at me blankly.

"I read her mind," I explain. "I saw what happened on Monday night. It wasn't an accident. The driver of that car meant to hit her."

Again, Scott says nothing. His face shows alarm and scepticism in equal measures, but the scepticism wins out. I forestall his objection by telling him what I witnessed in Cate's memories. "Cate got a look at the driver before the car knocked her down," I say. "The woman was smiling. There was"—I struggle for the rights words—"determination in her face. There was intent."

"What does 'intent' look like?"

I wish I had a good answer to that. I can picture the driver's expression, but describing it to Scott is another matter. Some things you just know when you see them. So I try a different tack. "Imagine you were driving and someone stepped out in front of you. You're going to be shocked, right? You're going to panic. But this woman's face showed nothing of that."

"Maybe the panicking came later. Maybe she didn't see Cate before she hit her."

"But she *did* see her. There was a second before the collision when their gazes met. And this woman didn't brake or swerve. She just came on."

Scott rubs his forehead with his hand. He is staring at me like I am a puzzle he can't solve. "There has to be another explanation," he says at last. "We know Cate took a bump to the head. Maybe it messed with her memories."

"If that were so, she wouldn't remember a thing. But her memory of the driver was sharp. She saw the woman's face as clearly as I am seeing yours."

"Then she must have made a mistake. You told me before that memories are unreliable. You said they don't show what we see, only what we think we see."

He is right, of course. When I first joined the Met, I went to a talk on the subject by an eyewitness expert. I can still hear the man's withered voice droning in my ear. He explained that our eyes collect light before turning it into nervous impulses that are sent to the brain. The brain then combines images with reasoning and expectation to form a perception. But that perception may be flawed. When visibility is limited, the eyes may transmit incomplete information, leaving the brain to fill in the gaps. The upshot is a perception founded as much on what the brain has added than on what is actually seen.

That could have happened in Cate's case. On the night of the collision, visibility was poor. Not only was it dark, but the car was moving quickly so Cate saw its driver for only an instant.

I try to look at this rationally. If Cate weren't my daughter, what value would I put on her memories? My starting point would be one of caution because I know how unpredictable eyewitness identifications can be. Human vision is fallible. Mistakes are made all the time. Plus, in this instance, my perception of events is second-hand. My belief that the driver tried to kill Cate is founded on my interpretation of the woman's expression—or rather my interpretation of Cate's interpretation. The dangers are obvious. It is like I am playing a game of psychic Chinese whispers.

But against my misgivings I must balance the clarity of Cate's vision. I myself am hopeless with faces. If you asked me to describe the nurse I just left in Cate's room, I would struggle to tell you if she had one head or two. Yet Cate's recollection of the driver was precise. In my daughter's mind, there is no question as to what she saw. And if she is certain, who am I to doubt her?

Something else strikes me then, and I wonder why I didn't think of it before. You don't mow down pedestrians on a whim; you need a motive. If the driver tried to kill Cate, the two of them must know each other. And if Cate knew the other woman, it stands to reason she would find it easier to recall her face—and perhaps interpret her expressions too.

When I put this to Scott, he sighs. I can see he remains unconvinced, but he asks, "Did *you* recognise the woman?"

"No."

"Then who is she? Why would she do this to Cate?"

And there lies the problem: I haven't got a clue. Cate has a mortal enemy and I wasn't even aware the woman existed. It leaves me feeling guilty because it shows how little I know about my daughter's life. As further proof, Cate has half a dozen bunches of flowers in her room, but I only recognise one of the names on the cards that came with them: Maddie, whom she went to school with. The other flowers must be from friends at university or work.

Thinking of work reminds me of the job Cate resigned or was fired from. Could the mystery of why she left Simpsons be tied in with the hit-and-run?

Outside, it has started to rain. I hear the patter of drops on the window, see them stream down the glass. The sky is leaden—a perfect match to my mood. Scott watches me. He opens his mouth, then closes it again, clearly building up to something.

Finally, he says, "I don't think you should read Cate's mind again."

My hackles rise. I know what he is thinking. Scott has long mistrusted my abilities because of the role they played in ending our marriage. After I spied on him the first time, I allowed it to become a habit. My trust in him died the death of a hundred cuts as I endured him eyeing up the shapely new intern or flirting with Jane from accounts. All completely harmless Scott would no doubt have told me if I had confronted him about it. But I never could confront him because I had promised not to spy on his memories. So instead my resentment festered.

Scott must have worked out why I became so cold. Whatever else he is, he is not stupid. And yet neither of us spoke about it, so nothing was resolved. After that, our breakup was just a matter of time.

But to use that as an objection to what I have done with Cate . . .

"I told Cate what I was going to do," I say. "If she didn't want to show me anything, she didn't have to. But why should she refuse? She had nothing to hide."

Scott frowns as if those last words were aimed at him. Perhaps they were. "That's not what I meant. When I came into Cate's room just now, why was the nurse here? It's because there was a problem, isn't it? It was because you read Cate's mind."

That is something I hadn't considered: that my asking Cate to relive the collision might have had an adverse effect on her—which it clearly did, judging by her elevated heart rate. But the ordeal was over quickly. And wasn't the stress of it worth going through if it meant I learned that someone tried to kill her?

"Don't you think Cate would want us to catch who did this?" I ask Scott.

"As far as she knew, we might have done so already. Now she will know we haven't."

"But she will also know we are on to the woman. That must be a reassurance."

"Maybe," Scott says. His gaze holds mine. "But when you chose to read Cate's mind, you didn't know someone had knocked her down on purpose."

It takes me a second to work out what he is implying. He is reminding me that my finding out about the attempted murder was unexpected. That I cannot use that to justify my decision to read Cate's mind, because I went into it believing she was the victim of an accident. And he is right. I was angry at Harman's lack of progress and at the thought of the driver getting away with their crime. I wasn't prepared to let that happen because catching the culprit would make *me* feel better, not Cate. I never stopped to consider what it would mean for my daughter.

Scott strikes a conciliatory tone. "It's great you were able to get through to Cate," he says. "And it's great that you saw the driver who ran her down. But there's something more important than catching the woman, and that's helping Cate get better." He hesitates over his next words before speaking. "I just think that from now on everything we do has to be what is best for Cate."

It is the mildest of rebukes, but still his words sting. I nod, and he smiles as if to draw a line under the discussion. He wants me to go further, I sense—to promise that I won't read Cate's mind again. But I cannot do that. The fact that I now know the hit-and-run was deliberate makes me more determined than ever to catch the culprit. Nothing aside from Cate's wellbeing is going to get in the way of that.

Nothing.

# 2

Thursday, 26 October
Afternoon

RANGER GRINDS THROUGH THE GEARS of the pool car, and the engine coughs and wheezes like an asthmatic. I have roped my partner into coming with me to the site of Cate's hit-and-run to see what there is to see. I worry this might get him into trouble with Mertin, but Ranger is too nice to turn down my plea for help, just as I am too hardhearted not to take advantage of that. I need Ranger to work out the truth of what happened to Cate; it is as simple as that.

It frightens me to think how much I will sacrifice to protect my daughter.

Earlier, I told Ranger about the driver who hit Cate. We had much the same conversation regarding the reliability of my daughter's memories as I had with Scott, just without the added guilt trip. Ranger trusts my judgement in a way my ex-husband does not. But that is probably because he doesn't know me as well as Scott does.

As we crawl through Battersea, Ranger stares at a restaurant on the left—an Italian joint by the name of Luigi's.

"You know that place?" I ask him.

"Uh huh. I did a stint there as a trainee chef—back in '99, just after I was a traffic warden."

It has become a running joke between us, all the jobs Ranger supposedly had before he joined the Met. I suspect more than a few of them are made up, but he always speaks with such sincerity that I cannot tell which are real and which are invented. Entertaining, for sure. But it also leaves me wondering how much of the real Ranger I have seen.

"You went straight into being a chef from being a traffic warden? Didn't you need training?"

"I got that on the job. Though a few customers didn't take kindly to me using them as test subjects."

We pass Luigi's now, and I look back at it in the wing mirror on my side. The sign above it looks like it was last painted when Ranger worked there.

"I'm still in touch with a couple of the guys I worked with," he continues. "We get together once a year and reminisce."

"You sound like you miss it."

"I do."

"So why did you leave?"

"Because of the head chef. The guy was a Gordon Ramsay fan. Thought the way to get the best from his staff was to give them the hairdryer treatment."

I regard him thoughtfully. I still don't know if he is telling the truth, but I *do* know he is enjoying himself immensely. "So you used to wear one of those chef's hats?"

"I've still got it," Ranger says. "I break it out every time I'm in the kitchen."

"Now I know you're taking the piss."

Ranger looks offended. "You don't believe me? You should come round when this is over, see for yourself. I'll rustle you up a carbonara, or a cacciatore, or whatever else M&S has got on special that day. What do you reckon, Sam? An offer like that, how could a lady say no?"

"Find me a lady, and I'll ask her."

Ranger laughs and pretends not to notice that I haven't given him an answer.

"So what do you think our chances are of finding Thornton's car?" I ask to change the subject.

"Pretty good, actually."

"I thought you said Thornton removed his licence plates so he didn't trigger any camera hits?"

"Or altered them, yes. But we can still check the video footage manually. And there are things we know that will help us track his movements."

"Such as?"

"We know his car's make, model and colour, and we know from his memories that it was dark when he pushed his Audi into the lake. That means he probably drove through the night to get to his destination—which in turn means he probably used motorways. Finding him on the cameras shouldn't be hard. And when we do, we can follow him to wherever he went and focus on lakes in the area."

"Sounds simple."

"It is. Unless you're the person who has to check through the cameras."

There is that.

"What's it like reading someone's mind?" Ranger asks me suddenly.

"How do you mean?"

"When you're around people, do you see their memories all the time? Or do you have to do something special to look at them?"

I glance across. "What's the matter? Worried I might accidentally eavesdrop on your own thoughts?"

Ranger chuckles. "I wish I had something worth eavesdropping on," he says in a voice that almost has me convinced.

"No," I reply in answer to his earlier question. "I only see people's memories when I want to. Fortunately."

"'Fortunately?' Don't you like the idea of everyone's secrets falling into your lap?"

"I'd rather they didn't keep them in the first place," I say, thinking of Cate's departure from Simpsons.

Ranger keeps his gaze on the road. "No one likes secrets, do they? Unless they are their own."

Outside, the first spots of drizzle fall on the car's windscreen.

# 3

THE RAIN HAS DRAWN A grey curtain across Brixton. As Ranger walks with me along Fletcher Street, water drips off his umbrella and is blown back into my face by the wind. I'm not sure what I hope to find here. No new evidence, certainly. But I want to see if there is anything that either supports or contradicts the idea that the hit-and-run was deliberate.

At the very least, I will get a feel for the place where the collision happened—and I may need it before I go to my next appointment. Because there has been one positive development in Cate's case since I spoke to Ranger this morning: a new witness has surfaced by the name of Paul Jorden. A reluctant new witness, judging by what my partner tells me, but Jorden's readiness to cooperate is neither here nor there. I am confident he will be forthcoming when I meet him later.

Fletcher Street is as dreary as the weather. I've never been good at dating architecture, but the houses around me unquestionably fall into the "seen better days" period. Beyond them are three-storey blocks of flats that look like something out of a Cold War spy film. This isn't the London I know, but then I have come to realise London isn't so much one big city as a hundred small ones thrown together.

I stop in front of a yellow witness appeal sign. When I speak to Ranger, I have to raise my voice above the drumming of the rain on his umbrella.

"This is where Cate was hit?" I ask.

"Yes."

I look around. This stretch of road is exactly as Cate showed it to me in her memory except for the parked cars. Through the standing water on the tarmac, I look for tyre marks. There are some to my right but none to my left, which is the direction from which the car came.

"No tyre marks before the point of impact," I say to Ranger. "Which means the driver didn't brake until after she hit Cate."

Ranger does not respond. I'm not telling him anything he doesn't already know. Or anything significant, frankly. The fact the driver didn't brake could fit with the idea the hit-and-run was deliberate, but it could also mean the woman didn't see Cate until it was too late.

The rain now seems intent on punching its way through our umbrella. With Ranger beside me, I walk down the road to the tyre marks. The gloom is gathering by the moment.

"Are we sure these marks are from the car that hit Cate?" I ask.

"Harman thinks so."

"Has she been able to work out what speed the driver was doing?"

"About forty." Ranger shifts his grip on his umbrella. "From the marks, Harman believes the car slowed but did not stop. That tallies with what the guy who called for the ambulance told us. By the time he got to Cate, the car was gone—so presumably its air bag didn't inflate, else the driver wouldn't have been able to go anywhere."

Again, the information is inconclusive as to whether the collision was premeditated. A failure to stop afterwards could be explained equally by the driver's panic as by malicious intent.

"The new witness," I say to Ranger. "Paul Jorden. Where was he standing when Cate was hit?"

"This way," Ranger replies, and leads me back along Fletcher Street.

"Earlier, you called him reluctant. What did you mean?"

"I mean, he'd rather we hadn't found him. Harman dropped in at the pub around the corner at lunchtime. She talked to some people and asked them if they'd seen the accident. Jorden said no, but then the girl he was with pipes up: 'Wasn't that the hit-and-run you told me about?' So then he has to come clean. It turns out that whilst he didn't see Cate get hit, he *did* see her lying in the road afterwards with some guy bending over her. Jorden claims he never came forward because he didn't think he could be any help. But Harman reckons he just didn't want the hassle."

My face twists. Hassle? I would hate for my daughter's attempted murder to inconvenience anyone.

Ranger stops in front of a three-storey house. The front yard doubles as a landfill site, and water spatters down into it from a backed-up gutter. On the frame beside the door are the numbers 110a, 110b and 110c, meaning the house has been converted into flats. Ranger tells me that our witness lives in 110b on the first floor.

I turn to survey the street. This is where Jorden was likely standing when he saw Cate. The place where she was hit is thirty metres to my left. From here, my view of the road is obstructed by parked cars. To make matters worse, after the collision, the car would have been travelling north along Fletcher Street—so away from us, not towards us. The chances of Jorden seeing anything useful are remote.

"We're wasting our time," I say, and Ranger does not deny it. This isn't some Scooby Doo mystery I can solve with a chase scene and a Scooby snack. I will still speak to Jorden, but I am swiftly losing heart.

Perhaps it is time to stop treading softly. I'm sure Harman has dotted all her *i*'s, but if she were investigating a suspected murder rather than an accident, she would be throwing a lot more resources at it. I should speak to Deputy Assistant Commissioner Abraham, or get my father to do so since the two of them are still friends. But would that achieve anything? No evidence in this case means no evidence. Drafting in another hundred officers won't change that.

"There's one thing we haven't tried yet," I tell Ranger. "I saw the driver's face in Cate's memory. If I describe the woman to an E-FIT operator, we can put together an E-FIT."

It's not something I have done many times before, because witnesses usually do the describing themselves. But I have had to fill in on occasion when people are too scared or too uncooperative to help.

Ranger's lack of enthusiasm is boundless. I know the recognition rate of the absurdly named *Electronic Facial Identification Technique* is low, but I sense Ranger's reticence has another source.

"If you do that," he says, "you'll have a hard job convincing Harman to use it. Officially, you shouldn't be anywhere near this case."

"What does that matter so long as I put her on the right trail?"

"Mertin won't see it that way."

"And who's going to tell him? You?"

Ranger looks away. "Mertin always finds out, you know that, Sam."

"Do you have a better plan? If we don't go with the E-FIT, what's our next move?"

Ranger does not respond. Maybe he has no answer, or maybe he is tired of arguing in the rain. "Let's go talk to this new witness," he says.

From his tone, it's clear he is not expecting to get much from Jorden. But I'll make sure the man tells us what he knows, even if I have to put my hand down his throat and drag out the words.

# 4

Thursday, 26 October
Afternoon

IT IS A TEN-MINUTE DRIVE to the workplace of Paul Jorden. Jorden heads up the Temporary Jobs Division at the imaginatively titled ABC Recruitment Agency. When Ranger and I enter its headquarters, we find Jorden at the reception desk, hard at work chatting up a receptionist. Jorden looks younger than me, but he is already bald, and his forehead reflects the glare of the ceiling spotlights. His shirt sleeves have been rolled up to reveal curiously hairless forearms.

Jorden makes us wait while he finishes the story he is telling the receptionist. Then he turns and gives us the once-over. The taller, broader, and infinitely better-looking Ranger immediately snares his interest. Jorden puts his hands on his hips. Here is a threat to his alpha-male status, and it is clear he means to defend it. I flash my ID and introduce myself and Ranger. Normally Ranger would take the lead, but he has told me he will keep a low profile at this meeting. Harman does not know we are here, and Ranger has come solely to make sure I behave.

"We need to ask you a few questions about the hit-and-run," I tell Jorden.

"Not that again," he replies. "I already told you people all I know."

"This will only take a few minutes."

Jorden folds his arms. "I got nothing more to say," he insists, glancing at the receptionist to make sure she sees him putting the police in their place. "If you need anything else, you'll have to speak to my lawyer."

It's an absurd thing to say, and everyone here knows it. How many people deal often enough with a criminal solicitor to be able to call them "my lawyer"? Aside from mobsters, that is.

"Who is this lawyer?" I ask. "In case we need to speak to him."

He doesn't exist, obviously. For a second, I see Jorden is tempted to pluck a false name from the air. Then sense prevails, and he says, "Just some guy."

"Some guy," I repeat. "Oh wait, I think I know him. Isn't he the one who works for some firm over in some place?"

The secretary hides a smile behind her hand, and Ranger is forced into his usual peacekeeping role. DI Irving once told me we have the "good cop, bad cop" act down to a tee. But he is wrong, since neither one of us needs to "act" our roles.

"Please, sir," Ranger says to Jorden, then sweeps out an arm, inviting the other man to lead the way to his office.

Jorden scowls at me before relenting.

His office is large enough to have its own echo. At the far side of the room is a desk with one chair behind it and six on this side. Evidently Jorden is used to preaching to an audience. On the walls are pictures consisting of seemingly random arrangements of lines, shapes and paint splatters. I can't decide if they are classics of modern art or something Jorden's child rustled up in the nursery.

Jorden sits in the chair behind the desk. He hastily hides an ashtray in a drawer as if he thinks we are here from health and safety. I'm not sure where he intends to hide the smell of smoke.

I sit opposite Jorden, Ranger beside me.

"I'm going to ask you some questions," I tell Jorden. "And I need you to think before you answer. Picture the scene in your mind. Close your eyes if it helps."

Jorden keeps his eyes open.

"Let's start at the beginning," I say. "Where were you at the time of the . . . accident?"

"Leaving my flat. I had to meet a friend at the Crown, and I was already late."

"The Crown? Is that the pub around the corner?"

He nods.

"Did the accident happen as you were leaving home? Or was it after?"

"It happened as I closed my front door. I remember hearing the lock click, then a bump from along the road."

"How far apart were the click and the bump? It's important."

It isn't important, actually. But by making Jorden focus on a detail, I hope to encourage him to tap into his memories. I want to check that things really did happen the way he says, and that he isn't hiding information to make his life easier.

When Jorden's memory comes, the first thing I see is his front door closing. He then turns away from his house, and I get a glimpse of the yard. Amusingly, it is empty of the rubbish I saw earlier. Either Jorden has forgotten it is there, or he simply does not see it when he passes. On Fletcher Street, there are parked cars on both sides of the road. To my left I can hear an engine turning over, but even as that sound registers, I hear another noise: the bump of a car hitting Cate. I shudder.

In answer to my question about the gap between click and bump, Jorden says, "Just a second or two."

"Did you know what the bump was when you heard it?"

"Nah, thought nothing of it. But I had to cross Fletcher Street to get to the Crown. And when I did, I saw this figure lying in the road."

"You saw"—I almost say *my daughter* but stop myself just in time—"someone in the road. But you didn't go to help."

Jorden shuffles in his chair. "Didn't see no point. Like I told the other policewoman, there was already a guy leaning over her. Looked like he was calling it in."

I can see the man in Jorden's memory. As Jorden claimed, he is standing next to Cate, holding a mobile phone. I can't make out his face because he is looking the other way. My gaze strays to the prone shape of Cate. At this distance, I cannot distinguish any details of my daughter. Perhaps that is a blessing.

The memory fades in Jorden's mind, and he looks at Ranger for support. "There was nothing I could do."

Ranger says, "What about the car that hit her? Did you see the number plate?"

Jorden shakes his head.

"Model? Colour?"

Another shake. "The car was gone by this time. All I saw was lights along the road."

"How far away were the lights when you first saw them? Think carefully."

A new picture forms in Jorden's mind. Once again, I see Cate lying motionless. The car that hit her is naught but a distant shadow. Interestingly, that shadow is closer to Cate now than it was in the first memory Jorden showed me.

"Fifty metres, maybe," he replies.

Fifty metres is a fair estimate, yet there is something wrong with the image I am seeing. When I grope for the reason, it eludes me. Something to do with the car? Perhaps I can prompt a sharper picture of it by asking Jorden specifics.

"How big was the car?" I ask. "Are we talking about a Mini or a people carrier?"

The shadow in Jorden's mind does not change. "Dunno," he says.

"What about its lights? Were they normal ones or those strip lights you get on the fancy cars?" Fancy cars. They'll have me on Top Gear next.

"Dunno," Jorden says again. "Seriously, I've been through all this before. There's nothing more I can tell you."

He pushes his chair back from the desk as if to signal the interview is over.

And that is when I realise what is wrong with the latest memory he showed me: Cate's helper with the phone is nowhere to be seen in it. But that makes no sense. In the helper's written statement—which I have read—he told Harman he stayed with Cate until the ambulance arrived. Yet he doesn't appear in Jorden's memory. Could he be lying? And if so, where has he gone?

I study again the picture in Jorden's mind. His vantage point has changed, I realise. In his first memory—when he showed me Cate's helper leaning over her—Jorden's house was visible ahead and to the left. Now, though, it is not in view. Based on how close he is to Cate, he is probably standing directly in front of it.

A coldness passes through me, for I understand now the significance of what I am witnessing.

"What happened next?" I asked Jorden, my voice barely a whisper.

He thinks I am referring to the movements of the car that hit Cate, so in his memory I watch its lights recede. But I have only half an eye on that. Instead I am watching my daughter, waiting for . . .

And there it is. In Jorden's mind, the helper rushes over from the right. He crouches beside Cate, shouts something to her, then pulls out his mobile phone.

The pieces come together.

"You lied," I tell Jorden.

He stiffens. "What?"

"You told me that when you first saw the woman lying in the road, she had someone with her. But the guy who phoned for the ambulance didn't come until later."

"That's not true."

"You walked away, didn't you?" That's why his vantage point changed between the two memories. "A woman lay dying, and you left her. You didn't even call for help."

"You've got it wrong," Jorden says. He sounds hurt rather than repentant. Plainly he doesn't think he has done anything wrong.

I struggle for calm. Ultimately it doesn't matter what Jorden did or didn't do, because another source of help—the man who phoned for the ambulance—was quickly on the scene. If Jorden had gone to Cate when he saw her, he would have reached her only a few seconds before her helper. Those lost seconds didn't cost Cate anything, so Jorden's inaction didn't cost her anything either.

But what would have happened if the other man hadn't been there? When Jorden left Cate in the road, he couldn't have known the Good Samaritan would be along moments later. Jorden could have been the difference between my daughter living and dying. And instead of checking on her, he fucks off to the pub?

I am on my feet. Jorden looks at me like he thinks I am going to hit him, and he is right to worry. If he hadn't put that ashtray in his drawer, I would be feeding it to him by now.

Ranger guides me from the room with a firm hand.

# 5

SITTING BY THE WINDOW IN Starbucks, I sip at the dregs of my coffee. I am supposed to be meeting Phoebe, the woman Cate's secretary described as her closest friend at Simpsons. Phoebe is already half an hour late, but I have to be patient. I am running short of options to advance my daughter's case. Unless another witness comes forward, I'm not going to learn anything new about the hit-and-run. I could speak to the man who phoned for the ambulance—and I may yet do so, if only to thank him. But he has cooperated fully with Harman, and thus there is little hope of extracting more information from him.

So I have decided to approach the problem from a new angle: namely, why did the woman in the car want to kill Cate? Does it have something to do with my daughter leaving her job at Simpsons after just two months? What prompted her departure, and why did she not tell me about it?

Across the street, I see the mountain of steel and glass that is Simpsons' HQ. Despite the late hour it is a hive of activity, with more people arriving than leaving. A woman wearing a trilby leads a line of younger suited companions inside like a mother duck leading her ducklings. I remember Cate's excitement the day she got a job at this place. Joining the working world meant moving on with her life, which in turn meant putting what had gone before behind her.

I felt much the same excitement when I started work at the age of twenty-six. My degree was in engineering, so naturally my first job was at a hardware store selling paint and tools and shit. Yes, I learned a lot from the experience. But it was the only work I could find offering hours that fitted in with Cate's nursery run. I recall the disbelieving looks I got from the Stepford wives on our street when I told them I was sending Cate to nursery—as if by doing so I was abandoning her. That wasn't how I saw it. After four years married to Scott, I was tired of being defined always by what I was to someone else—a wife, a mother or a daughter. I wanted something for me.

A young woman emerges from Simpsons and crosses the road. She must recognise something of Cate in my features for she waves to me through the window. It is Phoebe. I was expecting some dull-eyed, soul-drained, twenty-two-going-on-sixty-two-year-old. Instead, Phoebe skips into Starbucks like it is the first day of spring. Her hair is in bunches, her skirt is six inches short of decent, and she wears so much black eyeshadow she must have put on her make-up in the dark.

I like her already.

Phoebe sits across from me, then sing-songs a hello and puts her phone on the table as if it's a Dictaphone she means to record our discussion with. In reality, I know it is her signal that she is still on call and could be summoned back to the office at any minute. I have already decided how I will approach this conversation. I do not want to tell Phoebe someone tried to kill Cate, so instead I will confine my questions to why my daughter left her job and see what follows.

"How is Cate?" Phoebe asks.

I bring her up to date on developments. Before I came here, I phoned Scott to ask him to extend his shift at the hospital. He told me Cate woke up briefly while he was with her, but that she showed no more awareness this time than she did when I was there. Phoebe makes a glum face, yet it does not linger. It is not because she doesn't care, I sense, but rather because nothing can keep this woman down for long. She is like one of those helium balloons without someone to hold onto her string.

"Is it okay if I visit Cate?" Phoebe asks. She speaks so quickly, each second word comes out before the first has finished.

"I think she would like that," I reply. "Have you seen her much since she left Simpsons?"

"We tried to meet a few times, but one of us always had to cancel. Cate mostly. I wondered if she regretted changing jobs because she seemed to work harder in her new one than she did at Simpsons."

"Her new job at . . ." I pretend to forget the name of Cate's latest firm and wait for Phoebe to finish my sentence.

"She never said."

Damn. Frustrating as that is, though, I have still learned much from this exchange. If Phoebe thinks Cate might have regretted changing jobs, that implies she was the one who made the change. In other words, Cate resigned from Simpsons rather than being fired.

But when Phoebe speaks of a new job, does she know for a fact that Cate had one? Or has Cate been lying to her? The lie seems most likely. A new employer, after all, would have missed Cate by now and tried to find out what had happened to her. And that would mean calling me, since I am surely my daughter's emergency contact.

"This may be a strange question," I say to Phoebe, "but why *did* Cate leave Simpsons?"

I am on dangerous ground here. A mother should already know these things. Plus, if the circumstances surrounding Cate's departure were delicate, Phoebe might conclude Cate didn't tell me because she doesn't want me to know.

It seems that is not the case, though, for Phoebe says, "She hated the job. Hated it even more than the rest of us." She gives a lopsided smile. "Cate lucked out with her first seat and got a bastard for a partner. The Grinch we call her. I mean, all partners are bastards, but there are bastards and there are bastards, and the Grinch is a real *bastard*."

The word of the day is "bastard".

"Was it personal?" I ask. "Did the two of them not get on?"

"The Grinch doesn't get on with anyone."

"What about the other people in Cate's team? Was there someone else she didn't like?"

Phoebe raises an eyebrow. She is too smart not to realise something is amiss with my line of questioning. Sooner or later she will ask what is going on, but I reckon she should humour a grieving mother a while longer.

"Not that I know of," she says. "To be honest Cate and I didn't talk much about work. You know how it is. You spend all day working so when you get a break, the last thing you want to do is talk about more work."

This is getting me nowhere. I wonder what I am even doing here. No one from Simpsons would have wanted Cate dead. We are speaking about coworkers here, not drooling psychopaths. Also, Cate was only at Simpsons for a few weeks. Even if someone developed a grudge in that time, would they seriously settle it by running her down?

And yet can it be a coincidence that she mysteriously quit her job shortly before someone attempted to kill her?

I am missing something. If I am going to have any chance of finding out what it is, I need to keep Phoebe talking, so I ask, "Were you surprised when Cate left?"

When Phoebe nods, it sets her bunches bobbing. "Back in the summer after we joined, all the trainees went to a wine bar to celebrate surviving the first week. We did this thing where we had to say who we thought would make partner first, and Cate came top. She just seemed to fit in. We all got dropped in the deep end when we started, but Cate got it worst with the Grinch. Two all-nighters in the first week. A twenty-four-hour stint at the photocopier. But she never let it get to her. It was like she could close the office door at the end of the day and leave it all behind." She shrugs. "Until one day she couldn't. I guess it ground her down."

"You said 'one day'. Was it as sudden as that?"

"Well, maybe not quite."

"But it was just before Cate left?"

"I suppose."

It fits, I tell myself. Something happened to Cate a month ago. Something that meant she could no longer deal with the crap she had put up with previously. A mistake at work that could not be remedied, perhaps? Or a bust up with a colleague that could not be reconciled? Whatever it was, it must have been serious to leave someone contemplating murder.

But did this drama happen at Simpsons? Were Cate's issues at work the cause of her troubles or merely a symptom?

Phoebe picks up her phone and fiddles with it. I have probably got everything I am going to get from her, but if she can't shine a light on why Cate left her job, who can? Cate's secretary? The Grinch herself? I could talk to them, but they won't be as accommodating as Phoebe. They will want to know why I am asking questions, and I not prepared to give them answers.

Who does that leave? Cate's best friend Maddie? Maddie now lives in Bristol. I don't know how often she and Cate speak, but if Cate was going to tell anyone about her problems, it would be Maddie. There is also Cate's ex-boyfriend, Jake. He and Cate met five months ago at a mutual friend's party and split up only recently. They were together long enough for Cate to confide in him, and even if she didn't volunteer what the problem was, Jake might have detected the same change in her behaviour that Phoebe noticed.

I say goodbye to Phoebe. She gives me a hug, then bounces out of Starbucks and back to the office.

The moment she has gone, I pull out my phone and look up Simpsons' webpage on the net. I never got the Grinch's real name, but I suspect there aren't many female partners working in Cate's old department. Sure enough, I find only one: Jenni

Hagan. Her photo shows a woman in her late forties or early fifties. Fine-featured and rosy-cheeked, she looks much too cheery for her nickname.

She is also categorically not the driver I saw in Cate's memory.

As I rise to leave, I notice a copy of the Metro newspaper on the next table. It is open at page five, and I see there a photo of Lily—Thornton's daughter—along with half a page of text. I don't know what has happened to warrant such exposure for her disappearance, and I don't want to.

But whatever it is, it likely signals trouble for DCI Mertin—and thus for me too.

# 6

THE HIGH DEPENDENCY UNIT APPEARS deserted when I return to St Christopher's. The nurses' station is unmanned. It is only half past seven at night, yet it feels as if Cate's ward is sleeping. The floor has a just-mopped sheen, and the air is so heavy with disinfectant that my lungs get a scouring.

The door to Cate's room is closed, but I see movement through the half-open blinds. A nurse, perhaps? But then why are the lights off?

When I enter, I discover a man standing beside Cate's bed. He spins around as if I have caught him with his hand in my daughter's pocket. He is of an age with Cate and has blue eyes and shoulder-length blonde hair. Good-looking in a boy-band kind of way. He wears a suit, and on the little finger of his left hand is a diamond ring that would grace the hand of even the most demanding bride.

Behind him, Cate lies still. Her monitor seems to be beeping faster than usual.

"Who are you?" I ask the man.

"I'm Jake," he replies.

As in Cate's ex? What is he doing here? And how did he find out Cate was at St Christopher's?

Jake must have guessed my thoughts because he says, "I've been trying to get hold of Cate for a while, but my calls went through to voicemail. So I rang her office. Her secretary told me what had happened." There is a note of censure in his voice as if he thinks I should have contacted him myself. "And you are Mrs Greenwood, aren't you? I've seen you coming and going from the hospital."

Because that doesn't sound creepy at all. "I haven't seen you."

"No," Jake says. "I wasn't visiting Cate, I was, er, visiting someone else. I must have noticed you when I was on my way to see them."

"You've got two friends in the same hospital at the same time? Clearly you are a dangerous person to know."

Jake smiles, but the humour does not reach his eyes.

The silence stretches. I want to be alone with Cate, but I need to speak to this man. So I motion for him to precede me through the door, then lead him to the same empty room in which I spoke to Scott earlier.

Inside, I try to remember everything Cate told me about Jake. But aside from the fact that he is a trainee solicitor too, I know as little about him as I do about any of Cate's exes. I recall the first time she brought a boyfriend home to meet me—when she was studying at UCL. His name was Will, and he had a face full of piercings and a fondness for death metal music. I thought the encounter went well, but Cate was less convinced. Something to do with me extracting Will's surname from him, then phoning in a criminal record check before he had even left the house.

"Is Cate going to be okay?" Jake asks.

I give him an abridged version of events. The news leaves him looking more thoughtful than upset. I ask him if he and Cate kept in touch after the breakup. The way he scowls when I say "breakup" makes me wonder if, contrary to what I thought, it was Cate and not him who ended the relationship. He assures me that yes, they were still close before the accident, and that it was only a matter of time before they got back together, before adding that the split was mutual.

That settles it: it was definitely Cate who finished things.

"Earlier, you said you called her office," I say. "Didn't you know that she had left Simpsons?"

Jake does not answer immediately. It is clear that he didn't, but if he admits as much, it undermines his claim that he and Cate were still close. "No," he finally concedes.

I want to keep him on side, so I say, "It took me by surprise too."

"Well, it wasn't a surprise, exactly. From the day she joined Simpsons, she was always complaining about the job. The partners there worked her so hard that when she got out all she wanted to do was sleep. She even had to work at weekends. We started seeing each other less and less."

Not all bad news, then. "Was there any particular thing that got to her?"

"I don't think so. But at Simpsons there was a new drama every day."

"Such as?"

"I heard this rumour about someone getting caught taking drugs in the office. The girl was told to clear her desk, then marched outside by security. I asked Cate if it was true, but she wouldn't say. I guess her boss told her not to talk about it. But the fact she wouldn't tell me means something was going on, right?"

Not necessarily. At the station, there are a hundred such rumours doing the rounds every day. But since this is all I have to go on just now, I may as well find out more. "When did this happen? Was it around the time Cate left?"

"I don't remember."

Of course he doesn't. Since he wasn't even aware Cate had resigned, he couldn't possibly know about timings. "The girl who got fired, was she a friend of Cate's?"

"Yes."

"Did it affect Cate at all?"

Jake frowns as he thinks back. "Maybe. Something did, that's for sure."

"What do you mean?"

Jake begins turning the diamond ring on his finger. "I never really thought about it before, but it was around that time that she . . ." His words trail off. "I don't know, she just started acting differently. There was this call from the police, then—"

"The police?"

"Yes. Some detective, I think. Cate wouldn't tell me what he wanted. Said it wasn't important. But everything was a secret with her. There were days when I would phone her at work twenty times and still not get hold of her. And she would disappear at weekends without telling me where she was going, or meet people after work without asking me first."

I shake my head in mock sympathy. Cate didn't get his permission before going out to see friends? The cheek of it.

Jake warms to his theme. "Then she started calling these numbers I didn't recognise. Numbers with a weird code like 0176 or 0178 or something. It wasn't any of her uni friends either—I checked the contacts on her phone."

I don't know what to find more unsettling: Jake's revelations, or the fact that he has apparently been snooping on my daughter's calls. The two of them never lived together, so they wouldn't have shared a phone bill. Which means Jake must have peeked at Cate's mobile when she wasn't looking. When I focus on his thoughts, I get a glimpse of him sitting in a sushi restaurant. His table has one of those revolving metal plates at the centre for serving food. I see Cate's back as she disappears into the ladies. Before the door has closed, Jake starts rummaging in her handbag. He grabs her phone and—

I cut away. It feels as if I am intruding on my daughter's privacy.

I refocus on what Jake and I were discussing. Does any of Cate's behaviour genuinely count as suspicious? The call from the police is worth following up. Maybe Cate was sufficiently worried about the driver of the car that hit her—Mystery Woman as I have taken to calling her—to lodge a complaint. I will ask Ranger to do a check on the incident database and see if it throws up anything.

What about the rest of Jake's story, though? The unexplained absences he mentioned could simply have been Cate's way of putting some distance between them. As for the unfamiliar area codes, maybe Cate has friends that aren't listed on her mobile. Or she could have been phoning outside London to arrange a holiday, or for any number of other things.

That area code seems familiar, though.

"Did you ask her about these calls?" I say to Jake.

"No. There was never a good time."

"I can imagine. A thing like that might make it look like you were spying on her."

Jake's gaze is hard and flat. "I'm not the one asking all these questions," he replies.

Our conversation draws swiftly to a close after that. Jake departs with a promise that he will visit again soon, but it is wishful thinking on his part.

If I have my way, he will never again come within restraining-order distance of my daughter.

# 7

I SIT AT CATE'S BEDSIDE, watching her chest rise and fall. I am so tired, I wish there were another bed in her room that I could climb into. The beeping of her monitor sets my teeth on edge. But annoying as the sound is, I know it is infinitely better to the alternative of it flatlining.

I study her features. With each new discovery about her life, she becomes more of a stranger to me. The loss of her job. The call from the police. I used to be her confidante. When Scott and I lived in West Hampstead, we had a swing chair in our garden. Each day after school, Cate and I would sit on it and talk. We had our fair share of catfights in her teenage years. But Cate trusted me enough to tell me about her first kiss, her crush on her English teacher, and about how she once tried a cigarette at a friend's sleepover. She pretended not to like it, and in return I pretended not to be cross.

It all changed after the Lake District. Ben's death cast such a long shadow, we couldn't escape from it. Cate blamed herself for him falling in the stream, and for failing to rescue him afterwards. She tried to talk to me about it, but I was too busy wallowing in my own grief to listen. We drifted apart. Cate had a cancer scare over a lump in her neck that I didn't find out about until she got the all-clear. Then before I knew it, it was time for her to go to university. I allowed an emotional distance to develop between us that was not justified by the physical separation.

I let her down.

Neyland appears in the doorway and stops when she spots me. The lights in the room are dimmed, so she probably wasn't expecting Cate to have visitors. I see she is tempted to turn and walk out again. Then she puts on her business face and enters the room. She is dressed in green scrubs, and she is wearing her hair long. The style of it changes every day.

"Ms Greenwood," Neyland says. "Have there been any developments?"

I feel it should be me asking that question. "No."

"Give it time. It is still too early to read anything into Cate's inability to communicate."

But she *can* communicate, I remind myself. It's just that Neyland doesn't know that yet because I haven't told her I read my daughter's mind. "It's okay," I say. "I know Cate is in there."

Neyland's smile is noncommittal.

"Don't you see it in her eyes? There is awareness. There is . . . understanding."

No response.

Perhaps it is time I came clean. It will not be an easy conversation. On the few occasions I have revealed my psychic abilities to someone, their first reaction is usually to pull their children close and look for an exit. But if I need to tell the surgeon the truth for Cate's sake, I will do so.

"If you knew Cate was conscious, would it change anything?" I ask. "Would you treat her differently?"

"No. Though I guess we might investigate other ways of communicating with her."

I can breathe again. Thanks to my abilities, Cate already has a means of communication. "Is she in pain?" I say, glancing at my daughter's plastered legs.

"Unlikely. Even if she were awake, the morphine would take most of her discomfort away."

Of course, the morphine. I had forgotten about the painkillers. I wonder if they could be affecting Cate's mind—maybe even giving her visions. I need to know that in order to judge the reliability of Cate's memories, so I ask, "What effect will the drugs have on her?"

"I'm not sure I understand the question."

"Will they make her disoriented? Could she be hallucinating?"

If Neyland's eyebrows rose any higher, they would disappear behind her fringe. "It's unlikely."

"What about making her dizzy? Will she be . . . high?"

This is the final straw for the poor surgeon. Perhaps she thinks I mean to hook myself up to Cate's drip and get high myself. She makes her excuses and departs with such speed she leaves scorch marks on the floor.

# 8

PRU OWENS—THE THERAPIST CATE MENTIONED at our dinner on Monday—lives in a sprawling detached house within a stone's throw of Putney Heath. I telephoned her last night to arrange a meeting, and she has reluctantly agreed to spare five minutes of her time. As I approach her front door, she is already opening it. She is much younger than I am—maybe younger even than Cate. She wears a sombre trouser suit and has scraped back her hair off her face to give herself a severe look.

Pru's office reminds me of a headmistress's study. On a lacquered desk is a globe that dates to when Russia was still part of the USSR, while behind it is a floor-to-ceiling bookcase crammed with the sort of arcane books you can buy by the armful at a car boot sale. Pru sits behind her desk. There is no therapist's couch for me, just a huge leather sofa that threatens to swallow me when I sink into it.

I try a smile that falls on stony ground. "Thanks for seeing me," I say.

Pru folds her hands beneath her chin. "To be blunt, Ms Greenwood, I'm not sure why you insisted on coming. As I explained on the phone, the things I discussed with your daughter are confidential."

"But these are exceptional circumstances. Cate was hit by a car, and there are reasons to think it wasn't an accident. We need to find the woman responsible."

"Are you here in an official capacity, then? Or as her mother?"

"A bit of both."

Pru does not respond. She has a way of looking at me that says she is judging my every word and action. If so, I trust she will keep her opinions to herself. I am more than capable of assessing my own faults, thank you very much.

I wonder what Cate has told her about me. I wonder if my daughter judged me too.

"Cate is in a coma," I say. "Do you really think I would come here just to snoop on her secrets?" I meant to make a point not ask a question, but Pru seems to have to consider the answer. "Cate told me you were helping her come to terms with Ben's death," I continue. "I'm not interested in that. All I want to know is whether she said anything that could have a bearing on why someone would want to hurt her."

Still Pru keeps her silence. Perhaps she doesn't know what to say, or perhaps she just couldn't give a damn about Cate. I can't understand why anyone would want to use her as a therapist. Before I came, I pictured her as a woman with soft eyes and a velvet voice—the human equivalent of a warm bath and whale music. That's what a counsellor should be. But Pru is cool instead of calm, reserved instead of reassuring. If I ever had a session with her, I suspect I would leave it feeling worse than when I arrived.

Maybe I am being too quick to judge Pru, though. Maybe what I really don't like about her is the fact that Cate chose this woman to share her problems with rather than me.

"Did you ever have cause for concern about Cate's wellbeing?" I ask. "That much at least you can tell me."

"I didn't consider her a suicide risk or a danger to others."

"What about the risk from others *to* her?"

Pru does not reply. Instead she glances at a clock on her desk. If I drag this out long enough she might throw me a bone to get rid of me.

"Come on, Miss Owens," I say. "Help me out here. Please. You know I can get a warrant for the notes from your sessions with Cate."

"Then get one."

I hope it doesn't come to that. Pru's notes are "excluded material" under the Police and Criminal Evidence Act, so getting a warrant for them will be awkward. More importantly, the hit-and-run isn't my case, so the decision whether or not to obtain a warrant will be DS Harman's. And as yet she has no reason to seek one. As far as she is concerned, she is investigating an accident not an attempted murder. How could Pru's notes be relevant to that?

"I shouldn't need to get a warrant," I tell Pru. "Client confidentiality was never meant to cover a case like this. Would Cate object to you answering my questions? Or would she want you to help me find the woman who put her in a coma?"

For the first time, it looks like Pru's resolve may be wavering. She purses her lips as if she has to stop herself from saying something. When I tune into her memories, I see Cate sitting on the same sofa that I am. Cate is wearing the necklace and earrings I bought her last Christmas. I know this is just a memory, but it is good to see my daughter like this—alive and spirited instead of the broken figure I am used to seeing at the hospital.

"Cate left her job about a month ago," I say. "Did you know that?" Pru nods.

"Did she tell you what the problem was? Why she wanted to leave?"

"I can't think of anything that might be relevant to your enquiries."

Someone is choosing their words carefully. "Did you notice a change in Cate's behaviour at that time?"

Pru shifts her weight. It is the smallest of gestures, but since it is the only gesture she has made since we started talking, I fasten on it at once.

"Her friends claim she became more distant," I say. "More secretive. And something disturbed her sufficiently that she felt the need to go to the police about it."

"If she went to the police, shouldn't you be speaking to your colleagues instead of me?"

I wish it were that straightforward. But Ranger has searched the incident database and found nothing. If Cate did complain about Mystery Woman, either someone failed to record the issue or it was dealt with informally. "Was someone causing her problems?" I ask. "Someone she knew?"

The therapist's gaze remains flat. She is trying not to give anything away, but she is trying a little too hard. "Ms Greenwood—"

"There *was* someone, wasn't there?"

"I've told you all I can."

In Pru's memories, I see Cate again. Her shoulders are hunched, her face downcast, but when her lips move I cannot make out what she is saying. Pru remembers the conversation, not the precise words spoken. I take a calming breath. Why won't she cooperate? She knows what Mystery Woman did to Cate. She knows what is at stake here. Surely her professional conduct rules are less important than my daughter's life? "Who was it, Miss Owens?"

Pru rises from her chair and points me towards the door.

"What aren't you telling me?" I ask. "Who are you trying to protect?"

"I think it is time you left."

# 9

MY TREAD IS HEAVY AS I leave the sketch artist's room. I have spent the past hour putting together an E-FIT of the driver of the car that hit Cate. I still haven't asked DS Harman if she will use it, but I wanted to get the sketch done while Mystery Woman's face remained fresh in my mind.

Unfortunately, the image is barely recognisable even to me. Composite sketches, Ranger once told me, are entirely reliable in that you can rely on them always being wrong. When I look at the completed picture, each feature in isolation is precisely as I remember it. Yet somehow the overall package has come out looking like a cross between Cruella de Vil and the Wicked Witch of the West.

In the corridor outside the sketch artist's room is a burned electrical smell that suggests the computers here are as overworked as the people. To my left stands Ranger. He looks less than pleased to see me. He tries to mouth something to me, but my lipreading skills are rusty. Then I spot DCI Mertin approaching behind him, and I realise what Ranger was trying to warn me about.

"Ah," Mertin says. "Ms Greenwood. I am delighted to see you are ready to return to work."

He moves up to flank Ranger. With his hands on his hips, he is full of false good cheer. He looks from me to the door to the sketch artist's room, then back again. Clearly it is no coincidence that he—like Ranger—was passing at this moment. He knew of my appointment with the artist, just as he knows I am not really here to report back for work. There is a calculation in his gaze, and it dawns on me that he wants to make a deal. He is willing to overlook the fact that I am investigating Cate's case if I help him find Thornton's missing daughter.

Normally, a detective chief inspector does not need to ask those working under him for help. But with me it is not so simple. I am still on compassionate leave. I am also not officially one of Mertin's team; I am answerable to Deputy Assistant Commissioner Abraham, not the DCI. It is a state of affairs that dates back to when I first started working cases for the Met. Abraham moved me between units depending on where he thought my skills would be most useful. So I did spells with Homicide South in Lewisham, the Kidnap Unit at Scotland Yard, then the Special Enquiries team when a prominent politician was accused of running a paedophile ring from his constituency headquarters.

But I grew tired of being passed around like an STD. I was never in one place long enough to feel settled, particularly since I was told to keep my abilities a secret. That left the people I worked with suspicious as to my credentials and resentful of my interference. One DI asked me when my partner Fox Mulder would be joining us. Another accused me of being a mole for the Directorate of Professional Standards.

Then I was paired with DI Ranger to hunt down a rapist preying on joggers on Putney Heath. We hit it off straightaway. Ranger has a laidback streak wide enough for him to get on with Mertin. He is also not afraid to step outside the lines if it is necessary to secure a conviction. Once the Putney Heath rapist was caught, both he and I were surprised to find we weren't wholly dismayed at the prospect of working together again. So that is what happened. Unfortunately that means I now have to work with Mertin too, but I like working with Ranger more than I dislike being around the DCI. If that ever changes, I will ask for a transfer.

Mertin says, "Your daughter is making progress, I trust?" Then before I can reply he adds, "Since you're back with us, I guess you may as well dive straight into things. We've got Thornton coming in for another interview this morning, and I want you there. Ranger will brief you on developments, won't you, Inspector?"

"Sir."

"Excellent." Mertin casts another look at the sketch artist's door, then says to me, "I know this is a difficult time for you, Ms Greenwood. You look after yourself, okay?"

He makes it sound like a threat—which it probably is. I know Mertin would like to see me gone from his team for all that I have enhanced his clear rate. As far as he is concerned, I am an accident waiting to happen. At some point, the media is bound to learn of my role at the Met. When they do, our station will turn into a circus, and Mertin wants me gone before that happens.

While I am still here, though, it is clear he intends to get his pound of flesh from me.

Ranger wears a resigned expression as he leads me to his desk. There, he fills me in on the Thornton case. Thornton's car remains missing, but we now have an idea of its movements on the night Lily went missing. The Audi was spotted on traffic cameras on the M40 motorway near Oxford, then followed all the way north to the A591 west of Kendal. That means Thornton probably ditched his car in the Lake District. Alas, image enhancement has failed to show who was driving the vehicle. There is thus little point in confronting Thornton about our findings because he will claim his car had been stolen by this point.

Less progress has been made regarding his return journey to London. Ranger and his team have begun the torturous process of checking CCTV footage from mainline railway stations, but there have been no sightings of Thornton. In the meantime, enquiries of his neighbours in Earlsfield have achieved nothing but to draw his solicitor's anger. No one noticed Thornton's comings or goings on the night Lily disappeared. No one appears interested, either.

There have still been no withdrawals from Lily's bank account and no calls from her mobile—but then there probably isn't much of a phone signal at the bottom of a lake. Ranger has tried without success to contact her mother in Brazil. The only meaningful new development comes from a friend of Lily's called Olivia whom Ranger spoke to for the first time last night. Olivia claims that on Monday night—the night Lily went missing—Lily was with her at a housewarming party held by Olivia's brother. Whereas Thornton told us she had been shopping. It is a discrepancy worth following up, and that is why Mertin has called Thornton in again this morning.

Ranger finishes his update, then leans back in his chair. He asks me if I am ready for this. Apparently Thornton's lawyer, Stephanie Gale, is unimpressed by the conduct of our investigation to date, and in particular that someone told the press about the anonymous tip-off claiming Thornton had killed his daughter. She has also complained to Ranger about the manner in which I questioned her client at our last meeting.

Neither she nor Thornton will be pleased to see me again.

# 10

THE INTERVIEW TAKES PLACE IN the same room as last time. The only change is a stain on the floor near the door, together with a lingering smell of vomit that does nothing to improve the room's ambience. Gale is wearing her familiar white bow tie and practiced scowl. A stern-faced Thornton sits beside her with his arms folded.

Ranger tosses his file onto the table, then settles into the chair across from Gale. I take the remaining seat and shuffle back a short way as if to distance myself from proceedings. As I discussed with Ranger beforehand, I am going to pretend that I want to be here about as much as Thornton does—which isn't so far from the truth. With Gale unhappy at my methods, it makes sense for me to keep my head down.

"Thank you for coming in, Mr Thornton," Ranger begins. "I've had some new information about Lily that I was hoping you could shed a light on."

Thornton does not respond. I can feel his gaze on me.

Ranger opens his file and flips through some papers. "You know Olivia Webster?" he asks Thornton.

"I know the name."

"She's a friend of Lily. I spoke to her yesterday. She tells me that on the night Lily disappeared, the two of them were at the housewarming party of Olivia's brother."

Beside Thornton, Gale sits up straighter and glances at her client. Thornton says nothing, but his slowly released breath suggests relief at this line of questioning. For all he knew, Ranger might have called him here to tell him his car had been pulled from the lake. By comparison, any revelations Olivia Webster might have are sure to be tame.

"A party, Mr Thornton," Ranger repeats. "But you told us Lily had been shopping." He consults his notes. "That was why you gave her a lift. 'Lots of heavy bags', you said."

Thornton shrugs. "She must have gone shopping before she went to the party."

"Except that Olivia and her brother claimed she didn't have any bags with her that night."

"Obviously they were mistaken."

"Obviously. There's something else that puzzles me, though. You said you picked Lily up from the city. But the party was in Camberwell."

"Camberwell is in the city."

"It's in London, yes. But when people say *the city*, they usually mean the city centre."

Ranger leaves a silence for Thornton to fill, but the man says nothing. Beside him Gale taps her pen against her pad.

"Olivia also says Lily left the party at 9.45," Ranger continues. "Does that sound about right?"

Thornton shrugs a second time.

"In fact, Olivia told me she was certain about the time because she remembers trying to persuade Lily to stay. Your daughter refused, though. It was Monday night, you see, and she had lectures the next morning."

"If you say so."

"Help me out here, Mr Thornton. You live in Earlsfield. I'm guessing that's about a thirty-minute drive from Camberwell?"

Another shrug. Much more of this, and Thornton will strain his shoulders.

"So if you picked Lily up at 9.45, you must have got home at around 10.15. But the last time we spoke, you said you drove her to

Earlsfield station just before eleven. So she was home for forty-five minutes before heading out again?"

Thornton's face twitches. He is clearly uncomfortable about where this is heading, so I tune into his thoughts in the hope of catching a stray memory. But for now his mind remains blank.

"We might have left a little earlier," Thornton says.

"How much earlier? Five minutes? Ten?"

Finally, Gale enters the fray. "This is ridiculous," she says to Ranger. "I came here expecting a progress update on your search for Lily. Instead you continue to badger my client over irrelevant discrepancies in timing. I have to say I find this entirely unethical."

When a lawyer accuses someone else of being unethical, you know the conversation has gone to some weird places.

"These aren't irrelevant, though, are they, Ms Gale?" Ranger replies. "Our best chance of finding Lily lies in building up an accurate picture of her movements before she disappeared. Surely you can see that?" He looks at Thornton. "So, when did you leave for Earlsfield station?"

"I guess it could have been closer to 10.45 than 11."

Ranger pretends to consider. "Odd, isn't it? Lily leaves the party at 9.45 because she wants an early night, then an hour later she goes out again."

No response. With his story so comprehensively dismantled, you'd have thought Thornton would be shamed into confessing the truth. But I guess shame isn't something that troubles a man who is capable of killing his daughter.

Ranger checks his notes once more. "In our last conversation, you said you took Lily to Earlsfield station because she was going to see a film, correct?"

"Yes."

"And you dropped her right outside?"

"Yes."

"The reason I'm asking is, we checked CCTV from the station, and we can't find anyone matching Lily's description entering or leaving around 11."

Thornton says nothing.

"We looked for your car too. There's a camera outside an estate agent's that gives a perfect view of the approach to Earlsfield station, but curiously there is no sign of your Audi. No sign. We checked either side of eleven too in case you made a mistake about the timing—or another mistake, I should say. But we still couldn't find your car. It's almost as if you weren't there at all."

That provokes another outburst from Gale. The woman is everything I dislike in a lawyer. Her client's story is crumbling, yet still she retains a supercilious air. Throughout her tirade, Ranger sits unmoved.

It is time for me to risk an intervention. I catch Thornton's gaze and say, "We've got witnesses who claim they heard shouting from your house on the night Lily disappeared. This was after you collected her from the party."

This is a fabrication on my part. To my knowledge, no such witnesses have come forward. Yet it seems likely Thornton and Lily had a falling-out, because something must have stirred his blood enough for him to kill her. I see a memory of him and Lily inside their lounge. There is a worn floral carpet and a black faux-leather suite with mismatched paisley cushions. A pale-faced Lily stands with her hands clasped together as Thornton rages at her. He snatches up a telephone's receiver and waves it around before slamming it back in its cradle.

"Did you argue with Lily?" I ask Thornton. "Maybe she stayed at the party longer than you liked. Or you didn't want her going out again."

"We didn't argue," Thornton lies.

"And the raised voices the witnesses heard?"

"I must have had my TV on loud."

I leave a full thirty-second silence to express my scepticism, but Thornton stares coolly back at me.

"When Lily was home," I say, "did she contact anyone about meeting them in town?"

"I don't think so."

"And when you took her to the station, did she have a bag with her?"

"Just her handbag."

"So there's no way she could have been planning to stay with someone else that night?"

Thornton sighs before responding. I do not hear his answer because I am concentrating on a scene that has formed in his mind. Lily is in what must be her bedroom, stuffing clothes into a holdall. Is she leaving home? Was her row with her father that serious? Or was it her decision to leave that caused the row? If she planned to run away, she must have had somewhere to run to. And some*one*. A friend, perhaps? A boyfriend? If there is one thing sure to prompt an argument between father and daughter, it is a relationship that the father disapproves of.

In Thornton's memory, he watches Lily from her bedroom doorway. He is clutching a batch of papers. I try to read what is on them, but he lowers them from view and I cannot change the angle of the shot. This isn't a video camera that I can adjust to my liking; I see only what Thornton shows me. As Lily crosses to a chest of drawers, she turns her back on her father. He advances on her before the memory fades.

Ranger changes the angle of attack. "Why didn't Lily take her mobile phone with her when she went out?"

"What?"

My partner withdraws a piece of paper from the case file. "This is a signal-strength triangulation map carried out on Lily's phone for the period of 6.30pm to 11pm on Monday. It shows that her phone remained within the mobile phone cell covering your home for the whole of that time until it was turned off at 10.37pm."

Thornton stares at the map.

"In the days leading up to her disappearance," Ranger goes on, "Lily never went more than fifteen minutes without phoning or texting one of her friends. So why would she leave her phone behind on Monday? If she was heading into town so late, surely she would have wanted it with her in case there was a problem."

"She must have forgotten it."

"But Lily turned off her phone at 10.37. How could she turn it off one moment, then forget about it completely the next? And why turn her phone off anyway? That's something you do if you are staying in, not going out."

Thornton doesn't appear to be listening any more. In his mind, he is back in his car. Lily isn't sitting in the seat beside him, so this must be from a time after he killed her but before he reached the lake. Around him the city's lights are bright. I look for some landmark to orientate me, yet there is nothing except houses and street furniture. Ahead a traffic light turns red. The only other cars on the road are parked ones. Then for an instant Thornton's gaze flickers to his rear-view mirror, and I tense.

There is someone sitting on the back seat—a shadowy figure whose features I cannot make out. I am not even sure if it is a man or a woman.

What the hell? Who else could be in the car at this time? My first thoughts are of Mrs Thornton, but she left for Brazil before Lily vanished on Monday. Who does that leave? And why would they be in the car just as Thornton is going to dispose of his daughter's body?

There is only one explanation I can think of.

Thornton has an accomplice.

# 11

AS I ENTER THE RECEPTION at St Christopher's, my mobile rings. It is Ranger calling, but I do not pick up. I made it clear when I left the station earlier that I am now off the clock. Even so, I feel bad for my partner. Our interview with Thornton has thrown up more questions than answers. First there is Thornton's accomplice. Then there is the mystery surrounding Lily's decision to leave home. There is a line that connects all these dots into a coherent picture, but for now I cannot see it.

Perhaps the answers lie on Thornton's computer. On an unscheduled visit to his home yesterday evening, the eagle-eyed DC Underhill spotted a laptop that hadn't been present when the house was searched after Lily's disappearance. Thornton's work computer, it transpires. Ranger has asked Thornton to hand it over so we can check if Lily used it to make contact with anyone. But mainly we want to find out if the browsing history reveals any damning searches such as how to kill your daughter or where to access remote lakes in the UK.

Thornton refused Ranger's request, claiming Lily never used the laptop. But if he is reluctant to relinquish the thing, that just makes us more determined to get hold of it. Ranger is looking into obtaining a warrant.

I remember something I have been planning to do all morning, and I dial DS Harman's number. It is time I offered her my sketch of Mystery Woman. There is little chance she will use it if she finds out how I obtained it, but with her investigation going nowhere, I am hoping she will take any help offered. Ranger has warned me she is an abrasive character with language to match. Twice in the past she made inspector only to be busted down to sergeant when she stepped on the wrong toes.

She picks up the phone. "Harman," she says. Her voice is so proper, she sounds like the woman who hands around the scones at the Women's Institute meeting.

I introduce myself, but I get no further than my name before Harman explodes.

"Oh, for fuck's sake," she says. "First Ranger, now you. I can't even go to the ladies room without one of you climbing on my back. You think this is helping? You think if you keep chasing me I'll pull some new evidence out of my arse?"

As she continues her rant, I hold the phone away from my ear. But I make the mistake of moving it towards a young family on my right, and the mother shrinks away as if I am holding a spitting cobra.

When Harman exhausts her supply of swear words, I move my phone back to my face.

"Feeling better?" I ask.

"Much, thank you. Seriously, though, I'm sorry about what happened to your daughter, but there's nothing I can tell you that I haven't already told Ranger. I've hit a wall here. There are no witnesses. No evidence worth spit. And until that changes, this case is going nowhere as fast as my career is."

"Maybe I can help," I say. "I've managed to get hold of an E-FIT of the driver. I'll send it to you."

Harman is instantly wary. "Where did you get an E-FIT from? I haven't even found someone who can ID the car."

I make crackling noises down the phone. "Sorry, the line's breaking up. I didn't catch that."

"I said, where did you get—"

I end the call.

# 12

THE HOSPITAL CAFÉ SMELLS OF boiled cabbage and instant coffee. Earlier, I texted Scott to say I was on my way to St Christopher's, and he suggested we meet here. He sits a short distance away, wearing a suit and shirt but no tie. When he sees me, he surprises me with a 100W smile, and I look behind me to check he isn't directing it at someone else. As I approach his table, he half rises before settling down again. In front of him is a plate of chicken, chips, and mixed salad leaves that look like they've been scooped off the car park's tarmac. I take the chair opposite him.

Scott waves a fork at me and says, "Sorry, I couldn't wait any longer to start eating." It's like my dinner date with Cate all over again. "I got the chicken. And I can now strongly recommend everything else on the menu."

He pokes at his salad as if he fears something might be hiding in it. "I was in Cate's room when lunch arrived earlier," he continues. "A nurse wheeled a trolley in and asked Cate if she was hungry. When I explained she was comatose, do you know what the nurse said? 'Would she like a cup of tea instead?' Who knows, maybe she is used to patients feigning comas when the food comes around."

I force a smile. "How is Cate?"

"No change as far as I can tell. Neyland dropped by earlier to give me an update, but I left my medical degree at home today, so I ended up none the wiser. Maybe you can get more sense out of her."

"Has Cate opened her eyes?"

"No. She is probably saving that for you."

Because Cate is closer to me than him, is he saying? There is no denying that. With children, you get out what you put in. And where Cate is concerned, Scott has always been sparing with his attention. I am therefore surprised—and a little impressed—at how much time he has spent with her over the past few days.

Let's see how long that lasts.

I remember the time eleven years ago when our relationship was floundering and we resolved to make a new start. We moved from London to a village called Haddenham, changed our jobs, our friends, our working hours—changed everything, in other words, except the thing that most needed changing: us. Still, it worked for a time. We joined English Heritage and took Cate to every site within a hundred miles. We threw parties for our new neighbours and pretended to agree when they told us how lucky we were to be out of London. And in the evenings we scheduled "us time" complete with scented candles and other gimmicks I gleaned from Cosmopolitan magazine.

But the fault lines soon re-emerged. Why is it that when couples are struggling to get on, they think the solution is to spend more time together? Surely it should be less.

Six months later we were back in London.

When Ben came along, he represented yet another opportunity for us to start over. My pregnancy came as quite the surprise, since Scott and I had stopped trying for another child. Scott embraced his second chance at fatherhood. For men, a son holds a charm that a daughter never can. In Ben's short life, Scott spent more time with him than he ever did with Cate. Football in the garden. Football in the house. Scott used to say Ben was born with a pair of football boots on his feet, which explains the particular discomfort of my son's birth.

Cate was thirteen at the time I was pregnant—just old enough for me to have forgotten the loss of independence that parenthood brings, and to have reimagined bringing up a baby to be the magical time every mother pretends it is. And Cate had been an "easy" child. My friend Isabel once told me that girls make easy children and difficult teenagers, whereas with boys it is the opposite. Unfortunately, with Ben, I never got the chance to test that.

Scott has been chewing the same piece of chicken for the last two minutes. "So have you found out anything more about the accident?" he asks.

I spare him the details and say, "There's nothing to prove the driver meant to hit Cate, but there's nothing to prove the opposite either. If the hit-and-run was deliberate—"

"If?" Scott cuts in. "Are you starting to have doubts, then?"

I shrug. "The thing I can't see past is why anyone would want to kill Cate. What was Mystery Woman's motive?" I look around to check no one nearby is listening. "Did you know Cate left her job at Simpsons?"

Scott pushes his plate to the middle of the table. "No."

"It happened about a month ago. One of her friends claims Cate changed around that time, and her ex tells the same story."

"Changed how?"

"She became more fragile. More secretive. But I have no idea whether that had anything to do with the hit-and-run, or with her leaving her job for that matter." I eat a chip from Scott's plate. "How long had it been since you'd last seen Cate?"

"I don't know. Months? We arranged to meet up at my place a few weeks back, but Cate cancelled when something came up."

"Something work-wise?"

"She didn't say."

Was there an innocent explanation for this? Or is it part of the same pattern of elusiveness that Phoebe and Jake have already established? "When you spoke to her, did she seem okay? Was there anything different about her?"

"Not that I remember."

A member of staff comes to collect Scott's plate. On the next table, a baby stares at Scott with an intensity only the very young can muster. Scott pulls a face, and the baby smiles. He has always been best with the kids he can hand back at the end of the day.

"Where did we go wrong?" I ask him.

He looks at me.

"With Cate. She didn't tell me she had left her job. Instead, she came to dinner in her suit and pretended nothing had changed. Why would she keep that from me?"

"Why wouldn't she? Isn't that what kids do: keep secrets from their parents? On that basis I'd say we've brought her up to be entirely normal."

I frown. There is no issue that Scott won't seek to deflect with humour. Though when it comes to keeping secrets, I know neither of us is in a position to preach to our daughter.

Scott surprises me by reaching across the table and taking my hand. "You're being too hard on yourself. Cate wouldn't have kept something from you unless she had good reasons. When she wakes up, I'm sure she will tell you why."

I wait for a second, then extract my hand. In retrospect, I prefer the flippant Scott to the serious one.

"What's happening with the hit-and-run case?" he asks. "What is your friend Harman up to at the moment?"

"Oh, you know. Chasing her tail. The usual thing." I put on my innocent face. "Maybe you should give her a call and get the latest. I'm sure she would love to hear from you."

"What, now?"

"Why not?"

"Okay. What will you be doing in the meantime?"

"Waiting here. Patiently."

Scott shoots me the same look he used to give me when I went to the kitchen to make a cup of coffee and absolutely not to mix myself a gin and tonic. He knows I am thinking of reading Cate's mind again. What choice do I have, though? I could try to obtain Cate's therapy notes, or track down the detective who called her at home. I could talk to the man who reached her first after the accident, or investigate the calls she made out of London. But is it worth my time? I might spend weeks chasing down each lead only to find they ended in a cul-de-sac. Whereas there is one thing I can do that is guaranteed to identify the woman who ran down my daughter.

Scott studies me. I brace myself for a lecture, but it does not come. He knows the more he tries to talk me out of it, the more he will settle my mind. I have tried to do things his way, and they have brought me no closer to finding Mystery Woman.

"Be careful," he says at last. "If something goes wrong, I'm sure you wouldn't forgive yourself. I know I won't."

# 13

I SIT AT CATE'S BEDSIDE, reading to her from an Agatha Christie mystery. In the room with us is a cleaner with the longest nose I have ever seen. She has been mopping the floor for over ten minutes, and I can only assume she hasn't left because she is keen to know whodunit.

I am far more caught up in my own real-life mystery to care. I think about what Scott said at lunch regarding me reading Cate's mind. "If something went wrong . . ." But what *could* go wrong? I won't be asking Cate to relive her accident again. I just want to find out how she knows Mystery Woman. Cate won't be able to answer directly. But she can show me where she first came across the hit-and-run driver. And while she does so, I will listen out for the beeping of Cate's monitor, ready to end things if she shows signs of stress.

Finally, the cleaner leaves the room. I rise and close the door before returning to Cate.

Now that the time for action has come, I feel a sense of urgency. I worry Scott might reappear and try to stop me, but I will not turn back. Because contrary to what I suggested at lunch, there is no question in my mind that Cate's hit-and-run was deliberate. So I take her hand and explain the situation to her. I emphasise she must show me only the things she is comfortable with. Then I close my eyes and tune into her thoughts.

I feel a tug the like of which I have never experienced before, as if I am caught in a vortex. In Cate's mind, my daughter is walking along a hospital corridor so narrow that if she stretched out her arms to either side, she would touch the walls. Ahead is a door marked "Exit" in neon letters. Is she dreaming? Or is this a hallucination?

She continues to walk towards the door, yet it comes no closer. The image jolts and suddenly the door is not just in front of her but also above her slightly; the floor of the corridor rises to it. With every step Cate takes, the gradient increases until she is forced to advance on all fours. Then the slope becomes steeper still, and she slides back down the way she came. Doors and white walls flash past until Cate is deposited in her room—the same room the two of us are in now.

Another jolt, and she is back in her bed. She tries in vain to sit up. Beneath her hospital robe, I see her muscles bunching. My own stomach clenches as if her struggles were my own. The vision is painfully clear in its meaning: my daughter feels like a prisoner. Is this how she spends her time each day, trapped in unending nightmares?

I speak her name, hoping to wake her. She must be able to hear my voice because the picture shifts again, and I see myself in her vision, holding her hand as I am in real life. My face is drawn. Cate looks down at her right hand in mine. Her arm is shaking, and for an instant it seems like I am not so much holding her hand as gripping it to stop her moving. As if I am part of the problem.

The image blurs like a watercolour that someone has spilled water over. I experience a second of disorientation, then I am conscious again of my feet on the floor, my back against the chair. My body feels as stiff as it does after a long car journey. I shuffle in my seat, but I do not break my connection with my daughter because a new picture is forming in her head.

She is in a forest that looks like something from a Grimm's fairy tale. The trees are black, and each branch ends in a point that appears sharp enough to cut. The last rainfall has turned the mud to slop. Water drips from the leaves as if the trees are weeping. Is this one of Cate's memories or another vision? I experience a strange sensation like I am being watched. Like there is someone else in Cate's head with me. I should withdraw, I know. I asked Cate to show me information about Mystery Woman, and this is clearly not that. But something holds me.

Through the trees, I glimpse a stone building with a slate roof. I know now where I am. This is the cottage in the Lake District that I stayed in with Cate when Ben drowned.

I blink, and all of a sudden I am inside. The ground floor is one large open space complete with log fire, exposed beams and grandfather clock. My family is here—except for Cate herself, of course, since I am viewing the scene through her eyes. Scott and I sit in plush armchairs, each reading our own sections of the *Sunday Times*, while Ben pushes his Thomas the Tank Engine train around and around its track like he is caught in a time loop. The tension in the room is tangible. Scott and I are as grim-faced as if Ben had already died, and every tick of the clock falls as loud as a gong strike between us.

A weight settles on me, for this was not how things happened. That weekend in the Lake District was supposed to be an escape from the bleakness of London life. Scott and I had become consummate actors in hiding our struggles from our children. The "us" we presented to them was worlds apart from the "us" that existed in private. So why has Cate painted that day in such dark colours? Perhaps her memories have been distorted by the misery of what came after. Corrupted, if you will.

Or perhaps I am the one whose perception is skewed. Perhaps Cate was able even at that age to see through our pretence. I wonder if this is symptomatic of how she perceives her entire childhood. I also wonder, as I often have before, whether it is possible for me not just to view another person's thoughts but also to influence them. Imagine the possibilities. Change someone's memories and you change the person too. If I had the opportunity to rewrite Cate's thoughts, would I do so? Would I give her the perfect childhood I failed to provide the first time around?

The scene moves forward, and Cate and Ben are now outside. The only sound is the wind tangling in the branches. Every gust catches the water on the leaves and throws down a stinging spray in Cate's face. Ahead of her is the stream that ran beside the cottage—although it might be more accurate to call it a river such is its size and the speed of its flow. Upstream, it has burst its banks to flood the land alongside. But even around Cate the ground is a quagmire of muddy puddles.

Ben loves it, splashing along as if he were starring in an episode of Peppa Pig. Behind him, Cate picks her way through the trees. She is texting someone on her mobile. She never told me that she was on her phone when the accident happened. Instead she claimed she had been tying her shoelace, and that she had taken her gaze off Ben for only a second. No wonder she blames herself for his death. At the edges of her vision I see Ben clamber onto a tree trunk that has fallen across the stream.

I know what comes next, and I want to look away. I cannot watch. But I cannot not watch either.

The next few moments pass in a blur. There is a cry from Ben. Cate lowers her phone and spins around. Ben is in the stream, clutching a branch of the fallen tree. For a second he holds on.

Then the foaming torrent bears him away.

My blood has gone so cold it might be me in that water rather than him. Cate makes a sound that is half scream, half wail. She tears along the bank after him, feet slithering and skating in the mud, trees crashing and wobbling all about. A branch whips her face, but she barely registers it. The rushing of water is loud in her ears. Ahead is the wooden bridge where I played Pooh sticks with Ben the day we arrived. As Cate closes on it, she trips on a branch and sprawls in the muck. By the time she regains her feet, the stream has carried Ben under the bridge and out of sight. Cate screams again before turning back towards the cottage.

Then movement at the corner of her eye catches her attention. She looks across.

On the other side of the stream is a path. Among the trees beyond the path stands a figure—a woman wearing a hat, scarf and waterproofs. The scarf covers the lower part of her face, but there is no mistaking her all the same.

The bottom drops out of my stomach.

It is Mystery Woman.

# PART FOUR

# Dark Waters

# 1

Friday, 27 October
Evening

A FEW HOURS LATER, I am back in the hospital café. The shock of what I witnessed in Cate's mind is only now fading. I have heard from her before the story of how Ben drowned, but to see it through her eyes has made the wound feel fresh again. The . . . injustice of it all. If Ben had held onto the branch for a second longer, or if Cate hadn't tripped when she was chasing him, he could still be with us. On such fine margins are lives broken.

I suspect my daughter won't be the only one having bad dreams tonight.

I push the thought aside and reconsider what I saw in Cate's memories—assuming they were indeed memories and not just the conjurings of a nightmare-addled mind. No, I have been over this already. When I surfaced from Cate's thoughts, I discovered my daughter's eyes were open. She was awake, not dreaming. And when I read her mind again, I saw the same scene repeated over and over until Cate succumbed to unconsciousness. There is no question that the memory was real, just as there is no question that Cate wanted me to see it.

Beyond that, I can make no sense of things. What was Mystery Woman doing in the Lake District at that time? And what does it have to do with the hit-and-run? I have no answers.

That is why I have asked Ranger to meet me here. Right on cue, he enters the café with a Friday-feeling bounce to his step. When I see the Tesco carrier bag in his hand, my heart leaps to indecent heights. He sits across from me and produces four cans of pre-mixed gin and tonic. I want to kiss him, but I settle for a heartfelt thank you. I pop the first can's ring-pull and drain the contents in one go.

Ranger raises an eyebrow.

"What?" I say. "I was thirsty."

He looks at a water cooler to my left.

"It wasn't that kind of thirst."

"Uh huh. You know, I was lucky to smuggle those cans in at all. A security guard wanted to confiscate the bag."

"I bet he did."

"I had to show him my warrant card to make him back down. Urgent police business, I said."

"You were right."

He pauses. "I'm meeting up with some of the guys later for a drink. I know this isn't the best time, but if you feel like joining us . . ." When I do not respond, he continues: "It might do you good to get away from things for a while. Give the monkey on your back the night off."

"I'll think about it."

Ranger crosses his legs. "So, what's up?"

I launch straight into my story and watch Ranger's expression change from confusion to scepticism to outright bewilderment. After I finish, I try to forestall his inevitable first question by insisting the memory is genuine.

It doesn't work.

"Could the memory be wrong?" he says.

"I already told you—"

"I didn't say false, I said *wrong*. This was five years ago. Maybe Cate made a mistake about the woman's face. Maybe the stranger in the woods looked enough like the hit-and-run driver for Cate to mix them up."

I frown. This is not what I wanted to hear.

"Put it this way, Sam," Ranger says. "After Ben's accident, I assume you had to deal with the local police. Do you remember what the DI in charge looked like?"

"Bad example," I reply. "I remember the woman's face because I still dream of planting my fist in it."

"What about her sergeant, then? Do you remember him?"

I shake my head to concede his point.

"And you probably saw him a dozen times. Whereas Cate would only have seen Mystery Woman once, and at a moment of stress too. What are the chances she remembers the woman's face after five years?"

I open the next can of gin and tonic. "Maybe Cate didn't see her only once. Maybe she already knew her from earlier."

"Unlikely."

"Why?"

"Let me answer that with a question. What was this woman doing in the woods five years ago?"

I remain silent, not knowing what he is getting at.

"If she didn't know Cate," Ranger goes on, "then it was probably just a coincidence she was there. That makes her a random walker, minding her own business. Plenty of those in the Lake District. If she did know Cate, though, she must have followed her on holiday. But you lived in West Hampstead at that time, right? So this woman trailed you all the way to the Lake District from London? Why?"

When he puts it like that, it does sound silly.

"And that's not all," Ranger says. "Imagine Cate and Mystery Woman did know each other. Imagine there was bad blood between them. Why didn't Mystery Woman run down Cate five years ago? Why did she wait until now?"

"Because Cate was just a kid then?"

"So instead Mystery Woman harbours a grudge all this time? Does that sound right? Plus how would she have known where Cate lived now? Do you think she kept tabs on her for five years?"

I shrug before finishing my second gin and tonic. I swear each of these cans is smaller than the last. Maybe it is time I considered slowing down my rate of drinking.

There you go, it's considered.

"Okay," I say. "Let's pretend Cate didn't know the woman when she saw her in the woods. How does that help us?"

Ranger rubs his temples as if this is giving him a headache. "It has to be relevant that Cate showed you that particular memory," he says. "And that the woman was in the woods at that time."

"How do you mean?"

"I know this is stupid but say Cate keyed Mystery Woman's car at some point, and the hit-and-run was the woman's way of getting revenge. If Cate wanted to help us find her, wouldn't she show you a picture of the time she keyed the car? That way you would know what the history between them was, giving you a better chance of tracking the woman down. But instead Cate shows you that scene from the woods?"

He has a point. It's almost as if my daughter doesn't know who Mystery Woman is any more than we do.

Ranger strokes his sideburns. "Maybe the woman was doing something in the Lake District she didn't want anyone knowing about. Maybe she'd just buried someone in a shallow grave or something."

"Maybe. But that doesn't explain why she tried to silence Cate now. If the police hadn't caught up with her after five years, she must have known she'd gotten away with it."

"Maybe she didn't want to take a chance on Cate talking."

"Maybe."

We seem to be dealing exclusively in that word.

I open a third can of gin and tonic and take a sip. Already the alcohol is singing in my veins. Through its song, a thought tugs at me—something Jake said when I spoke to him yesterday. "Cate's ex told me Cate changed before she left Simpsons. That she became more distant, more secretive."

"So?"

"So what if she ran into Mystery Woman around that time? That could have unsettled her enough to explain how she changed."

"Unsettled her enough to make her leave her job?"

"Why not? If the blood between them ran bad enough for the woman to try to kill Cate, wouldn't Cate have been freaked out by her reappearance?"

Ranger's nod is half-hearted.

An old man with a Hitler moustache walks past the café. He sees my drink and tuts. Ranger raises the unopened fourth can of gin and tonic and gives him a mock toast. The old man sniffs and turns away.

"So what will you do next?" Ranger asks me.

"Start digging around," I reply. "When I spoke to Cate's ex, he mentioned her calling some numbers with a strange area code."

"You think it might have something to do with Mystery Woman?"

"It's worth checking out. If the numbers are still in Cate's call log, I might be able to retrace her steps. Maybe she started asking questions about her past. Maybe those questions are the reason she got run down."

"But questions about what?" Ranger says.

I shrug and take another drink from my can.

There is only one way to find out.

# 2

WHEN I SHOW UP AT Casey's wine bar later, Ranger looks equally surprised and pleased to see me. Casey's is one of those swanky places on Putney High Street where the tables have bowls of olives, and the prices are the best-known cure for alcoholism. With Ranger are DS Napier, DC Vickers and four women from Westminster CID whose names I forget as soon as I hear them. Ranger asks the people on his bench to shuffle along. One of the women ends up practically in Vickers's lap, but neither looks disappointed at the development.

I nurse my gin and tonic and listen to the others talk shop. Westminster CID is on the trail of a man who assaulted a criminal defence barrister, and the Senior Investigating Officer is deciding whether to continue the hunt or send a "Thank You" card to the culprit. Whenever Ranger contributes, he looks my way in an effort to draw me into the conversation. Normally I would be in the thick of the banter, but today I am content to let the waves of chat break over me. And try not to feel guilty about enjoying myself while Cate lies alone in the hospital.

Half an hour later, I have barely said a word. The conversation moves on to the violence at last week's student march over tuition fees. I offer to get the next round in, then weave my way to the bar.

When I finally catch the eye of the barman, I have to repeat my order three times before he hears it.

"Need help carrying?" Ranger says from behind me.

He ferries our companions' drinks back to the table, then settles himself on a stool next to mine. A burst of laughter comes from our group. There is now plenty of room on the bench that Ranger and I have vacated, but Vickers and his female friend remain pressed together.

Ranger follows my gaze. "They seem to be getting on well," he says.

"I thought Vickers was going out with Angie from technical support."

"So did he, until he walked in on her on Tuesday and found her being overly friendly with one of the trainees." He sips his Peroni. "The story has been causing quite a stir. Not only was the guy ten years younger than Angie, he was also a family friend. Apparently, she called in favours to get him placed with her. Now we know why."

"Ouch."

"That's what the guy's family thought when they found out. They pulled him out of there so fast he got whiplash. It may go down as one of the shortest traineeships in the history of the Met."

"Nice," I say. "It's too bad I wasn't around when the story broke."

Ranger nods. "If anyone else has a scandal in the offing, I'll ask them to hold off until you're back."

At that moment his phone rings. He checks the number but doesn't take the call.

"Don't tell me," I say. "Mertin?"

"No." When I give him a questioning look, he goes on, "My parents. They're coming down to visit tomorrow. Even taking me to see a game at Highbury. But it's just an excuse for them to ask me for more money."

"Money for what?"

"Good question. A while back they told me they were struggling to pay their mortgage, so I agreed to help out. After the third time, though, I got suspicious. That's the problem with being a copper:

you never stop asking questions. So I looked up their house at the Land Registry. Turns out they don't even *have* a mortgage any more." He shakes his head. "Doesn't say much for their opinion of my detective skills if they thought I wouldn't find out."

"So where is the money going?"

"No idea." There is just enough hesitation in his answer to leave me wondering if that is the whole truth.

"What about you?" he asks. "Things alright with your family?"

"Fine." I'm not sure why, but people always seem to assume I have skeletons in my childhood. "I'm an only child, so growing up was an uneventful affair. And my parents assured me it was nothing personal when they emigrated to the opposite side of the world."

Ranger starts peeling the label from his beer bottle. "They left three years ago, right?"

"Three and a half."

"Did you consider going with them?"

"Maybe."

At the time, my divorce from Scott was dragging on. I had a new house to find, a new life to build. The temptation to put a few thousand miles between me and my troubles was strong. But Cate had no interest in moving, so that was the end of that. Plus if life has taught me anything, it is that the faster I run away from one problem, the sooner I run into the next.

"Have you ever thought of leaving the Met?" I ask Ranger. "Just giving Mertin the finger and taking off somewhere?"

"All the time. I've got a friend whose job took him to San Francisco last year. He can't stop talking about the beaches and the cable cars. They've even got a half-decent football team, even if it is of the American kind."

"So what's stopping you?"

Ranger shoots me a look, then shrugs. "If I work that out, you'll be the first to know."

# 3

Saturday, 28 October
Morning

EIGHT O'CLOCK NEXT MORNING, AND I have already taken my first steps on Mystery Woman's trail. As I scroll through Cate's mobile phone log, I am relieved to find that the numbers go back several months. I remember my conversation with Jake about Cate's mysterious calls. "A weird code like 0176 or 0178," he said. I'm not sure why those numbers should be any weirder than others, but I guess to some Londoners any code outside the capital counts as odd.

I quickly discover what I am looking for: a string of numbers that begin with 017687. Cate started calling them on the fourteenth of September. Now I need to learn which region that code belongs to.

I switch on my computer and wait for it to clear the sleep from its head. Then I open up the internet browser and put the first 017687 number into Google. It brings up a reference to a place called Clearview in Keswick. It sounds like a nursing home, but when I click on the link I find it is a guest house sporting four en suite bedrooms. The next few numbers in Cate's phone log are more guest houses and B&Bs. Perhaps she called them because she was arranging a stopover in the Lake District, but I consider that unlikely. If you are planning a relaxing weekend away, the last place you choose is the place where your brother drowned.

This must have something to do with Mystery Woman, but what? I work through the options. Let's say Ranger and I were correct in thinking Cate didn't know the woman when my daughter saw her in the woods. If Cate wanted to find out who she was, what would she do? All she had to go on was the stranger's face and the fact that Mystery Woman was in the Lake District when Ben died. If the woman wasn't a local, she would have had to stay somewhere in the area. Hence Cate's calls to the guest houses, perhaps? Was she trying to find out if they kept records from five years ago that showed whether Mystery Woman had been a visitor?

I do a search of the next numbers on the call log. Google gives me nothing for the first couple, but the third comes up as the Cumberland & Westmoreland Herald. One of Keswick's local newspapers. Just reading the name now is enough to bring a heat to my face. After Ben's accident, there was an opinion piece about him in that newspaper. It was written by a man called Iain Ritchie—his name is imprinted on my memory—and the gist of it was that Scott and I should be locked up for neglecting Ben. His death was no mere accident. By letting him out of the house with Cate, we had invited tragedy. We *deserved* what happened next.

The article generated a flood of letters from likeminded readers. I don't understand how people can be so heartless, but then no one believes in forgiving mistakes until they make one themselves.

Why would Cate contact the Herald, though? What does the paper have to do with Mystery Woman?

I return my attention to the guest houses. There is something I am missing. I picture Cate picking up the phone to the guest houses' owners. What would she say to them? "Hi, I'm trying to track down a woman whose name I don't know and who may or may not have stayed with you five years ago. Can you help?" I can imagine the owners' reactions. In fact I don't need to imagine it, because if I listen hard enough, I can still hear the echoes of their laughter from all the way down the M6.

An idea surfaces, and I scroll through Cate's call log again. Around the time she phoned the guest houses there are several calls to London numbers. I type them into Google. Most come up blank, but I find a link to a Chinese restaurant as well as to a nearby off-licence on Coldharbour Lane.

That's my girl.

Then I strike gold. The next number belongs to a portrait artist in Streatham called Martha King. I open her website. On the front page is a pencil sketch of a bride with the strained smile of someone having second thoughts about her happy day. I click on the bio of the artist. As expected, Martha King was once a forensic artist—with the Met, no less. She retired nine years ago. The pieces come together. Cate must have used King to put together a sketch of Mystery Woman. She could then take that sketch to the Lake District and see if it jogged someone's memory.

I call King's number but am redirected to voicemail. No surprises there, since it is the weekend. I hang up without leaving a message. Maybe on Monday I will try to get in touch with her again, but for now I reckon I can do without King's sketch of Mystery Woman.

I already have my own E-FIT, after all.

# 4

FAST FORWARD TWO HOURS, AND I am in Cate's ground-floor flat in Brixton. Her heating has been off since the hit-and-run, and there is a dank smell to the place that makes it feel like I am deep underground. I have come to check her computer's browsing history in case it lists any illuminating websites. But when I turn on her laptop, I find it is password protected. If this were the movies I would now type in a random combination of birth dates and lucky numbers, then act surprised when I cracked the code first time. Instead I spend ten minutes making ever-more elaborate guesses before finally conceding defeat.

Determined to leave with something useful from my trip, I search Cate's flat. On a bookcase in her bedroom I discover a folder containing bank and credit card statements. I skim through them. It turns out that reading through someone else's financial affairs is no less tedious than reading through your own. Together with the Sainsbury's bills and the Netflix subscription I see payments to Martha King and to Clearview—Cate must have stayed at the guest house when she visited the Lake District. But among the lines of text there is no smoking gun.

In my daughter's bedside locker I find a blue address book. Most of the names inside mean nothing to me, but I take it anyway . . .

My breath catches. For beneath the address book is a rape alarm and a can that looks like a deodorant but is instead labelled "self-defence spray". I shake the can to see if it has been used before. It appears to be full. Did Cate buy the spray and the alarm merely as a precaution? Or did she feel she was in imminent danger? The fact the can is in her bedside locker rather than in her handbag suggests the former. But clearly she must have felt threatened if she saw the need to buy the spray and the alarm.

My mobile phone rings, and I recognise Scott's number. He has probably arrived at the hospital and is wondering why I am not there. I take the call.

"Hi," I say.

"Where are you?"

"At Cate's."

Scott pauses. "Anything I should know?"

I take a breath then tell him everything, from what I saw in Cate's memories, to my discussions with Ranger, to what I have learned this morning. When I finish, he says nothing. I sense he wants to tell me how crazy this sounds, but his silence makes the point eloquently enough.

"Can you look after Cate for a couple of days?" I ask.

It is time I paid a trip to the Lake District. I don't want to leave my daughter, but I tell myself Cate would understand my absence. Moreover, she would *want* me to do this else she wouldn't have shown me the scene of Mystery Woman in the woods.

"You're going to Keswick, aren't you?" Scott says. There is a cold-ness in his voice, and I remind myself that the place holds no less painful memories for him than it does for me.

"I have to."

"What are you going to do there?"

"Take Mystery Woman's E-FIT and show it around. Cate must have been on to something when she went there otherwise the woman wouldn't have tried to kill her. All I have to do is retrace Cate's steps and see where they lead."

When it comes to finding Mystery Woman, I will have one important advantage over my daughter: since she trod this path before me, I can also take a photo of Cate along and ask people if they recognise her. Maybe no one will remember seeing Mystery Woman, but they might remember speaking to Cate, and that will help them recall whatever questions Cate asked them on her visit.

"Retrace her steps," Scott repeats. "You do realise those steps may have got Cate put in hospital? What if the woman you're looking for tries to do the same to you?"

I hadn't considered that. The prospect doesn't overly concern me, though. If Mystery Woman wants to come after me, she will first have to crawl out from under whatever rock she is hiding. And when she does, I will be waiting.

"I'll be careful," I tell Scott.

It isn't the first lie I have told him, and I suspect it won't be the last.

I hang up and return to the lounge. I've got a long drive ahead of me, but I need to tidy up the mess I've made in Cate's flat . . .

A shadow falls across me, and I glance at the window. The Venetian blinds in the lounge are half closed, but between the slats I see a blur of movement, a glint of light on metal. As quickly as it comes, it is gone.

My mind takes a second to catch up to what my eyes are telling me. Someone is out there. And the fact they took off so swiftly suggests they didn't want me knowing they were watching. A nosy neighbour, perhaps, keeping tabs on what I am doing? Or something more sinister?

My Spidey senses tingle.

I cross to the window and seize the cord to the blinds. In my haste I fumble it, but I grip it on the second try and yank it so hard the slats swish to the top in a single motion. The window looks onto Maycross Street. In front of me is a strip of mud and moss posing as a lawn, then a low wall before the road itself. I look left and right along the block of flats. No sign of the Peeping Tom or Thomasina. They could be hiding behind a parked car on Maycross Street, but did they have time to reach it before I reached the window?

Maybe they are crouching behind the boundary wall. Or maybe they are closer than that—just on the other side of the wall I am standing next to.

My tingle is back. I press my forehead to the window and attempt to look along the wall, but such is the angle of my view, someone could be waiting with their back to the bricks just a few feet away and I wouldn't see them. I grab the window's handle and try to turn it, but it won't move. The damned thing is locked. I search for a key behind the plant pots and photo frames, knowing the spy could even now be making their escape.

To hell with this.

It takes me five seconds to reach Cate's front door, another ten to reach the main door to the block of flats. As I crash through it, I almost collide with a young man laden with Tesco bags. Outside, I am greeted by the smell of wet grass and diesel fumes. Cate's lounge window is to my left. There is no one standing beside it. In fact I can't see anyone nearby except a boy riding a bike and a window cleaner working on the upper windows of the next block of flats. I run down the path to the road and spin around, looking for any shady characters.

Nothing.

I walk along the pavement until I am level with Cate's window. In the muddy ground beneath it are what appear to be fresh footprints. The building ends a dozen metres away, so I trot to the corner and glance around it. Still nothing. What if I was right about the spy hiding behind a parked vehicle? I am about to drop to my knees and look beneath them when I hear voices behind. I turn to see two girls walking towards me, taking turns eating chips from a McDonalds carton. When I ask if they've noticed anyone acting suspiciously, they look at me like I am talking a foreign language.

I try again. "Did you see anyone running from that building?" I ask, pointing to Cate's block of flats.

"Er, you?" the taller one replies, earning a snigger from her companion.

Great.

A final scornful look from the girls, then they depart arm in arm. A Smart car trundles past. The window cleaner descends his ladder.

This is hopeless. Whoever was outside Cate's window is long gone. I head back to the door to my daughter's block of flats.

And try to convince myself I didn't imagine the whole thing.

# 5

Saturday, 28 October
Afternoon

BLOODY TRAFFIC. THANKS TO A jam north of Birmingham, I have already been on the road for six hours, yet I am only just approaching Preston. In an effort to keep myself alert I have set my car's fan to blow cold air in my face. But still my thoughts wander. I have been thinking of Cate—and trying not to think of her. With each mile that I draw closer to the Lake District, the sun sinks farther and the darkness closes around me. It seems fitting considering where I am going and what happened there five years ago.

When I flick through the radio stations I get a dozen different DJs all admiring the sound of their own voices. So I turn on my Gorillaz CD and listen to the music while I watch the milometer tick over. Normally I enjoy driving. I recall travelling to Paris once for the wedding of a friend from university. I loved that trip—and not just because it was a chance for Scott and me to recreate our happy days at King's College. Having the distances measured in kilometres instead of miles made it seem like you were travelling so much faster for the same speed.

Talking of speed, I stir from my reverie to find my car's speedometer is touching eighty.

Whoops.

I put my foot down and accelerate to a more comfortable ninety.

In my rear-view mirror, I see a set of headlights that has been trailing me since Manchester. I remember Scott's warning about Mystery Woman. This isn't the first time I have wondered if I am being followed, but on each previous occasion the car in question turned off at an exit or overtook me when I slowed. I am being foolish. How could Mystery Woman know I am going to the Lake District? How could she know I am trying to find her? It's not as if she has been staking out my flat for the past week.

Although if she was the one spying on me at Cate's house . . .

I check the clock and curse. I had hoped to arrive in Keswick by evening so I'd have time to make some calls. Tomorrow is Sunday, and it will be harder then to contact the people I want to talk to. True, all the guest houses will be open, but what about the Cumberland & Westmoreland Herald? Slim chance anyone there works on a Sunday. They probably aren't even in the office now, but I have to try calling, don't I? So I pull off at the next services and look up the paper's number on my phone before dialling its switchboard.

Remarkably, a woman answers. A helpful woman. I don't know who Cate talked to when she contacted the paper, so I pretend I am my daughter and play stupid. It is a role that comes easily to me. I tell the receptionist I spoke to someone there a month ago, but can't recall the person's name. Can she ask around, please, and see if one of her colleagues remembers talking to me?

Shortly afterwards I am put through to a man called Peter McGrath. I explain who I really am, and we agree to meet after lunch tomorrow. Yes, McGrath remembers speaking to Cate, and yes, he is intrigued to know why I want to talk to him now.

# 6

Saturday, 28 October
Evening

TWO HOURS LATER, I PARK my MX-5 outside a guest house known as Firwood Cottage and get out. I would have been here sooner but for an unfortunate diversion when my satnav tried to take me through the middle of Derwentwater. Judging by the temperature, I am somewhere north of the Arctic Circle. It is drizzling, and the wind feels harsh enough to scrape the flesh from my face.

Before setting out this morning, I counted on Cate's phone log the number of calls she made to each guest house. Firwood Cottage received the most, so that is where I am starting my enquiries. As I reach the porch, I get a whiff of the honeysuckle covering the building's frontage. Inside, the natural stone of the reception hall makes the room as gloomy as a cave. Behind a desk is a young woman in a pencil skirt and a snow-white shirt. She is serving an elderly couple wearing matching tartan coats and with a suitcase the size of a double wardrobe. While they fill in a form, I introduce myself to the receptionist and show her both a photo of Cate and the E-FIT of Mystery Woman.

"You speak to manager," she says in heavily accented English before banging on a door behind her marked "staff". "Meester Bailey!"

From the other side, a male voice unleashes a stream of four-letter words that turn the air blue.

The receptionist does not seem to notice. She grabs a key from a hook on the wall, then sets off to lead the elderly couple to their room, tugging their suitcase behind her.

I feel like I have stumbled into a Fawlty Towers remake.

The moment I am alone, I head for the staff door and open it without knocking. I find myself in a windowless room just large enough for an armchair and a table with a box TV on it. In the armchair sits a man wearing a crumpled tee-shirt and a waistcoat too small to button across his gut. He is watching a game of rugby on the TV.

"You shouldn't be in here," Mr Bailey says without looking up. His voice is so deep, it measures on the Richter Scale.

I am reluctant to play the "police card" outside London, but with this man I have no choice.

"Police," I say, flashing my ID. Such is Bailey's inattention, he can't have noticed that I am from London or that my ID is not a warrant card. "I need to ask you some questions."

Bailey doesn't respond, so I step between him and the TV.

"Five minutes is all this will take," I say. "Now, do you recognise either of these women?"

Bailey glares at me, but he does eventually look at the photo and the E-FIT. His gaze lingers on Cate. In his memories, I see a flash of my daughter. She is standing at the desk in the reception area. Bailey has made her hair too dark, and she is six inches too short. But on the plus side, he has recalled her bra size perfectly.

Bailey points at Cate's photo. "Her," he says. "She was around here a few weeks back asking about my records."

"Your records?"

"Something about an old guest. I don't remember what she wanted exactly, but I know my answer was no."

"No, as in you wouldn't help? Or no, the woman was never a guest here?"

"I wouldn't help, obviously. I can't give out guests' information."

From the TV behind me comes a burst of noise. Bailey cranes his neck to look around me, but I move to block his view again.

"This woman," I say, gesturing to Cate's photo. "Did she come in with a sketch to show you, or did she give you a name?"

"A name."

Interesting. So Cate must have found out who Mystery Woman was before she came here. "What name?" I ask Bailey.

He shrugs.

"Short, long? Local, foreign?"

Another shrug.

"Was there anything else you remember that might be helpful? Something the woman said, maybe? Like where she was planning to go next."

"Not that I recall. Now, if you don't mind . . ."

I leave him to his game. I could try to force him to help me further, but for the time being my task is to retrace Cate's steps, not set off on a new path entirely. And it is clear that whatever she found out about Mystery Woman, she did not discover it here.

On to the next guest house.

# 7

Saturday, 28 October
Evening

I PUT MY NEXT DESTINATION into my satnav and set off. It is now so cold I am losing sensation in my toes. In the distance, the brooding shadows of the hills are a deeper darkness in the gloom. The drizzle has turned the roads greasy, and the glow from my headlights wavers and sparkles on the tarmac. Such is the weight of blackness around me, it feels like I am driving with a sheer drop to either side, and a moment's carelessness could send me spinning off the road and over a precipice.

That is why I am only doing fifty when the other car comes roaring up behind me. Its driver seems intent on setting a new land speed record, and I hear a screech of brakes as he slows to stop driving into the back of me. If this boy racer wants to drive himself into an early grave, who am I to get in his way? But there is nowhere for me to pull over, and the road is too twisty for the driver to risk overtaking. So instead he sounds his horn in an effort to make me go faster.

I maintain my speed.

In front, standing water has collected in a dip in the road. My car ploughs through it, throwing up spray. The back wheels start sliding out to the right before I tug on the steering wheel to correct them. I hadn't thought it possible, but the car behind me comes still closer to my rear bumper as if its driver wants to climb into my back seat. For an absurd moment I think he is going to ram me.

And yet is that so absurd? Maybe the driver is not a "he" but a "she"—Mystery Woman to be precise. Maybe she has located me before I could locate her. We are alone on the road, and the driving conditions make this a perfect spot for an "accident". The slightest shunt could cause a crash. My heart beats a quickstep. I look in the mirror to see who the driver is, but I can't make out anything through the glare of the car's headlights. It edges out as if to overtake. This is a good sign, I tell myself, since if the driver wants to pass, she cannot also mean to bump me.

Unless she intends to hit me from the side.

My foot hovers over the brake pedal. As the road climbs towards a blind crest, dry-stone walls rise up to either side, hemming me in. Behind, my tormentor starts flashing her headlights as if she thinks I might not have got the message from all the beeping.

My petrol warning light chooses that moment to come on.

Then I drive over the rise, and the road levels out and straightens. I slow down and indicate left to pull in. There is a twinkle of light in my side mirror, then the other car streaks past with a final blast of its horn. Inside, I see two shadows instead of the one I was expecting.

Not Mystery Woman after all.

I take a breath and let it out. Now that the danger has passed, my fear turns to irritation. I am annoyed as much at myself as at the other driver for making a big deal out of nothing. Part of me wants to chase after the car and give its driver a taste of his own medicine, but he is the one who is supposed to be the arsehole. His taillights disappear over the top of the next incline.

There is a glow on the skyline indicating the lights of a village beyond. I check my satnav and set off again. My destination—the Posthouse—is apparently just ahead, yet strangely the map shows it as an isolated building rather than part of a settlement.

Then I reach the crest and know instinctively that I have found what I am looking for—the place where Mystery Woman must have stayed five years ago.

For one side of the Posthouse is enveloped in flames.

# 8

Sunday, 29 October
Morning

I HAVEN'T DARED OPEN MY curtains yet. I spent the night in a B&B on the edge of Keswick. My room is a shrine to blue gingham and has a ceiling that slants down at one end. No doubt the owners market it as a feature, but I have already banged my head on it twice.

I pace the room, my thoughts tripping over one another. On local radio this morning I heard reports of the fire at the Posthouse. No one was hurt in it, but otherwise no information has been released by the police. Could it have been started accidentally? What are the odds of that happening on the day I paid a visit?

The only alternative, though, is that Mystery Woman is responsible, which would mean she must have known I was coming here. But how? There are two options. First, she saw me leaving London—leaving Cate's flat, probably—and followed me. Since she knew which guest house she stayed in five years ago, she was able to go there directly and start the fire while I wasted time at Fawlty Towers.

Second, someone warned her I was coming. But who did I tell? The only people I mentioned it to are Scott and the journalist Peter McGrath. The idea of Scott conspiring with Mystery Woman against Cate is ridiculous. What about McGrath, though? Cate spoke to him when she came here last month, so maybe he told

Mystery Woman my daughter was on her trail. It makes a certain sense. Mystery Woman had to find out from *someone* that Cate was hunting her.

The problem is, I telephoned McGrath only yesterday afternoon, just a couple of hours before I saw the Posthouse burning. Imagine he called Mystery Woman immediately after putting down the phone to me. If she lives in London—which I assume—there is no way she could have gotten to the Lake District in time. Maybe she is a local, then. But if so, why would she have stayed in the Posthouse five years ago? Has she moved to the area recently? Or did someone else start the fire in her place? McGrath himself, perhaps? Or another accomplice?

This is nonsense. I am turning this into a grand conspiracy. Hell, maybe everyone is in on it except me.

So what's my next move? I still intend to keep my afternoon appointment with McGrath. Maybe he *is* in league with Mystery Woman, but since we have arranged to meet in a coffee shop, I can't see how he poses any danger. And if he does know my target, I might learn something useful from his memories.

How should I pass this morning, though? Previously I had planned to visit more guest houses, but there seems no point in doing so now. I could try to speak to the Posthouse's owners and find out if their records survived the fire. Yet I doubt they will be in the mood for questions while the ashes of their livelihood are still warm. Perhaps I will summon up the courage to visit the cottage I stayed in when Ben drowned. If I look around, I might see something to explain what Mystery Woman was doing in the woods five years ago.

I peek through a gap in the curtains into the B&B's garden, half expecting to see Mystery Woman looking at me from behind a tree. The place is deserted, but I cannot shake the sense that hidden eyes are watching me.

On a whim, I call Scott. He answers on the second ring.

"How are things?" he asks.

"There's been a fire," I say.

"What? Where? Are you okay?"

From the shock in his voice, it is obvious he knows nothing about the Posthouse, and thus he couldn't have been the one who told Mystery Woman I was coming. Not that I doubted him, of course. I ignore his questions and ask about Cate. He tells me her condition hasn't changed, and that he is on his way to St Christopher's now. Apparently Phoebe from Simpsons visited Cate yesterday—wearing lederhosen, no less. Jake called by too, but Scott sent him packing.

"Now," he says. "What's this about a fire?"

# 9

THE WIND HAS RUFFLED THE surface of Derwentwater to waves. In the distance, hills rise to brush the sky. To my right, a path winds through woods that extend to the edge of the lake. The holiday cottage I stayed in five years ago is a stone's throw behind me. I walked this way with Cate one morning, watching the coots bob on the water around Lord's Island until the cold chased us inside.

Memories press in upon me from the day Ben drowned: I remember shouting Ben's name as I stumbled along the path with a hysterical Cate in tow; tripping over a root in the failing light and spraining my ankle; feeling so sick I vomited on Scott's shoes. That sickness stayed with me throughout the sleepless night that followed. The next day, while everyone else searched for Ben's body in the shallows, I called to him as if he might have survived the swollen stream and a night in freezing temperatures. Even now I have to stop myself calling to him.

I head back along the path towards the holiday cottage. On the way, I see the bridge that Ben was swept under in Cate's memory. Erosion of the banks has caused the supports on the opposite side to slump, and the bridge is now cordoned off with fluttering red tape. Like a crime scene.

Twenty more paces bring me to the point where Mystery Woman stood when Ben toppled into the water. The fallen tree that he was clambering over is visible upstream. Tied to it are the remains of a bunch of flowers—Cate's probably, from when she came to Keswick. The petals have long since fallen off to leave a handful of withered stalks that look like something from The Blair Witch Project.

I gaze around. What was Mystery Woman doing here that she didn't want anyone knowing about? There are no shallow graves in sight, no chalk outlines of bodies on the ground. I leave the path and walk a short distance into the woods. The trees thicken. My steps leave impressions in the mud that are quick to fill with water. I wander around for a full ten minutes, but whatever I was hoping to find, it isn't here.

By the time I return to the path, my shoes are caked in muck. I consider following the path farther from the lake, but I have already checked its course on a map, and I know it leads precisely nowhere.

I shouldn't have come here.

Through the trees to my left, I catch sight of the holiday cottage. The owners have given the walls a fresh coat of paint, and the flowerpots around the porch give it a picture-postcard feel. In a window I see a woman in a white dress with skin so pale she looks like a ghost, while out front is a man smoking a cigarette. He wears a three-piece suit as if he has stepped out of a boardroom, yet he has tattoos extending up both sides of his neck. He watches me as I watch him.

A final puff on his cigarette, then he flicks the butt into a flowerbed and calls, "Can I help you?"

I shake my head.

I wonder if anyone can.

# 10

Sunday, 29 October
Afternoon

IT IS DRIZZLING AGAIN AS I hurry along Station Street in Keswick towards the Costa coffee shop. Every third building is a tearoom or an estate agent renting out holiday cottages. Even in the October rain, there are groups of hikers tramping along in their home-knits. Madness. Scott loves it here. As a child his family used to come to the Lake District for walking holidays, but for me "walking" and "holiday" are two words that should never be in the same sentence.

I open the door to Costa and am greeted by a wall of heat. Sitting at a nearby table is a man who rises as I enter—Peter McGrath, no doubt. He wears a shiny suit, a stripy tie, and he has a beard so thick it must serve as an extra layer against the cold. I remind myself this is the man who may have warned Mystery Woman I was coming to Keswick. I look for any hint of nervousness in him, but his gaze is steady and his smile is assured.

"Samantha Greenwood?" he asks.

I shake his hand. "I should have worn a red carnation so you would recognise me."

When McGrath laughs, the sound comes all the way up from his feet.

I order a cappuccino, then sit opposite my companion. His legs are so long I have to angle my own to find space. McGrath takes out a notebook and puts it on the table. The implication is plain: he has sniffed out a possible story here and wants information from me as much as I want it from him. To break the ice, I ask him if Iain Ritchie—the man who wrote the venomous opinion piece on me and Scott five years ago—still works for the Herald, but McGrath tells me that he has moved on. To the next circle of hell, presumably.

"So how are you finding the Lake District?" he asks.

"It's nice."

McGrath gives me a knowing look. "High praise indeed. I must admit, it took me a while to warm to the place when I first moved here. But it's not so bad when you get used to the wind, the rain, and the crushing sense of isolation and despair."

I give a tight smile, still wary of my host. "You're not from Keswick originally?"

"God, no. I grew up in Hastings but studied at Lancaster. It was as far away as I could get from my folks without crossing a national border." McGrath fiddles with his notebook. "So how is Cate?"

"Not good," I say. "She got hit by a car. She's in a coma." If Neyland were here she would object to my use of that word, but I am not about to launch into an explanation of vegetative states and minimally conscious states.

McGrath frowns. "I am sorry to hear that."

Is he less surprised than he should be? Less sympathetic? It is difficult to read his expression through his beard. And why isn't he asking about Cate's prognosis? I tune into his thoughts in case they hold the answer, but for now there is nothing there to see.

"You're probably wondering why I wanted to speak to you," I say.

McGrath nods.

"Before Cate's accident, she and I started a conversation we never got to finish. She told me she'd spoken to you a while back about a woman she was trying to find."

If McGrath is working with Mystery Woman, now is the time I will see her in his memories. Instead, I glimpse Cate sitting across from him at a table like this one. A different coffee house, perhaps?

Cate looks gaunt and grave. Strange how the people I have spoken to recently all perceived her in a different light. Between McGrath, Jake, Cate's therapist, and the owner of Firwood Cottage, I have seen all my daughter's different faces.

"I remember," McGrath says. "She showed me a sketch of a woman."

"What did the woman look like?"

He blows out his cheeks as he thinks back. And finally an image of Mystery Woman forms in his mind. It is not her real face, though, but rather a sketch of it. Cate's sketch, probably. I am as certain now as I can be that McGrath isn't in cahoots with Mystery Woman. This comes as both a relief and a disappointment since it means I can't use him to find her. "Long hair," he says. "Dark eyes. About your age. That's all I remember."

I pull out my E-FIT of Mystery Woman. "Is this her?"

McGrath holds the E-FIT at arm's length and peers at it. "Maybe. These pictures all look the same to me."

"You don't know the woman, then?"

"No."

I tilt my head. Something in McGrath's voice tells me that is not the end of the story. "But?" I say.

The journalist warms his hands on his coffee cup. Behind me, the shop's coffee machine steams and hisses. "But my dealings with Cate didn't end there. She asked me if the Herald kept copies of its old articles. She wanted to see if there were pictures of the woman from around the time when your son died. I pointed her in the direction of the microfilm archive at Penrith library."

"Did you ever speak to her again?"

For a while I fear McGrath won't answer. I can almost hear the cogs whirring in his head. He must be wondering what is so important about Mystery Woman that it could have dragged me away from Cate's bedside.

"Do you mind if I ask what this is about?" he says at last.

"That's what I am trying to work out. If I can retrace Cate's steps, I may have a better idea."

McGrath's look suggests he knows this is an evasion, but he answers my earlier question nonetheless. "Yes, I spoke to her again a few days later. She didn't find anything useful at the library. So instead she wanted to know about the police officers who ran the case into your son's death."

McGrath is watching for my reaction, but I'm not sure what to make of this revelation. Why would Cate be interested in the police? Perhaps when McGrath couldn't help her, she considered other people who might recognise Mystery Woman. And the police officers working at the time Cate first spotted her would be a good place to start.

McGrath adds, "Cate got her hands on a copy of the coroner's report into your son's accident. She was particularly interested in the parts about the lead officer, Detective Inspector Hewitt. You remember her?"

I nod. Hewitt was the woman who left Scott and me wanting to punch her. Lazy and confrontational, she was as sympathetic to our loss as if we had lost a set of keys instead of a son.

"Then you will also remember," McGrath says, "how the coroner tore strips off Hewitt in his report. Delays in arranging divers and search parties. Lost witness statements." He ticks them off on his fingers. "Apparently an inquest's worth of papers was put in the wrong file and never seen again. Hewitt tried to blame it on one of her juniors, but the coroner gave that short shrift. And yet for reasons I never understood, the DI escaped the affair with only a rap on the knuckles from her superiors."

This is all news to me. I never read the coroner's report into Ben's death. But I have no trouble believing the worst of Hewitt.

"Do you think Cate went to speak to Hewitt after she called you?" I ask McGrath.

The journalist raises an eyebrow. "I hope she had more sense than that," he says.

# 11

THE SUN IS SETTING AS I turn my car onto the road out of Keswick. I am on my way back to the Posthouse. I have already driven there three times this afternoon, only to continue past the guest house when I saw police cars outside. On the radio earlier, I learned that DI Hewitt of all people is investigating the fire, and that she is treating the circumstances as suspicious. Has she already identified Mystery Woman as the culprit? What a pleasant irony it would be if Mystery Woman were to be caught for one crime—the arson—while trying to cover up her involvement in another—Cate's hit-and-run.

I am not going to wait on Hewitt's enquiries before proceeding with my own. That is why I am returning to the Posthouse after hours—so I can show the pictures of Cate and Mystery Woman to the owners without Hewitt looking over my shoulder. According to radio reports, only part of the guest house was damaged in the fire. If the living areas were untouched then the owners might still be on site.

It is fully dark when I pull up on the Posthouse's forecourt. There is no damage to this side of the building; evidently the fire was started around the back. As I hoped, the police cars have gone. Unfortunately, all of the other cars have gone too, and not a single light shows in the guest house's windows. The place is deserted.

So what do I do now? Come back tomorrow? The owners will likely return in the morning, but so will the police. Maybe there is a sign in the window with the owners' contact details—for guests arriving now with reservations. If so, I might still be able to speak to them tonight.

I kill the headlights and get out of the car. On the air is a sour-sweet scent like burned honeycomb. As I cross the Posthouse's forecourt, gravel crunches beneath my feet. Somewhere a door or a panel has come loose; I can hear it thudding against a wall. A line of police tape surrounds the building, but I get close enough to observe there is no sign in the guest house's porch.

Square one, it is good to see you again.

I pace along the frontage and look through a window, but the blinds have been closed. It is the same in the next room I come to. I find myself wondering if the Posthouse's owners kept their old records on paper or computer. If on paper, where would they be stored? In a filing cabinet? Or out of the way in a cellar or garage? In either case, there is a good chance they escaped the blaze.

If they are kept on a desktop computer, things get trickier. Even if the computer survived the fire, it is unlikely the damaged guest house will still have electricity. The only way to see what is on it would be to break in and steal the computer to check through later.

Which I would never do, of course.

The banging of that loose panel starts up again. Perhaps it offers a way inside if I were minded to use it.

There is a path leading around the building. Reaching it would mean crossing the police tape, so instead I enter the garden. The rain has turned the lawn into a sponge. I can feel the wet soaking into my shoes as I squelch around the side of the guest house. The wind probes every gap in my clothing, and the chill is like needles across my skin.

I have to clamber over a low stone wall to reach the back garden. Here, I get a better view of the damage caused by the fire. In the roof is a jagged hole that looks like some monstrous creature has taken a bite out of it. Beneath the windows the ground is sprinkled with broken glass, while the windows themselves have been boarded up, as has a door to my left. Is that where the fire was started? The stonework around the door is blackened. With no time for anything fancy, Mystery Woman probably poured petrol on the door and set it alight. That would explain why the damage is not as extensive as I expected.

I place a hand on the police tape, still undecided on what to do next. From the hole in the roof rise tendrils of smoke that are shredded by the wind. The smell of burning has grown stronger, and I have a greasy taste in my mouth. Where is the loose panel I heard banging? I can't make it out in the darkness, but it must be close.

Am I really going to break in, though? Leaving aside the fact that I will be disturbing a crime scene, what are the chances of me finding what I'm looking for? Plus I might leave behind my fingerprints for Hewitt to—

I freeze. On the glass of an upper-floor window I see a glimmer of light. Before I can focus on it, though, it is gone. Just my imagination? There is no movement at the window to suggest someone is inside. It's possible what I saw was instead a reflection of something behind me. But when I glance around to check, I see nothing of interest. The garden stretches away before me. At the bottom, trees sway in the breeze, while beyond are the distant shadows of nameless hills. This place makes the middle of nowhere feel crowded.

I return my attention to the guest house. From inside I hear a creak of timbers. A footstep, maybe? Or a crossbeam settling down for the night? I cock my head to listen, but all I can make out now is the whistle of the wind and the rustle of leaves. It is probably nothing. If someone else were here, I would have seen their car on the forecourt as I arrived.

Unless they parked on a nearby road and walked the final distance. That way, they wouldn't have given away their presence. Like I have done, stupidly, by leaving my car out front.

I whisper a curse. I have had my fill of adventure for one night. What was I thinking coming here? Sneaking around a creepy burned-out house in the dark with a would-be killer on the loose . . . what could possibly go wrong?

I slip and stumble back the way I came, my senses straining for any sign that I have company. My breath plumes in the cold. When I reach the wall, I scrape my knuckles climbing over it—

A shadow looms out of the darkness in front of me. I stagger back against the wall, the air crawling in my throat. One of the stones in the wall shifts under my weight, and my first thought is to pull it loose and use it as a weapon.

Then a torch shines into my eyes. I blink against the glare.

"Well, well," a man's voice says. "What have we here?"

# 12

THE INTERVIEW ROOM IN KESWICK police station has the look of a nuclear bunker, and the hostile expressions of the two detectives sitting across from me only add to the bleakness. I have already revealed to them my position at the Met; my ID lies on the table between us. But it seems professional courtesy in these parts extends no further than providing me with a cup of muddy water masquerading as coffee.

On the right of the two sits Detective Inspector Hewitt in a polo-necked sweater and tracksuit trousers. She hasn't aged a day in the past five years. As she chews a stick of gum, she makes no effort to keep her mouth closed.

Beside her sits the young man who surprised me at the Posthouse earlier—DC Daniel Knox. Knox has a heart-shaped face and floppy hair, and his round, wire-rimmed glasses make him look like a university lecturer. His crumpled suit and crooked tie suggest that he, unlike his boss, has put in a full shift today.

The silence drags out. Hewitt must have spent too much time reading the Idiots' Guide to Intimidating Interviews, for she glares at me as if she expects me to crumble under the weight of her gaze. In reality I am grateful for this pause because it gives me a chance to consider how I will answer her questions. She won't believe I am chasing a woman from Cate's memories. But whilst telling the truth is out of the question, I don't want to get caught in an outright lie either. That leaves me a narrow line to tread, especially since I have no idea how much the detectives already know about my reasons for coming to the Lake District. Was it bad luck I bumped into Knox at the Posthouse? Or did McGrath tell him I was in town?

Knox sneaks a look at his watch. Apparently, I am not the only one with places I would rather be. Hewitt hasn't arrested me, so I am within my rights to get up and leave. Yet I know I must be on my best behaviour. I may not have broken any laws at the Posthouse, but Hewitt could make my life awkward for as long as I remain in Keswick. In any case, if I play this right, I could learn what she has found out about Mystery Woman.

Finally the DI tires of her own game. "Mrs Greenwood—" she begins.

"Ms Greenwood," I correct her.

"You're divorced? Oh, I am sorry to hear that. Aren't you sorry, Constable?"

Knox nods.

I take a breath and count to ten. Best behaviour, remember. "Thank you."

"So, *Ms* Greenwood," Hewitt continues. "It's good to see you again after all these years. What brings you to the Lake District?"

Predictably, she hasn't dived straight into what I was doing at the Posthouse. First she will no doubt lay a trap for me. "Unfinished business," I reply. "It was the anniversary of Ben's death a few days ago. I came to pay my respects."

Hewitt shakes her head in mock sadness. "A tragedy, that affair. Don't you think it was a tragedy, Constable?"

Knox nods again.

I count to twenty this time. At this rate we could be here for a while.

"Is that when you came to Keswick?" Hewitt asks. "A few days ago?"

"No. I arrived yesterday."

"Yesterday," Hewitt repeats. From her tone you would think I have admitted something unsavoury.

"You know, the day before today," I say.

Okay, so that one slipped out.

Hewitt shows no reaction. "Was that why you were at the Posthouse earlier? Because you were looking for somewhere to stay?"

I'm guessing the DI already knows the answer to that, so I say, "I'm staying at the Old Rectory."

"Is that so? It's odd, then, that Knox should find you at the Posthouse earlier. Unless you had some other reason for being there . . ."

She leaves the sentence hanging.

I do not respond straight away. What can I say I was doing at the guest house? "I was curious."

"Curious?"

"About the fire. I heard about it on the radio and thought I'd take a look." I shrug. "I blame my police background."

Hewitt reaches for my ID on the table. "Yes, about that," she says. "This isn't a warrant card, is it? It says you're a consultant for the Met."

"That's right."

"What do you consult on?"

"Advanced interrogation techniques." It's the answer I usually give when I don't want people knowing about my psychic abilities.

"Wow, sounds impressive. Are you impressed, Constable?"

Another nod from Knox.

"But you're not actually a policewoman, are you?" Hewitt says. "You haven't taken the oath."

"No."

"So to suggest to someone you *were* a police officer . . . well, that would be wrong, wouldn't it?"

"Correct." I wonder where this is heading. Somewhere with a hidden pit and spikes, most likely.

"The thing is," Hewitt goes on, "DC Knox here spoke to Ron Bailey at Firwood Cottage earlier. Just checking in with the other guest houses after the fire, you understand. Seeing if the owners had noticed anything unusual. And the only unusual thing Bailey could remember was you. He said you told him you were police."

"I said I was *with* the police," I respond. I don't know if that is true or not, but it's my word against Bailey's.

"He also told us you were looking for two women. Which is funny because you said you were here because of your son."

Hewitt leaves a silence for me to fill, but I say nothing. Since she hasn't asked me a question, I am not about to volunteer information.

"Who are these women you are looking for?"

I reckon I have humoured her long enough to warrant asking a question of my own. "May I ask why this is important? I'm not even clear why we're speaking now."

"Really? Well, let me put it this way. Twenty-four hours ago you arrived in the Lake District and started asking questions at Firwood Cottage. Half an hour later a different guest house goes up in flames. Then today we find you sneaking around the Posthouse for reasons I can best describe as flimsy. And you're telling me there is no connection to any of this?"

"Are you accusing me of starting the fire?"

"Did you hear me accuse her of anything, Constable?" Hewitt asks Knox.

The nodding dog shakes his head for a change.

"Then who did start the fire?" I say.

"I'll ask the questions," Hewitt replies. She sets her fists on the table. "What were you doing at the Posthouse?"

I keep silent.

Hewitt smiles as she chews her gum. "Exercising your right to silence, eh? Let me try you with an easier question, then. Where were you at 8pm yesterday?"

Hewitt says it casually, but I notice Knox go tense. His anticipation is tangible. He thinks he is about to catch me lying, and that must mean he and Hewitt already know the answer. But how? "I had just left Firwood Cottage," I tell Hewitt. "I was probably on the road to the Posthouse at that time."

A pursing of the DI's lips betrays her disappointment.

And then I see it. "You were in the car behind me," I say. "You were the one who almost ran me off the road." The timing makes sense. The Posthouse was in flames at that point. Hewitt and Knox must have been in the area when they received a call to investigate. A glimpse at Knox's memories confirms it. He is sitting beside Hewitt in the front passenger seat of a car, watching my taillights swerve and bounce through the darkness. I look from Knox to Hewitt, then back again. "You remember my car, don't you? Did you recognise it when you saw it at the Posthouse?"

It is the detectives' turn to stay silent.

"Well, this is a stroke of luck," I say. "I couldn't ask for a better alibi."

"How's that?" Hewitt snaps.

"When you overtook me yesterday, I was driving towards the Posthouse. If I had started the fire, I would have been heading in the opposite direction—away from the scene of the crime."

The DI shrugs as if that means nothing. Clearly she isn't about to let a small thing such as facts get in the way of her theory. "And why were you going to the Posthouse? Why did you go back there tonight?"

I do not reply.

We repeat the same conversation three times before the DI loses patience and bangs her hands on the table. My cup of muddy water jumps but does not spill. I get the impression Hewitt knows I didn't start the fire, but she also knows I am holding something back. She jabs a finger at me and says, "I'm going to nail you to the wall, *Ms.* Greenwood. You hear me?"

"To the wall. Got it."

Hewitt storms out and slams the door behind her.

I think that went well. I wait a few seconds, then get up to leave.

DC Knox raises a hand to forestall me. He shoots a glance at the door before speaking for the first time. "We're not finished yet," he says.

# 13

Sunday, 29 October
Evening

KNOX BEGINS BY TREATING ME to another dose of the silent treatment. A minute goes by. Two. I pass the time by counting off my hairs as they turn grey.

"Well, this is cosy," I say. "We must do this again sometime."

Knox gives a ghost of a smile. "When I spoke to Mr Bailey earlier, he said you showed him a photograph and an E-FIT. May I see them?"

I can't think of a reason to refuse him. I pass them across the table. Knox looks at the photograph of Cate, then at me.

"Hmm," he says. "I noticed the likeness the first time I saw you. The woman here, she's your daughter, isn't she?"

I blink. He recognised me at the Posthouse? Before I had even showed him Cate's photo? But that must mean ... "You know Cate?"

"I do. She came to see me a few weeks ago. We also spoke a couple of times on the telephone. She never explained where she got my name. But she told me she had been looking at old newspaper articles about your son's death, so maybe I was mentioned in those." He pushes his glasses up the bridge of his nose. "She showed me a sketch of a woman she was looking for. A woman who bears a remarkable resemblance to the one in this E-FIT."

I wonder if Knox is the mysterious detective Jake remembered Cate speaking to—the one I tried in vain to track down. But I have more important questions on my mind at this point. "And did you recognise the woman?"

He wags a finger at me. "Not so fast. I have talked for a while, now it is your turn. Who is the woman in the E-FIT?"

I study him for a second. Is he playing me straight? What if Hewitt is in the corridor outside, listening at the keyhole? Maybe she always intended to stamp off and leave me with Knox. Maybe this is her plan B in case she failed to bully the information out of me. "Are we off the record?" I ask Knox.

"We are."

I'm not sure I believe him, but I judge it is worth the risk. "I don't know who the woman is. If I did, I wouldn't be showing her E-FIT around."

"Then why are you looking for her?"

"Because Cate was."

Knox is unimpressed. "If it were that simple you could have asked your daughter about her. Why travel all the way to Keswick?"

"Because Cate was knocked down in a hit-and-run a week ago. She's in a coma."

The DC responds with the resignation of a man who frequently receives bad news in his work. "I'm sorry."

His sincerity makes a welcome change from the indifference I have received lately from the likes of Cate's secretary and her therapist. "Thank you."

"That's not the whole story, though, is it?" Knox continues. "You wouldn't leave Cate and drive three hundred miles out of curiosity alone. What is so important about this woman that you have to find her?"

I copy his wagging-finger motion. "Not so fast. I've talked for a bit, now it's your turn."

Knox's half-smile is back.

"Were you able to identify the woman in Cate's sketch?" I ask.

"I think so. It is five years since I last saw her, and that was only for a short time. But I believe she is one of the people who saw your son drown." He watches my reaction—or lack of it—then adds, "Well, well. Thank goodness you are sitting down. I can see my news has come as quite a shock."

It isn't a shock, of course. I knew from Cate's memories that Mystery Woman was present when Ben fell in the stream. "Did Cate say why she was looking for this woman?" I ask.

"She did not. But then your daughter was almost as evasive as you are."

I am beginning to like Knox. A pity. It will make it harder for me to deceive him when the time comes.

"All Cate would say," he goes on, "is that it was imperative she found her. She wanted me to give her the woman's name and address from our file."

"Which you wouldn't do."

"Actually, I did give her a name. There seemed no harm. But the address was more complicated. I don't know how much you remember about the time after Ben's accident, but the investigation ran into a few setbacks."

I recall my discussion with McGrath about the coroner's report. "Delayed search parties," I say. "Missing evidence."

Knox gives a stiff nod. He is looking defensive all of a sudden.

I play a hunch. "You are the one Hewitt tried to blame for everything, aren't you?" That is probably the only reason he is talking to me now, and why he was willing to accommodate Cate's request for a name.

"I was," he replies. "At that time I had only just joined Hewitt's team, so I made for an easy target." He tries to sound offhand, but there is a sharpness to his gaze that betrays his resentment. "The evidence of the woman you are looking for was one of the things that went missing. I remember speaking to her on the day of the accident, then preparing a written statement. But there isn't a signed copy on the file. So either she never did sign it, or we lost her details before she could do so."

"Did the draft statement have an address on it?"

"It did not."

"What was the woman's name?"

Knox holds up his hands. "Woah, there. It's your turn again. Why are you looking for her?"

"Because it's possible she was involved in Cate's hit-and-run."

"Involved how?"

"She was the driver. The E-FIT I brought with me came from an eyewitness description." I do not mention, obviously, that the eyewitness is me.

Knox is silent, considering. I can see the thoughts flitting behind his eyes. Doubtless he has already grasped the implications of my words, but it cannot hurt to spell them out.

"That's right," I say. "My daughter comes here to find Mystery Woman, and a few weeks later the woman runs Cate down in her car. Then yesterday I come to retrace my daughter's steps, and within an hour of me arriving a guest house is set on fire."

"You believe we are looking for the same woman?"

"It makes sense." I reach for my cup of coffee before thinking better of it. "What have you found out so far about the fire?"

"Little that I can share."

"Oh, come on, you can do better than that. I already saw the damage to the back of the Posthouse."

"Then you will know this was a petrol-and-match affair. Strictly an amateur job."

Are there professional arsonists, then? I wonder what the starting salary is. "Did anyone see who did it?"

Knox's shrug leaves me none the wiser.

"And the Posthouse's records? Were they destroyed in the blaze?"

"They were. But that may not be the end of the matter. Because after I spoke to Mr Bailey at Firwood Cottage, I also spoke to the owner of the Posthouse. I wanted to know if you had paid him a visit as you had Mr Bailey. He said no, but he remembered talking to your daughter a few weeks ago. Apparently she managed to persuade him to check his records and see if a certain woman had stayed at his guest house five years ago."

I suppress a smile. Some men cannot say no to a pretty face—though all men believe they are in the minority that can.

"His records went back five years?" I say.

"Six, actually. Something to do with the Statute of Limitations."

"And was Mystery Woman an old guest of his?"

"She was. Cate left with a copy of the form the woman filled in when she arrived, complete with her address and other details."

It is the breakthrough I have been waiting for. This form must be why Mystery Woman set fire to the Posthouse. But where is Cate's copy? In her flat, probably, since she won't have thrown it away. I will have to search her place again when I get back to London.

What if I can't find it, though?

I meet Knox's gaze and hold it. When I asked him earlier what Mystery Woman's name was, he didn't say he did not know; he just refused to answer. I need that information now in case Cate's form has gone missing. At least then I will have something to go on.

"What was the woman's name?" I ask.

"Vicky Evans." Knox watches me to see if the name means anything, but I have never heard it before.

"Thanks," I say.

He nods. "And if you should happen to find a copy of that form . . ."

"I will let you know."

Knox helps himself to my E-FIT of Mystery Woman, then stands to indicate the interview is over. I do not follow his lead immediately.

"Is your boss going to cause me more trouble?" I ask.

"Almost certainly."

"You're not a fan?"

He crosses his arms. "Hewitt's not so bad when you get to know her," he says, before adding in a low voice, "Said no one, ever."

I laugh.

"Just don't leave town until the DI gives you the nod, okay?"

"Whatever you say."

Twenty minutes later I am in my car on the A5271 out of Keswick, heading back to London.

# PART FIVE

# Karma

# 1

Monday, 30 October
Morning

AS I READ TO CATE in the hospital, I listen to the hum of her machinery. So much happened in the Lake District, yet here it feels as if time has stood still. Cate remains in precisely the same position that I left her. Her monitor beeps its endless rhythm. Indeed the only thing that has changed is the yellowing of her facial bruises. I can't deny a sense of disappointment. Pursuing Cate's trail to Keswick made her feel more alive somehow. Yet now when I look at her, she seems to belong more to the ranks of the dead than the living.

I finish a chapter in her book and set it down. I got back from Keswick at 1am, so my eyes are too gritty for reading. Instead I talk to her. Before her accident, the two of us could go for weeks without speaking, but now after just two days apart I find I have missed our chats—however one-sided they may be. I don't want to tell Cate about my trip to the Lake District. This is a chance for me to forget about the trauma of the past week before I throw myself into the investigation once more.

So I tell Cate about happier days. I remind her of our summer trip to the Cornish coast in '99 when we caught a lobster in the rock pools at Treyarnon Bay. And the time three years later when I fell asleep on a beach on the Île d'Oléron and woke up looking like a cooked lobster myself. Good memories—though I may not have thought so when I was buying a shop's supply of aftersun the next day. Time can play such tricks on the mind.

From outside Cate's room I hear raised voices. A glance through the internal window reveals Jake at the nurses' station. Scott told him we would contact him when we have information about Cate, so I don't know why he is here. Fortunately the nurses stop him coming through. I have asked them not to let him disturb Cate in future, and he takes the news with the lack of grace I expected.

My mobile buzzes. It is probably a message from Scott or Ranger—both have been in touch this morning to ask about my trip to the Lake District. When I check my phone, though, I find a text from DCI Mertin telling me it is CRITICAL that we meet. And since he has put it in capitals, it must be true. I reply to say I will come in this afternoon. First I must finish my shift with Cate, then go to her flat and look for the form that Mystery Woman filled in at the Posthouse.

I am close to finding her; I can sense it.

I wonder if she can too.

# 2

Monday, 30 October
Afternoon

FROM THE FLAT ABOVE CATE'S, I hear the clump of footsteps, while through the bedroom wall comes a thumping techno beat that sounds like the artist's impression of a migraine. I am trying to think where Cate might have put Mystery Woman's form, but the noise makes it difficult to concentrate. A single piece of paper could have been slipped into any of her files, and I spend twenty minutes flicking through them without success.

Where else could it be? Cate wasn't a spy that she would have hidden it under a loose floorboard. Nor did she have a flatmate from whom she needed to keep it out of reach. I check her bedside locker, her laptop case, the boxes under her bed. Here I find old books, bags of summer clothes, albums of photos from Cate's university days, but no form. Then I notice that her wardrobe has a drawer at the bottom, and I pull it out.

Beneath Cate's collection of shoes is a brown manila folder. I open it and take out its contents. Bingo. There are dozens of newspaper articles about Ben's accident—some photocopies, others printed off the net. Most are marked with a highlighter pen, and several have handwritten annotations in their margins. I also find Cate's sketch of Vicky Evans, a copy of the coroner's report into Ben's death, and a handful of unsigned witness statements including the one from Evans. Why did Knox never mention giving these to Cate? Is it possible she obtained them from another source?

I spread the papers out across Cate's bed. It must have taken her weeks to put this information together to the point of it becoming an obsession. But why? What drove her determination to find Evans? None of the scenarios I have envisioned previously account for this. I had thought Evans was in the woods on the day Ben drowned because she was doing something she shouldn't have been. Cate was a witness to her presence, and thus Evans wanted to silence her. But if that were so, Evans would have been looking for Cate, not the other way round.

Near the bottom of the folder I find Vicky Evans's form from the Posthouse. There is a coffee-mug stain in the top right corner, but it doesn't obscure any of the words. Scribbled on the form is Evans's address: 34 Randolph Mews, London. There is no district mentioned. No postcode. I cross to the bookcase and grab Cate's A-Z. Thankfully there is only one Randolph Mews in the capital—in Maida Vale.

I snatch up my car keys and head for the front door.

# 3

Monday, 30 October
Afternoon

I CRUISE ALONG RANDOLPH ROAD, looking for the turning into Randolph Mews. In Maida Vale, the pavements are barely visible beneath piles of fallen leaves. Every house has bay windows and mock pillars, and every parked car has that fresh-from-the-show-room feel. I love this area. I have a friend who lives close to the BBC studios on Delaware Road. After Scott and I sold our house in West Hampstead, I tried to buy a flat here with my share of the proceeds.

I still remember the pained expression of a local estate agent when I told him my budget.

Eventually I reach Randolph Mews. The road is barely wide enough to accommodate a car, so I park on Randolph Road and continue on foot. Now that my target is close, I find my anger building. I remind myself that I am here to scout the lie of the land, not to seek a clash with Vicky Evans. It is five years since she filled in the form, so she may have moved house since. My plan is simply to walk past number 34 and see if I can glimpse anyone through a window. I will also look for a car outside with a dented bumper.

I am definitely not going to burst in and confront her.

The houses on Randolph Mews consist of brick terraces adorned with potted plants and window boxes. One has a table and chairs outside it as if it doubles as a café. Opposite is a line of white garages. Since the houses are only on one side, their numbers rise sequentially. An old woman with a blue rinse watches my every move from the window of number 3. Her gaze prickles my back after I pass. I reach number 12, then enter a passageway that takes me under the first floor of two linked buildings that front onto Randolph Avenue. I emerge at the other end . . .

And stop.

Ahead are gates marked with the words "Robert Close". To my left, Randolph Avenue stretches into the distance; to my right, it extends a short way before meeting Blomfield Road. So where is the rest of Randolph Mews? Where is number 34? Beyond the gates? Behind the garages I saw earlier?

I turn back the way I have come, then understanding hits me.

There *is* no number 34. Evans has given a false address.

# 4

Monday, 30 October
Afternoon

I AM FASHIONABLY LATE FOR my meeting with DCI Mertin at Wandsworth police station. As soon as I arrive at his office, he ushers me inside. Papers are stacked on his desk with geometric precision. Beside them are the leftover crumbs of his lunch, and he sweeps them into one hand before depositing them in the bin. The lingering smell of warm bread makes my stomach grumble.

Mertin sits straight in his chair. There is an air of formality about him. Perhaps I should be worried about what this portends, but I am too busy fuming over Vicky Evans's bogus form. I was so close to finding her! Now everything I have worked towards has come to nothing. I will not abandon my search, though. Having started on this path, I must follow it to its end, no matter where it leads. I owe Cate no less.

"I had Inspector Hewitt on the phone earlier," Mertin says. "She tells me you're a suspect in an arson enquiry. Claims you've been tramping around her crime scene and generally being a pain in the arse. I told her not to take it personally since you're a pain in the arse to me as well."

I nod. It is good to know Mertin has my back.

He watches me expectantly. "Well?" he says.

"Well what?"

"What were you doing in the Lake District? You may not have to tell Hewitt, but you damn well have to tell me."

The truth won't serve me any better here than it would have done in Keswick. So I say, "I was catching up on some holiday."

"Holiday," Mertin repeats. He rises from his chair before turning to look out of the window. I don't know why—he can't see anything through the drawn blinds. The DCI is silent for a while. I am beginning to think I am dismissed when he asks me, "What's the last you heard about the Thornton case?" The change of subject takes me aback, but before I can respond Mertin continues: "I'm guessing you haven't checked in with Ranger since you interviewed Thornton on Friday. Why should you? Your daughter is in hospital. You are on leave." The DCI faces me again. "And it is fair to say I have accommodated you on that, right? I haven't pressured you—I haven't *obliged* you—to return before you are ready?"

"No."

Mertin scowls. "And this is how you repay me?" He jabs a finger at me. "Given that you travelled to the Lake District, you obviously felt able to leave your daughter's side. But did you come in to help with the Thornton investigation? Of course not. Instead, you buggered off to Keswick and messed up Hewitt's crime scene. What's the matter? Isn't ours good enough for you?"

I do not respond. No matter what I say it will be the wrong thing.

"Oh, I know what you're thinking," Mertin goes on. "You're thinking, we don't have a crime scene here. We don't even *have* a body. And whose fault is that?"

I stare at him.

"Yours, of course! You're the one who gave us Thornton pushing his car into a lake. But can we find the car? No. Then you gave us a mysterious accomplice sitting behind Thornton in his car. But can we find that accomplice, or a reason why they would help Thornton dispose of his daughter's body? No again." Mertin's voice is rising by the second. "Could that be, perhaps, because neither the lake nor the accomplice exists? Did you even stop to consider that possibility?" He makes a chopping motion with his hand. "Thornton has had us chasing shadows from the start. And you played right into his hands!"

My head is spinning. Does the DCI think that Thornton tricked me? That he invented the memory of the lake to make me believe he had killed Lily? But that would mean he knew I was a psychic. And neither he nor his solicitor gave any hint of that.

"You think Lily is alive?" I ask.

Mertin throws up his hands. "How would I know? The only reason we thought otherwise was because of what you saw in Thornton's memories. Even if he did dispose of his car like you say, it doesn't prove Lily is dead." He tuts his disgust. "You just assumed she was in the boot."

And what else was I supposed to think? Plus I wasn't the only one to reach that conclusion. Mertin was as guilty as me of adding two and two to get five. I push the thought aside. Could Lily really be alive? Is it possible we have been looking at this wrongly from the start? It always surprised me that Thornton lawyered up from day one. All he achieved by doing so was to make himself look guilty. But what if he wanted to look guilty? What if he wanted us to believe Lily was dead?

I shouldn't be getting mixed up in this. My hands are already full with trying to find Vicky Evans, yet I cannot deny the case has got me interested. "If Lily is alive, where is she?" I ask Mertin.

The DCI is a long time in answering. "My guess? In Brazil with her mother. Did you know Ranger spoke to Mrs Thornton at the weekend? Her daughter is missing, but she hasn't returned to London. And according to Ranger, her display of concern at Lily's disappearance was about as convincing as your story about holidaying in the Lake District."

I let that one go. "Did you find Lily's passport when you searched Thornton's house?"

Mertin shakes his head. "We've put out a port alert, and we're checking with the London airports to see if she flew out from there. But no hits yet. We're also checking Thornton's work laptop.

He wiped his search history, so it'll take the techs time to piece together what he's been up to."

"Let me speak to him again—"

"No!" Mertin cuts in. "You stay away from Thornton, understand? We need to give the techs time to do their job. Until then I don't want you anywhere near this case. The only reason we're in this mess now is because you rushed—you *blundered*—into Thornton's first interview without the full facts."

I cannot believe he said that. If I had had the full facts, I wouldn't have needed to speak to Thornton at all. That's what police do, isn't it? Question suspects to solve crimes. But I don't push it. If Mertin wants me not to do any work, that is one order I am happy to follow.

And yet the irony isn't lost on me. When he wanted my assistance, I couldn't give it. But now that I am offering to help, he says no. It makes me wonder why he called me in here. I have spent the last week doing my best to avoid the Thornton case; now he summons me to tell me to do just that?

I take my cue to leave and cross to the door. Mertin's voice draws me up short.

"Oh, and you're to have no further contact with DI Ranger, am I clear? I have told him the same. I don't know what you've got yourself involved in with your daughter, but you keep Ranger out of it. For his sake if not for yours."

# 5

Monday, 30 October
Afternoon

I FIND RANGER SITTING AT his desk—or at least I assume there is a desk under all the files and scraps of paper scattered across it. Normally my partner is as organised as Mertin, so the sight of this clutter leaves me feeling unsettled. Ranger stares at his computer screen as if it holds the answer to the meaning of life. At the next desk DC Underhill is engaged in a heated call with forensics over how quickly they can turn around fingerprint results.

I wave my hand in front of Ranger's face to catch his attention. "You survived the weekend, then?" I say.

He looks at me. "I suppose. I was in here for most of it. When I did get to see my parents, I spent the whole time waiting for them to ask me for money, and they probably spent the whole time waiting for me to offer. In the end, no one said anything." He picks up a paperclip and starts bending it out of shape. "They looked old. My dad in particular must have aged a year for every week since I last saw him."

I nod. I am worried I'll think the same when I set eyes on my own parents tomorrow. They have texted to tell me they are flying out from Auckland later. I haven't seen so much as a photograph of them since they emigrated three and a half years ago, so I suspect my first sight of them will come as a shock.

"By the time Saturday night came," Ranger goes on, "I got to thinking one of them had cancer or something, and that they needed the money for treatment. Maybe that was why they invented the story about mortgage payments—because they didn't want me knowing the truth."

"Time for some more detective work?" I ask, remembering his enquiries at the Land Registry about their home.

"I've got enough going on with this," Ranger says, gesturing to the papers on his desk. "Did Mertin fill you in on Thornton?"

"Just the basics."

"Media coverage over the weekend has prompted a flood of calls from people who claim to have seen Lily. Probably false alarms, but we've got to check them out. And while we're doing that, we can't be doing proper work."

"Such as?"

"Such as confirming the timeline for when Thornton really *did* pick up Lily on Monday night. There are only so many roads he could have taken from Earlsfield to Camberwell, so his car must appear somewhere on CCTV. But as yet we've found nothing." Ranger tosses the mangled paperclip into the bin. "We also need to get to the bottom of that anonymous tip we received at the start of the case. You remember it? The one that said Lily had been murdered? The speech analyst now reckons Thornton might have made the call himself. But apparently he muffled his voice somehow, so we can't be sure."

I voice the question I have been mulling over since I spoke to Mertin. "Why would Thornton want us to think Lily was dead?"

"To protect her from something, maybe?"

"But what?"

"We're still working on that. Are you here to help?"

"No. Mertin told me he doesn't want me involved. He says I'm to blame for everyone thinking Lily was dead. In fact it seems everything that's gone wrong with the case is my fault."

"Sounds reasonable." Ranger is trying to make a joke of it, but behind his light tone I can sense his disquiet. He appears more worried about my future in Mertin's team than I am.

"Any word from Harman?" I ask.

"Nothing you'll want to hear. She says she can't use your E-FIT of Mystery Woman because you won't tell her how you got it. Aside from that, the only new development is a kid who claims he saw a car with a dented bumper driving along Abbeville Road after the accident. He wasn't sure about the model, though. 'A big, dark car' was all he could say."

That narrows it down.

"What about your weekend?" Ranger says. "How did things go in the Lake District?"

"Fine," I reply, conscious of Mertin's warning not to involve Ranger further in my investigation.

Ranger shoots a meaningful look at the DI's door. "Fine, eh?" he says. "I feel reassured already."

# 6

IT IS DARK BY THE time I arrive at St Christopher's. I have visited Cate so many times here, I could find my way to the HDU with my eyes closed. But I have never known the hospital to be as quiet as it is tonight. From the rooms to either side I hear muted conversations and the drone of equipment, but the doors are closed as if their occupants have locked themselves in for the night. I feel an urge to step softly so as not to disturb the silence.

My thoughts keep returning to Vicky Evans. I am still smarting from the false address on her form from the Posthouse. But I have other options to find my target. Cate's laptop may contain clues to Evans's identity, so I could take it to our tech people to break the password. I also need to go through her papers again in case I missed something on my first flick-through. Then there is the Posthouse fire. Knox may have found a link between Evans and the blaze, so I need to speak to him again. And hope he isn't bitter over me leaving Keswick so abruptly.

I pass a cleaner mopping the floor and give him an apologetic shrug as I walk across the lino he has just washed. Then, as I reach the Sexual Health Clinic, I take my usual peek through the window in the door in case I recognise someone inside. From behind me I hear the tread of rubber soles, but when I look around there is no one there. I feel like I am in a Hammer horror film, pacing the corridors while I wait for the jump scare.

On reaching the HDU, I ring the bell at the entrance and am buzzed through. Immediately I sense something is amiss. There is a charge to the air that spells trouble. From the direction of the nurses' station I hear the slap of running feet, agitated voices. Shadows gather on the walls. A phone rings, but no one answers it.

I break into a half jog. This might not have anything to do with Cate, I tell myself. There are plenty of other patients in the HDU, and it doesn't always have to be my daughter suffering the emergency.

But deep down I know it is.

Around the corner, I see nurses scattering in every direction like birds startled by a handclap. Beyond, the blinds to Cate's room are open, and through them I glimpse Neyland leaning over my daughter. Cate's monitor beeps away like R2-D2 on speed. I rush for her door but don't make it that far. A nurse, in her keenness to intercept me, almost tackles me to the ground. She presses me to the wall.

For a second I struggle against her, but her grip is iron.

# 7

Monday, 30 October
Evening

BESIDE CATE'S BED, I SLUMP into my chair. Adrenaline has carried me along for the past half hour, but now it sets me down with a bump. Cate lies motionless beneath her faded green blanket, exactly as she always does, making it easy to believe tonight's crisis never happened. I'm still not clear what *did* happen, but just as the thought comes to me, Neyland strides into the room.

"Ms Greenwood," she says. "It's good to see you again." She has dialled up her sincerity to eleven, so there must be bad news coming.

I push myself to my feet. "Is Cate going to be okay?"

"Yes. There was a problem with her syringe driver—"

"Her what?"

"The pump that controls her flow of morphine. Unfortunately, she was given too high a dose."

"How?"

Neyland clasps her hands together. "We're not sure. Most likely one of the nurses misread the machine's readout when she operated it. But there's nothing to worry about. The excess morphine caused Cate's breathing to slow, triggering an alarm on her monitor. That alerted us to the problem, so your daughter would only have been on the high dose for a few minutes."

Nothing to worry about? I must have imagined the shrieking monitor and the flustered nurses, then. And of course Cate is in no position to tell us what effect the drugs had. I ask Neyland about the risks associated with excessive levels of morphine, and she concedes that overdoses can be fatal. Then she spends the next five minutes informing me how easily mistakes like this can be made, and why the hospital is not to blame.

When she finally departs, a nurse enters to check on Cate's equipment. As I watch her go about her business, I wonder if she was the one whose carelessness put my daughter in danger. I should be angry, but all I feel is relief. It is hard to believe I persuaded myself last week that it would be better if Cate had died in the hit-and-run. My reaction to this evening's events proves how wrong I was. I am not ready to let my daughter go. I never will be.

The nurse leaves, and I close the door behind her. In the HDU outside, the clamour has died down. I check my watch. It is only eight o'clock, yet it feels as if half the night has passed. I squeeze Cate's hand and feel a pressure back. Just an instinctive reflex, probably. When her eyes flicker open, though, my heart stutters.

I keep a tight rein on my excitement. She has opened her eyes before and shown no signs of awareness. My hopes have been dashed too many times for me to fall prey to them again.

Sure enough, when I move into Cate's line of sight, her gaze does not track me. The bruising around her eyes has diminished, and the red stain to the left one is fading. I search for something encouraging to say, but the words won't come. Is Cate aware of what happened to her earlier? In case she remains oblivious, I have no intention of enlightening her.

Her gaze holds me. It carries the same intensity I remember from the first time I read her mind—when I found out the hit-and-run was not an accident. I realise with a start that she wants to tell me something.

I hesitate, then close my eyes and sink into her memories.

Cate shows me the same hospital room we are in now. It stretches taller than I perceive it, but perhaps that is because Cate has only ever seen it from her bed. The marks and scratches on the ceiling are testimony to how intimately she has come to know her surroundings. Is this a memory from today? The dark window suggests it is night-time—so just a short while ago?

Then in Cate's mind I hear the click of her door opening and closing. Muffled steps are followed by movement in my daughter's peripheral vision. A face comes into view, and I half expect it to be my own.

But it is not me. It is Vicky Evans.

# 8

Monday, 30 October
Evening

I LEAN ON THE WALL next to the door to the hospital's security room. Inside, I hear Ranger speaking to a guard. When I called Ranger earlier to ask for his help, he didn't mention Mertin's prohibition on him getting involved. I feel bad for taking advantage of my partner again, but I need him to get me access to the hospital's CCTV footage. If I can prove Vicky Evans was in the HDU earlier, it will put me on a firmer footing when I ask Neyland if the accident with Cate's syringe driver might have been sabotage.

And what else could it be? Cate didn't actually see Evans tamper with the machine, but it is fair to assume the woman didn't drop by to check there were no hard feelings for the hit-and-run. It would have been easy for her to meddle with Cate's equipment, then slip away with no one seeing. I guess I should be grateful she didn't smother Cate with a pillow. If she had done that, though, she would have flagged her guilt to the police. This way she has made the incident look like an accident because the only witness—Cate—can't tell anyone what happened.

Except she has told someone. She has told me.

The thought of Evans being alone with my daughter leaves me feeling like I have a dozen spiders crawling in my gut. Foolishly, I believed Cate was safe in St Christopher's, but if Evans was prepared to kill her in a hit-and-run, why shouldn't she try to sneak in and finish the job? It seems so obvious now, I wonder why I didn't consider it before.

Ranger emerges from the security room and closes the door behind him. He is holding his warrant card, and he waves it under my nose.

"Sometimes I think this is all I am to you," he says, but he smiles to take the edge off his words.

I do not respond. He has been a better friend to me than I deserve.

"I have spoken to the security guard," he adds. "The guy was a bit jumpy. Kept asking me whether a crime had been committed, because if so he had to report it. I told him we were looking for a"—Ranger makes speech marks with his fingers—"*person of interest.* He shouldn't give you trouble."

"Thanks."

Ranger studies me for a moment. "Do you know what you're doing?" He isn't talking about me checking the CCTV, I know; he is referring to my pursuit of Vicky Evans.

"Not a clue," I reply.

"That's what I thought." He points to the door. "You'd better get in there. I'll sit with Cate until you're done."

The security room is as small as a miser's tip. Behind a desk to my right are three huge screens each showing a grid of nine CCTV images from cameras around the hospital. At the desk sits a man in a brown uniform. He has a birthmark on his forehead and a stomach so ample his belt is straining to contain it. On noticing me, he leaps to his feet and stares at me as if I am the first woman he has ever set eyes on.

Ken, as he introduces himself, tells me where the hospital's cameras are sited, how long the images are stored, and so forth. When he moves on to the legalities of recording patients receiving medical treatment, I feel like I do when someone mentions pensions. There is no camera in Cate's room, Ken explains, but there *is* one at the entrance to the HDU, as well as in the waiting room and at the nurses' station. I ask Ken to begin the search with the camera at the entrance—from 7.30pm, when I arrived at the ward.

Soon, I am looking at a picture of myself on the screen. Clearly Evans must have arrived before I did, so Ken pushes a button to rewind the image. Among other visitors to the HDU, I see a boy on crutches, a woman pushing a buggy, an old man staggering along the corridor as if the hospital were at a tilt. Then I notice a middle-aged woman in a red coat, and I ask Ken to pause the footage.

I study the figure. Strange. I saw Evans in Cate's memories just an hour ago, yet I am struggling to recall her face. Eventually I decide the woman is not Evans, for whilst they share the same nose and pencilled-in eyebrows, the woman in the picture is too old to be my target.

The next possibility is a nurse I haven't seen before. She bears a passing resemblance to Evans, but do I seriously think Mystery Woman has impersonated a member of staff? Nurses don't leave their uniforms lying around for strangers to steal, and it's not as if Evans could have picked one up at a costume shop. The uniforms in such places are meant less to fool hospital staff than they are to impress a partner in the bedroom.

Or so a friend tells me.

After a while, I sense Ken losing interest. Judging by the time-stamp on the video we have gone back more than three hours. But it is possible Evans entered the HDU earlier than that and waited for the right moment to creep into Cate's room. If this were a formal investigation, some constable would have to wade through—

A new figure appears on screen.

"Stop," I tell Ken.

The image freezes.

In the picture is a woman wearing a Nike baseball cap. Beneath it she has wavy blonde hair that hangs loose to her shoulders—like Evans. But what sparks my interest most is the fact that she keeps her head down as she approaches the HDU. Admiring her shoes, perhaps? Or deliberately hiding from the camera?

Ken moves the image forward a frame at a time, seeking a better view. I watch the woman lean down to speak into the HDU's intercom. Then she pushes open the door and enters the ward. In all this time I don't get so much as a glimpse of her face.

"Are there cameras in the corridor outside as well?" I ask Ken. As I see it, the woman might have hidden behind her cap from this camera, but she can't have crossed the whole hospital with her gaze on the floor.

Ken nods and presses some more buttons. The timestamp from the HDU footage has given him a point of reference, so he is able quickly to find the woman on another camera. This one is outside the door to the Immunology Unit. I see "Evans" pass by with a sprightly step. Her chin and mouth are visible, but the rest of her face is concealed by her cap. She moves out of shot.

Damn.

There are other cameras I can try. I will start with the ones in the HDU's waiting room and nurses' station. And if Evans doesn't show up on those, I understand from Ken there are dozens more scattered around St Christopher's, covering everything from the car park to the main foyer.

Sighing, I pull out a chair and sit down.

I hope Ranger has made himself comfortable in Cate's room.

# 9

Tuesday, 31 October
Morning

I AM WOKEN BY A tap on my shoulder. I prise my eyes open. Scott stands in front of me, looking dispiritingly bright and energetic. He is humming a tune that sounds like a song by the Killers, but there are so many wrong notes I can't be sure. As I groan and stretch, he gives me a cautious smile. I have spent the night sleeping in Cate's chair, and it has left creases in me that will take time to iron out.

In Scott's hand is a plastic cup of coffee from the hospital's café. He looks at it wistfully, then offers it to me. I decline.

"Late night?" he asks.

"You could say that."

I didn't disturb him yesterday with news about Cate's emergency, but there is no putting it off now. I rise and motion for him to join me at the window. From the courtyard outside, I hear the buzz of an air conditioning unit the size of a nuclear reactor. Keeping my voice low, I tell Scott about the syringe driver and about my trawl through the hospital's CCTV footage.

As I finish my story, Scott shakes his head in disbelief. "This is crazy."

I don't like the way he looks at me when he says it. "Which part?"

He ignores the question. "Did you find anything on the security tapes?"

"Nothing definitive." I spent two hours with Ken looking for the woman in the cap. The clearest shot we found was from the main entrance, but even then my target's features were in shadow. And by this time my eyes were so scratchy I had to hold my eyelids open with my fingers. I am pretty sure it was Evans in the picture—but then I am also pretty sure I spotted Elvis, along with Donald Trump and the Ghost of Christmas Past.

"What does Neyland have to say about your sabotage theory?" Scott asks.

"I don't know. I haven't seen her this morning."

"You must have spoken to her yesterday, though. How did she say Cate's morphine levels got elevated?"

"One of the nurses made a mistake when she increased the dose. But then Neyland had no reason to suspect foul play. And if a button can be pressed accidentally, it can also be pressed deliberately."

I wish I had thought to get the syringe driver dusted for prints. I could still do so now, but I don't know any scene of crime officers well enough to ask them to do a bit of moonlighting. And even if I did, how would I explain a CSI's presence to the nurses? Would they even allow an investigator in the HDU without going through official channels?

Scott purses his lips. "So the only reason to believe Evans was here at all is because you saw her in Cate's memories."

"You think Cate is making this up? Or that I am?"

"Of course not."

"Then what are you saying?"

"I just find it hard to believe . . ." Scott stops himself and starts again. "Maybe Cate sensed something was wrong when her monitor started beeping. Maybe her fears came out as a nightmare, and she imagined Evans in the room."

"I know the difference between a memory and a nightmare."

"Really? How many times have you read someone's mind while they were sleeping? Or while they were comatose?" I start to reply, but Scott speaks over me. "I've been researching Cate's condition on the net. No one knows what's going on in the heads of coma patients. How can you be sure what you saw in Cate's mind was real?"

"She wasn't dreaming!" I snap. "Her eyes were open. And you didn't see the way she looked at me. She wanted me to read her thoughts."

"Maybe. Or maybe you assumed she did because that was what *you* wanted." Scott puts his coffee down on the windowsill. "You didn't ask her this time if you could read her memories, did you? You just went ahead and did it."

My frustration boils over. "What does that matter?" It is clear Scott still harbours a grudge against me for the times I read his thoughts without permission. He is making this about us. But there hasn't been an "us" for four years.

"What exactly did Cate show you in her memory?" Scott asks. "Did you see Evans tampering with the equipment?"

"No. But Cate can only see what is right in front of her."

"So there's no proof the woman did anything to the syringe driver."

"Proof? This isn't a fucking courtroom."

"You know what I mean." Scott gestures to the equipment around Cate's bed. "How would Evans even know which machine to mess with? I don't understand what half these things do. Do you?"

"Maybe she's been doing research like you have."

Scott snorts.

"Why is this so hard for you to believe?" I ask. "Evans has already tried to kill Cate once. Why shouldn't she do it again?"

Scott does not answer, and I realise he has doubts not only about the syringe driver, but about everything that has happened this past week. He still thinks the hit-and-run was an accident. I try to see things from his perspective. I have yet to come up with any hard evidence against Evans, nor do I know of any reason why she should want to kill my daughter. But what other explanation is there for Cate's memories of the woman, and for the fire at the Posthouse on Saturday?

When I put this to Scott, his expression softens.

"I have no idea what is going on," he says. "But whatever the explanation is, it can't be any weirder than what you are suggesting."

# 10

Tuesday, 31 October
Morning

I ARRIVE HOME IN TIME to meet the postman on my doorstep, and he hands over the latest batch of bills for me to ignore. Inside, I take off my shoes and sling my coat over a chair. The gin bottle on the kitchen table is tugging at me like it exerts its own gravity, but for once I manage to resist. I have just two hours before I am due back at the hospital. Cate needs someone with her around the clock now. And since I am not going to convince my superiors to provide her with police protection, I will have to spend more time at her bedside.

But for how long? I can't watch my daughter forever. How soon before Evans tries to kill her again? How soon before she sneaks past my guard?

I have to find her.

On a table in my lounge sits the folder of papers I discovered in Cate's flat. I snatch it up and open it. On the top is a collection of newspaper articles from five years ago. I hadn't appreciated at the time how much coverage Ben's drowning received in the national press. There is a piece in the Guardian blaming his death on abnormally high rainfall—and by implication global warming. The Scotsman, meanwhile, has an editorial bemoaning the state of national flood defences. Unsurprisingly, both papers have used Ben's tragedy to advance their own agendas.

Next, I find an article from the Cumberland & Westmoreland Herald written by Peter McGrath. It talks about search parties and police divers, and includes a picture of Ben—the one I gave to DI Hewitt after his accident. It was taken at Legoland on Ben's third birthday and, in the background, there is a life-size Lego statue of a moustachioed pirate. Ben is giving his toothy, for-the-camera smile as he holds me in a joyful headlock. Not that you can actually see me in the picture, of course; I have been cut from the other half. It was the perfect snap of Ben, yet I succeeded in spoiling it by closing my eyes at the wrong moment.

I had forgotten about that day. Perhaps I made myself forget. That was a mistake, I now know. By failing to deal with my grief, I allowed Ben's death to rob me not just of his future but also his past.

Beneath the article is an unsigned police witness statement from a man called Uwais Fairall. I skim its contents. Fairall is the guy who tried to save Ben. He swam to where my son was flailing in Derwentwater, only to return with nothing more than Ben's bobble hat. There is another statement from his girlfriend Danielle Cooper giving the same information.

Next comes the coroner's report. Most of it is taken up by such scintillating subjects as the topography of the Lake District and the inclemency of the weather. But there is also a summary of the police witness statements in the case, as well as a page slating DI Hewitt's handling of the investigation. The harshness of the criticism is wince-inducing—the words "breathtaking incompetence" in particular draw my eye. It is almost enough to make me feel sorry for the inspector.

Almost.

But predictably the report contains nothing to help me find Vicky Evans.

I set down the document and look at the gin bottle in the kitchen. Perhaps it would be okay to have *one* drink.

Then my gaze falls on the form Vicky Evans filled in at the Posthouse. Maybe I should double-check the address in case I misread the house number. But no, when I look at it again it is definitely 34. I think about the road name: Randolph Mews. If I had to invent a false address, I would choose something common like Main Street or Queen's Road. Why did Evans pick Randolph Mews? Does she live in Maida Vale, or has she done so recently?

Something else about the form bothers me. I understand why Evans put the wrong address on it—if she was up to no good in the Lake District, she wouldn't want anyone using the form to track her down. Hell, maybe the name Vicky Evans is made up too. But if *all* of the information on it is false, why did she want to destroy it? Why risk setting fire to the Posthouse and being done for arson?

I scan the form again. In Cate's flat, I merely glanced at it because I was only interested in Evans's address . . .

My heart skips a beat. There it is: along with Evans's name and address, she has given her car's licence number.

Of course, the number could be wrong like the address is. But what if it isn't? The last hotel I stayed in wanted my car's registration so they could ensure only paying guests used their car park. Maybe that is why the Posthouse's owners asked for the information as well. Maybe they have problems with day trippers exploiting their facilities. If Evans didn't want to get clamped, she might have had no choice but to put her correct licence number on the form. And that would explain why she wanted to burn the thing before I could get my hands on it.

I call Ranger, and he agrees to run a check on Evans's number plate.

I wet my lips with my tongue. The gin is calling to me again, but I ignore it. Instead I search through Cate's papers for Evans's witness statement. The first thing I notice is that whilst Evans's name is at the top, the rest of her personal information is missing. It strikes me as odd that the woman gave a statement to the police. I have been working on the presumption that she tried to kill Cate because she didn't want my daughter reporting her presence near the cottage. But if that were the case, why didn't Evans flee the scene immediately? Why hang around to be interviewed?

Knox has already told me that Evans's statement includes testimony about Ben's drowning. As I read the document, though, I get another surprise. The account makes no reference to Ben falling in the stream. Instead Evans says she was walking beside Derwentwater when she saw my son washed into the lake. Most likely she lied because she wanted people thinking she was by the lake instead of in the woods. She describes seeing Ben thrash in the water, about hearing his cries for help—

The phone rings, and I grab the receiver. It is Ranger.

"I've got those details you asked for," he says. "The car is a 2008 Peugeot 407. Black. But there is no record of a Vicky Evans ever owning it."

I swear under my breath. So either Evans is a false name, or she gave a false number plate on the Posthouse's form. Or both.

"Who was the car registered to five years ago?" I ask.

"Ashleigh Imbriano."

It is a moment before I can speak. Imbriano. That is a name I haven't heard for years, and one I hoped never to hear again. My stomach feels like I have swallowed a lump of ice. When Ranger next talks, I barely hear his words.

"Sam?" he says. "Are you still there? Sam?"

"I'll speak to you later," I reply and put down the phone.

# 11

Tuesday, 31 October
Morning

MY CONNECTION TO ASHLEIGH IMBRIANO did not start with the car in the Lake District; it began nine years ago when Scott went on a corporate bonding weekend with some work colleagues. You know the sort of thing: where people get better acquainted while building log rafts and sailing them over waterfalls. When Scott returned home the following Monday, he was unusually preoccupied. Then the next day, as he came out of the shower, I noticed a suspicious mark on his neck. It looked like a bite, and not of the mosquito variety.

My doubts festered. I hadn't read Scott's mind for months, but one morning as he drank his coffee at the breakfast table, I succumbed to my temptation.

Then wished I hadn't.

Because it turned out that on his corporate bonding weekend, Scott and a female colleague had taken the "bonding" part too literally. The woman was called Yasmin—a girl fresh out of university who wore enough makeup to launch her own Avon catalogue. Yasmin was the one who gave Scott the mark on his neck. He was reliving that moment when I eavesdropped on his memories.

I doubt it was the first time he had strayed. Before we moved to Haddenham, there was a time when Scott came home at an

unearthly hour from an impromptu client dinner. It was only
when I read his memories later that I learned the dinner had been
a candlelit affair with a woman in a dress so revealing its creator
must have run out of material before he could finish it. Fiona she
was called. I never challenged Scott about the incident because it
might have been innocent. Plus I knew from past experience how
much he hated me spying on him.

But then the people who squeal loudest about their privacy are
always the ones with something to hide.

On the day I found out about Yasmin, I was initially too shocked
to confront Scott about her. I sleepwalked through the morning.
On the school run I drove into the back of a 4x4 and gave it a dent
to remember me by. Later, after a liquid lunch, my numbness gave
way to a rage that coiled tighter and tighter about me until I could
scarcely breathe. And I decided to get back at Scott in the worst
way possible: by doing to him what he had done to me.

At this time I was working as a teaching assistant at a Hampstead
primary school called St Joseph's. Luca Imbriano was one of the
Year Five teachers. In spite of his Italian name and parentage
he was born and bred in London, yet he tried to give himself a
Mediterranean mystique by adopting an accent straight from the
Dolmio adverts. Ever since I joined St Joseph's he had had his eye
on me. True, he never expressed his interest openly, but it was
obvious from the not-so-subtle glances across the staffroom and
the "chance" encounters in the playground at break times.

When I discovered Scott's infidelity, I arranged for Cate to go to a
friend's house after school, then asked Luca out for a drink. We met
in the bar at a nearby Premier Inn where I knocked back enough
gin and tonics to drown my mounting reservations. After that . . .

Well, the alcohol has taken away most of my memories of what
happened next. And it is welcome to keep them, too.

It was the worst mistake of my life. Now, as well as feeling angry
at Scott, I felt angry at myself. How could I challenge him about
Yasmin when I was as much in the wrong as he was? So the next
day I sloped into school and tried to forget all about it.

Except that Luca wouldn't let me. Maybe he had hoped our liaison would lead to something more. Or maybe he couldn't handle the fact that I was the one who ended the affair. For two weeks he pestered me for a repeat performance. I explained, I apologised, I insisted he back off, but to no avail.

So I walked out of St Joseph's and never looked back.

That should have been the end of the matter. But somehow Luca got my mobile number from school and continued to harass me. His stream of texts and voicemails would eventually have drawn Scott's suspicion, so one Saturday I went into town and dropped my phone in the Thames. That stopped the calls. Or maybe it didn't, who knows?

I never knew Luca was married. But to my shame, I never stopped to ask either. And Ashleigh has to be Luca's wife, right? She must have learned about our affair and decided to confront me about it. That is why she came to the Lake District five years ago.

But it leaves other questions unanswered. For example, if Ashleigh lived in London, why did she trail me all the way to Keswick instead of tackling me at home? More importantly, would she really stoop to murder because I slept with her husband? It seems unlikely. And even if she were sufficiently unhinged to do so, why target Cate in the hit-and-run and not me? And why wait so long after my affair with Luca to act?

Something is not right.

I turn on my computer. The quickest way to solve this riddle is to speak to Ashleigh herself. I open the BT Phone Book page and type "Imbriano" into the search box, but there are no hits in London. Not one. I go to the St Joseph's school website and find Luca isn't listed among the staff. He must have moved away from the area. But what about Ashleigh? Has she left London too? Or is she living here under her maiden name?

I call Ranger again. When he answers the phone, I hear bedlam in the background.

"What's happening?" I ask.

"We've caught a break in the Thornton case."

"Oh?" I can't say I'm interested, but I know I don't enquire enough about Ranger's concerns. I am so wrapped up in my own problems I have stopped considering anyone else's.

"Lily's been spotted on CCTV in the Eurostar terminal at St Pancras," Ranger explains.

"She's alive?"

"She was last Tuesday morning—the day after she disappeared. Cameras show her boarding the first train to Paris at 05:40. And it was Thornton's laptop that led us to her. Our techs found a link on it to the Eurostar schedule, as well as searches for flights from Paris to Rio. We're checking to see if Lily boarded one."

And why would Lily fly to Rio from Paris instead of London? Because by doing so she made it harder for us to track her movements, of course. If she had flown from London, we would have found that out as soon as we put out a port alert. Whereas by flying from Paris she kept her departure from the country secret for longer. Even I know you can travel on the Eurostar without the UK authorities checking your passport.

"What is Thornton saying about this?" I ask Ranger.

"Not much. But his solicitor is enjoying herself now that Lily is apparently safe. She says we would have found her days ago if we hadn't been so intent on pursuing her client."

"What about Mertin?"

"Mertin wants to close the investigation down. It's not a crime for Lily to leave the country. And whilst we might get Thornton for wasting police time, there's no appetite for that. The DCI just wants the case to go away."

I don't need to tell Ranger how stupid it would be to let this go. Lily wouldn't have gone to the trouble of sneaking out of the UK unless she had something to hide. Something big. We can't let her get away with a crime just because we don't yet know what that crime is. "What about Thornton's missing car?" I ask.

"Mertin is working on the assumption that it was stolen like Thornton said."

Because Thornton has proved such a reliable witness to date. I do not press the point, though. Ranger is not the person who needs convincing.

"I need you to check something for me," I say.

There is a pause. "Is Ashleigh Imbriano your Mystery Woman?"

"That's what I'm trying to find out." My mobile buzzes to tell me I have a text, but I ignore it. "Ten years ago, her husband Luca worked at St Joseph's school in Hampstead, but he has moved on. Is there any chance we could track him down through the local education authority, then use him to find his wife? Or ex-wife, if that's what she is now."

"Maybe. Do you know this Luca Imbriano?"

"I used to."

Ranger waits for me to explain, but I keep my silence. I am not going to share my tainted history with him unless I have to. "Are you going to tell me what's going on?" he asks at last.

"When I know myself."

He gives a weighty sigh. Over the clamour at his end, I hear his chair creak. "If I help you, it's on one condition: when you go to speak to Ashleigh, I go with you. Agreed?"

"Agreed." I would have asked him to come anyway, so it's not as if I am conceding anything.

"I'll make some calls," Ranger says. "But it might take a while. This Thornton business is keeping everyone busy."

"Understood."

I hang up and check the text I received earlier. It is from Scott. He needs me at the hospital urgently. He doesn't say what it is about. He doesn't even say there is cause for concern, but my heart sinks nevertheless.

I have learned that news these days only comes in shades of black.

# 12

IT TAKES ME TEN MINUTES to find a parking spot at St Christopher's, then the same again to fit my car between the white lines. Inside the hospital, my shoes squeak on the lino floor. As I turn into the corridor to the High Dependency Unit, I almost bump into a nurse coming the other way. He shoots me a glare as if it is my fault I cannot see around corners.

My phone rings and, assuming it is Ranger, I answer it without checking the number.

"Ms Greenwood?" a man's voice says. "It's DC Knox."

Shit. "I can't talk now."

"You don't have to talk, just listen. DI Hewitt wants to see you."

"Great. I have an opening in my diary next Monday."

"No, today. And here."

Hewitt wants me to go back to the Lake District? So she isn't willing to waste her own time travelling, but she is more than willing to waste mine. "That could be a problem," I say. "You know how it is, busy, busy."

"Really?" Knox replies. "Because when I spoke to DCI Mertin just now, he told me your workload is thin at present."

The constable sounds a lot less friendly than he was when we spoke on Sunday. Maybe he copped the blame for my premature return to London. Hewitt certainly has form when it comes to finding scapegoats.

I earn a second glare from another passing nurse—this time for using my phone in the hospital, perhaps.

"Can we cut the bullshit?" Knox says. "Someone called our operations room yesterday to say they saw an MX-5 leave the Posthouse after the fire. An MX-5 with a registration that starts KJ21. Ring any bells?"

Surprise, surprise, my number plate begins KJ21. "Let me guess, the tip was made anonymously. And by a woman."

"You got it."

Knox is smart enough to know that Ashleigh is trying to set me up. But DI Hewitt won't care about that. She has an excuse now to make my life awkward, and she will no doubt take full advantage.

"How is your investigation coming along?" I ask Knox.

"You know I can't talk about that. But speaking hypothetically, it is possible another woman was seen leaving the Posthouse after the blaze started. It is also possible she looks a lot like the woman in the E-FIT you gave me."

"Did anyone get a look at her car?"

"No comment. On a completely separate note, have you managed to find the form your daughter was given by the Posthouse's owner?"

I am silent, considering. I don't want Knox to get to Ashleigh before I do, but that is unlikely without my information about Luca Imbriano. Also, telling him about Ashleigh might get him off my back for a while.

"Yes," I say. "But she gave a false address on her form, so her name is probably false too."

"And?" Knox prompts. He must know I am holding something back.

"Her licence number was also on the form. Maybe we can use that to find her."

I hear the click of a pen. "What was it?" Knox asks.

I tell him. I have committed Ashleigh's registration to memory.

"I'll look into it," Knox says. "In the meantime, Hewitt is expecting you."

I have barely hung up before my mobile rings again. This time I check the caller first and see that it is DCI Mertin. So I don't answer. If I wasn't expecting to hear from Ranger at any moment, I would turn the thing off. Seconds later Mertin sends me a text saying, "Answer your phone!"

I wish I could, but my hands are tied. Hospital rules, and all that.

In the corridor, I pass Ken the security guard. He waves me a cheery hello as if we are best friends.

My phone rings again, and again I let it go to voicemail. When Mertin's next text arrives, I can feel the anger radiating from it.

"Get your arse up to Keswick!" it says. "That's an order!"

Or, rather, I presume that's what it says because I haven't read it, remember.

That's my story, and I'm sticking to it.

# 13

IN THE HDU, IT IS someone's birthday. Along the corridor from Cate's room, I see a window filled with balloons and hear "Happy Birthday" being sung in the strained tones of people who have nothing to celebrate. I shake my head. Who could work in a place like this? Who could handle the misery every day? My mother once asked me the same thing about my job in the Met, but it is more difficult for doctors and nurses. To be good at their job, they have to truly care, and the more they care, the more it hurts.

As I reach Cate's room, I notice a change to the rhythm of beeps that has become the soundtrack to my life. Scott stands on the other side of her bed. Behind him, light streams through the window, casting his shadow across Cate. Scott hums as he holds her hand. There is something about the way he grips it . . .

Understanding comes to me, and I stumble to a halt. He is not just holding her hand. *She* is holding *his* too.

Cate's head turns a fraction, and her gaze finds mine.

"Hi, Mum."

A tingle like pins and needles goes through me. She is awake. *Properly* awake. Four strides bring me to her bedside. I sit on the blanket and hug her. Tears sting my eyes, as they have so often of late. If I'm sad, I cry; if I'm happy, I cry. How unfair is that?

Cate returns the gesture with the briefest of hugs before her arms drop to the bed again. She feels so thin and frail, I suspect I could snap her in two if I tried. Then it dawns on me I am squeezing her too tightly considering her broken ribs. I release her and draw back so hurriedly I bang my head on the monitor arm extending over her bed.

"Steady there," Scott says to me before glancing at Cate. "Looks like your mum has designs on that bed when you're finished with it."

It is the feeblest of jokes, yet I laugh like he is the next Ricky Gervais. And of course that sets off my tears again. Cate tries a smile, but manages only the slightest curl to her lips. Her eyes have a haunted cast to them. She is clearly still hurting, and her movement remains limited. I feel my excitement start to drain away, yet I fight to hold it in. For once, the "buts" can wait. I want to enjoy this moment while I am able.

I grab a tissue from my handbag and dab my eyes. The silence draws out. Cate is too weary to speak, and Scott has doubtless exhausted his topics of conversation while waiting for me to arrive. There are so many questions I need to ask Cate about the revelations of the past few days, but this is hardly the time. I try to think of something to say that will not lead me into a discussion of the hit-and-run, or Cate's injuries, or my misadventures in the Lake District. In the end I prattle about the roadworks on the Kentish Town Road and the antics of the DIY enthusiast who lives in the flat above me.

I am boring even myself, so it comes as no surprise when Scott starts fiddling with his phone and Cate's eyelids droop.

I clasp my daughter's hand as she drifts off to sleep.

Scott motions me outside, and I follow him to an empty room along the corridor. Inside, the floor has been freshly mopped, but there is a stink in the air as if someone has hidden a body under the bed. Scott looks tired. His skin is pale, and his shirt hangs from his shoulders as if he has lost as much weight as Cate has. He embraces me. For a second, I think he means to kiss me too, but sense prevails. My memories of Yasmin and Luca have left me wanting to keep my distance from him.

"I spoke to Neyland a while ago," he says. "She gave me the same message she always does: Cate could go on to make a full recovery, or she could be disabled for the rest of her life. It's a positive sign that she has woken up, but we still don't know the extent of her brain injuries."

I nod. The woman sure does find the fence comfortable to sit on.

"Cate will need physiotherapy and psychotherapy and who knows what other therapies if she is going to recover fully," Scott adds. "So she'll have to stay in hospital for some time." He gives me a pointed look. "And that means we'll have to be here to help her through it."

I know where he is going with this. He's about to ask me to abandon my search for Ashleigh, but that is unthinkable when I am so close to finding her. I could get a text from Ranger at any moment with the woman's address. "We've been through this before," I say.

"We have, but Cate waking up changes everything. It's time to put this business with Mystery Woman behind us. When Cate is able to talk, you can ask her what happened in the hit-and-run. In the meantime—"

"In the meantime her would-be killer is on the loose."

"Which makes it all the more important you stay here and don't go wandering around the country again."

I open my mouth to speak, but Scott gets in first.

"Look, I'm not asking you to forget this completely. I'm asking you to shelve it until you've had a chance to talk to Cate and confirm that what you saw in her memories was real."

"It could be weeks before she is ready for that."

"So it takes weeks. Whoever this Ashleigh woman is, she's not going anywhere. Just consider it, would you?"

I take a breath and abruptly realise I am as tired as Scott looks. I cannot deny a part of me has had enough of this business. Cate needs me. A week ago, I berated myself for neglecting her before her accident. Yet thanks to my trip to Keswick, Scott has probably seen more of her this past week than I have.

Perhaps it is time for me to hand over the investigation to Ranger. If I really am close to Ashleigh, my colleague can take things from here. I trust him to finish the job in spite of Mertin's ban on him getting involved. Once Ashleigh is in custody, Cate can ID her as the hit-and-run driver. I can also get Harman to match Ashleigh's car to the paint and glass samples she obtained from the crime scene.

Job done.

I don't need to be there when Ashleigh is arrested. I still have questions I want to ask her, but do I seriously believe she will oblige me with answers? And anyway, Mertin won't let me come within scratch-your-eyes-out distance of the woman.

As for revelling in her downfall, I can save that pleasure for her day in court.

The idea seems more and more appealing.

Then a new thought occurs to me, and I focus on Scott again.

"How did you know the woman's name was Ashleigh?" I ask him.

# PART SIX

# Sirens

# 1

Tuesday, 31 October
Afternoon

THE TEMPERATURE IN THE ROOM has cooled a degree, yet Scott is suddenly sweating; I can smell it coming off him.

"What?" he says.

"Ashleigh. You said her name a moment ago."

"I must have heard it from you when we spoke this morning."

"Impossible. I only learned about her myself a couple of hours ago."

"Then you must have mentioned it just now."

I might have believed him if his expression didn't say so clearly he was lying. "No, I didn't."

Scott stays silent.

"It was you, wasn't it? You told Ashleigh I was going to the Lake District. That's how she was able to get to the Posthouse so quickly." I considered the possibility at the time, but dismissed it as crazy. It still *is* crazy. Yet it explains why Scott has been so keen for me to abandon my search for Ashleigh. And why he has consistently cast doubt on Cate's memories.

He glances at the door as if he wants to make a dash for it. His shaved head glistens. I tune into his thoughts. If I get a glimpse of Ashleigh, that will be enough to confirm my suspicions. But Scott has blanked his mind. I need to rattle his cage to see if I can shake something loose.

"What else did you tell her?" I ask. "The best place to run down Cate? Or when she would be alone in the hospital?"

Scott stabs his mobile at me. "Are you listening to what you're saying? I would never hurt Cate. In case you've forgotten, she's my daughter too."

"A fact you only seemed to remember when she got injured. You've had nothing to do with her for twenty-two years."

"We can't all be model parents like you."

His barb finds its mark, but I won't be distracted. I know he is lashing out because he wants to move the conversation away from Ashleigh.

"Did she tell you to keep an eye on Cate?" I ask. "Is that why you've spent so much time with her recently? So you could monitor her progress and report back?"

Scott says nothing.

"No wonder you never showed any interest in finding Ashleigh. You knew all along where she was."

His voice is cold. "I've told you already, Ashleigh has got nothing to do with this."

And finally I get the memory I've been waiting for. In Scott's mind, I see Ashleigh standing outside Moorgate tube station. She is wearing sunglasses and pulling a cigarette out of a packet of Benson & Hedges. As he approaches her, she gives him a coy smile.

"So you do know her," I say.

For a second I think Scott is going to deny it, but he must realise the game is up. His features relax, and he shrugs. "Fine," he says. "I know Ashleigh. She contacted me a few weeks ago at work. Said she had some information for me. Said it was only fair I knew. You see, it seems she and I have something in common." He pauses. "She told me about you and Luca. How you cheated on me."

My feelings of guilt are back, but I will not let him take the moral high ground. "And what about the times you cheated on me? What about Yasmin, and Fiona, and all the others I don't know about?"

Scott's look is unapologetic. He is plainly one of those men who thinks that if a woman has an affair she's a bitch, but if a guy does it he's Casanova. Or maybe he believes the fault here is ultimately mine for spying on his memories when I promised not to. Perhaps he is right. Perhaps we are both to blame.

Or perhaps he knows more than he has said so far.

My pulse is racing. Yes, I can see it in his eyes.

Sure enough: "But that's not all Ashleigh told me," he says. "It's true, isn't it? Ben was Luca's son, not mine."

It is the moment I have been dreading for the past nine years. And yet I feel relief that the truth is out. I have never told anyone this before—not my parents, and not Cate. Especially not her.

I always suspected that Ben was Luca's son from the timing of my pregnancy. But a suspicion is all it was until he was born. Then the truth became undeniable. Ben had Luca's dimples and dark eyes. And as he grew, he developed his father's curly hair and earnest expression. Every time I looked at him it felt as if fate were laughing at me. I wanted to forget my infidelity, but the memory of it—through Ben—would now follow me around forever. Here was justice.

I never arranged a DNA test to prove Luca's paternity because I never saw the need. A part of me didn't want to accept the truth. I hid behind excuses. I told myself I was blameless because Scott had strayed first. But things were not so simple. I never told Scott the truth about Ben. I wanted to. Indeed sometimes I think I started drinking in the hope the gin would lend me the courage to come clean. Instead I let Scott bring up Ben believing he was his son.

A while ago, I condemned Scott for keeping secrets from me, yet I was never brave enough to tell him mine.

I wonder how Ashleigh worked it out. Luca couldn't have known Ben was his son because he never saw him. Maybe Ashleigh pieced it together on the day she saw Ben drown. What if that was the reason for everything that came after? What if Ashleigh ran down Cate as a way of getting revenge? The thought makes me want to vomit. What if I am responsible for Cate's injuries?

"Is that what this is about?" I ask Scott. "Did Ashleigh try to kill Cate to get even with me?"

Scott shakes his head. "You're not listening," he snaps. "Ashleigh had nothing to do with the hit-and-run."

My anger returns. "Would you bet Cate's life on it? Oh no, wait, you already have. When you failed to turn in Ashleigh after the hit-and-run, you gave her the opportunity to mess with Cate's syringe driver."

"You're wrong. She swore to me she was in Edinburgh when Cate was run down."

"And you believed her?"

"Of course I did. Ashleigh's not like that."

"How would you know? You only met her a few weeks ago." I am almost shouting now. "Why can't you see the connection? A stranger appears in your life, then shortly afterwards Cate is attacked. Ashleigh used you to find her."

Scott does not respond, but his expression remains defiant. My gaze flickers to the mobile in his hand. I wonder if Ashleigh's details are on there. If Ranger can't use the woman's name to track her down, maybe I could use Scott's phone instead.

"Where is she?" I ask him.

Again, he does not reply.

"Where is she?"

I grab for Scott's phone, but he snatches his hand back. With his other hand, he pushes me. The shock of it, rather than the force, makes me stumble. I topple backwards and crack my head against the frame of the empty bed. It shifts on its wheels. My vision swims.

At that instant, the door to the room opens. A nurse enters—a matronly woman with a hint of a primary school headmistress about her.

"What in the name of all that's holy is this racket?" she begins.

Then she stops when she sees me on the floor.

Scott takes a step back. I shake my head to clear it.

The nurse looks from me to him. "I'm calling security," she says.

# 2

Tuesday, 31 October
Afternoon

I PACE BACK AND FORTH across Cate's room in time to the beeping of
her monitor. I am ten-cups-of-coffee twitchy, and my head throbs
from where I hit it on the bed. It might even hurt as much as I made
out to the security guard, Ken, when I gave him my version of my
clash with Scott. Now Scott is in the security room, taking his turn. I
pity Ken for having to try to make sense of the mess Scott and I have
made of our lives. If he has any ideas, I hope he shares them with me.

Cate shifts in her sleep, and my thoughts turn to Ashleigh. By
now, Scott will probably have warned her about our conversation.
How will she react? Will she panic? Is she desperate enough to come
after Cate again? No, after her failed effort with the syringe driver,
she will know I am expecting that. Plus the last time she sneaked
in here was at night. During the day, there are too many people
around the HDU to repeat the feat.

My phone buzzes to tell me I have a text. I am expecting another
rocket from Mertin, so I am pleasantly surprised to see it is from
Ranger. His message reads simply:

Ashleigh Walker, 315 Saltram Crescent, Maida Vale. Meet you
there in an hour.

Ashleigh Walker, not Imbriano. As expected, the woman has
reverted to her maiden name.

I hesitate. If I am going to get to Maida Vale in an hour, I will have to set off soon. But that would mean leaving Cate alone. Okay, it will only be for a short time. Earlier my parents phoned to say their plane had landed at Heathrow and they were on their way here. The journey should take them forty-five minutes at most, and there is little chance of trouble reaching Cate before they do.

But what is the rush to confront Ashleigh now? Even if she knows I am on to her, what can she do? Run away? People don't drop their lives at a moment's notice. The daily grind will have forged a dozen leashes around her neck, and trying to flee will only make them pull tighter. And where would she go that Ranger or Knox could not find her? Unless she has been training to be the next 007, she has no hope of evading the police.

I phone Ranger to push back our rendezvous at Ashleigh's house, but he doesn't pick up. So I wait two minutes and try again.

Still no answer.

What do I do now? Leave him a message? If he is on his way to Maida Vale, he may not receive it until he arrives. Which means a journey wasted. I can't do that to him after he has stuck his neck out for me like this. And what if he decides to speak to Ashleigh without me? I don't want him hearing her side of the story before he hears mine. She might even give him the truth.

I stop pacing. I have a chance to end this. To get answers from Ashleigh to the questions that still plague me, such as why she targeted Cate instead of me, and how she likes her prison food served.

My decision made, I seek out the matronly nurse and ask her to keep her eye on Cate until my parents arrive.

Five minutes later, I am in my car and heading for Maida Vale.

# 3

ON THE APPROACH TO THE Holland Park roundabout, the traffic is so bad there is a queue for the queue. I stare at my car's clock. It is half an hour until I am supposed to meet Ranger, yet it feels like I have been in this jam for twice that time. A bus blocks my view, so I cannot see what is causing the holdup. Behind me, a taxi driver leans on his horn, but amazingly this doesn't make the traffic move faster.

When I reach the head of the queue, I see a Volvo has demolished the wing mirror of a Range Rover. The drivers have exited their cars and are engaged in a healthy exchange of opinions. One of them—a woman in a headscarf—is waving an umbrella around as if she means to go into battle with it. After I pass her, I watch in my rear-view mirror as she gestures with the umbrella to her damaged car.

That is the first time I notice the old-style Merc a short distance behind me. It only catches my eye because it has edged out from the other cars to give the driver a better view along the road. Probably just keen to know what the delay is, so I think nothing of it.

Until a few minutes later, when I check behind me and see the Merc is still three cars back. I squint in an effort to see the person at the wheel. But the glare off the Merc's windscreen makes that impossible, and my trying causes me briefly to lose focus on the road in front. I almost hit a suited cyclist when he cuts me up without signalling. I beep at him, and he graciously apologises by giving me the finger.

As I turn onto the Westway, the traffic begins to flow more freely—only to snarl up again when I take the Paddington exit. On Warwick Avenue, I power through the lights as they are changing. The drivers of the two cars immediately behind me must be colour-blind because they manage to squeeze through after.

The Merc runs a red to keep up.

I frown. At any normal time I would think nothing of this. Bad driving in London is the rule, not the exception. But these are not normal times, and there is a simple way to determine whether the Merc is following me.

I take the next left onto a sleepy avenue and watch in my rear-view mirror as the first car behind me continues along the main road. The second—a Ford Focus—turns with me, as does the Merc.

Another left, then I pull up thirty metres along and look back. The Focus drives over the junction, but the Merc slows and stops.

That settles it: the car is definitely trailing me. The driver must have spotted my parked car and realised they'd been rumbled.

*Ashleigh.* It has to be her. No doubt she was following me in the hope she would get a chance to shunt me into moving traffic. Or maybe she planned to wait until I got out of my car so I could have a similar "accident" to the one Cate had.

For ten seconds, she and I hold our positions, each waiting for the other to move first. I consider driving away. But I am not going to run. I was driving to Maida Vale to confront the woman. If she has come to me instead, that saves me a journey.

I do a swift five-point turn that finishes with me mounting the kerb. On the pavement, a woman pushing a double buggy stops to admire my driving skills. By the time I am facing back the way I came, the Merc has gone.

I press the accelerator, and my car lurches forwards to the junction. To my left I see a trail of black exhaust fumes. The Merc is disappearing at speed. With any luck some learner driver will arrive on the scene to impede her flight. But then I remember that the slow ones only ever get in *my* way.

I set off in pursuit, crunching through the gears. My speedometer touches fifty. Houses and parked cars flash by on either side. The way the vehicles are parked bumper to bumper stirs a memory in me of Fletcher Street where Cate was hit.

Reluctantly, I ease off. However much I want to catch Ashleigh, I can't risk this chase ending with me scraping some unfortunate soul off my bonnet.

It is clear Ashleigh doesn't know this part of London from the way she slows at every turning to see where it leads. Eventually she takes a right. By the time I reach the junction, she is fifty metres ahead. The new road has a liberal scattering of speed bumps, and I go over the first one fast enough to make my stomach flip. In front, the Merc approaches a green light at a T-junction. I glare at the light and will it to turn red.

It does!

Ashleigh takes a second longer than is prudent to brake. She is obviously tempted to run this light as she did the one before, but the traffic on the main road has already started moving. The Merc's tyres squeal in complaint, and the back wheels swerve and slide as if the street is covered in ice. Ashleigh comes to a juddering halt level with the lights.

Got you.

As I pull up behind her, I get a glimpse of her blonde scalp over the driver's headrest. I jump out of my car and approach the Merc on the right, behind the driver. The Merc edges forwards, but there is nowhere for Ashleigh to go. She revs her engine, then bangs her hands against the steering wheel in frustration. I reach for the driver's door handle. My blood is up. I have no idea what I am going to say to Ashleigh, but I doubt it is anything I would repeat in polite company.

A voice in my head urges caution. I know this woman is dangerous. She won't have a gun, but what if she is carrying a knife?

I yank open her door, ready to slam it closed again if she tries anything.

Then stiffen.

Because it isn't a "she" in the driver's seat, it's a "he". Cate's ex, Jake, to be precise. Dressed in jeans and a Lacoste polo shirt, he looks as sheepish as a rack of lamb.

It is a moment before my mind starts to function again. The Merc's interior stinks of fresh leather. I stare at Jake. His Adam's apple bobs as he swallows.

"What the hell are you doing?" I say.

Jake won't meet my gaze. When he speaks, his voice is barely a whisper. "I left messages for you at the hospital. You never got back to me."

"So you thought you would follow me?"

"I wanted to know how Cate was doing. The nurses wouldn't let me see her." Jake's sheepishness has gone and he now looks as petulant as a five-year-old brought to heel. "They said you told them not to."

"And why is that, do you think?"

No response.

My thoughts burn. I want to shake some sense into Jake, but that would mean touching him. I knew he was a creep and a pest, yet his actions here promote him into stalker territory. They also shine a new light on some of the events of the past week. Like that time at Cate's flat when someone was spying on me. I thought it was Ashleigh, but what if it was Jake? If he followed me today, why not on Saturday too?

There is also my conversation with Cate's therapist, Pru. When I quizzed her about a change in Cate's behaviour, and about whether someone was causing my daughter problems, her reply was guarded. "I can't think of anything that might be relevant to your enquiries," she said. I thought she was protecting Mystery Woman. But what if she knew nothing about Cate's quest to find

Ashleigh? What if instead Cate had told her therapist about a more mundane problem such as a troublesome ex? Pru would have been justified then in not sharing the information with me.

My theory even explains the rape alarm and the self-defence spray in Cate's bedside locker.

I search for calm. Maybe I am leaping to conclusions. Maybe Jake is guilty of nothing more than caring too much for my daughter. It would be unreasonable to condemn him without first giving him a chance to justify himself.

I am in no mood to be reasonable, though.

Jake has left his car's engine running. Since I am on the driver's side, the key ignition is in easy reach. I grab the keys, then hurl them back along the street.

# 4

I HAVE PARKED OPPOSITE ASHLEIGH Walker's house in Maida Vale. Her fake address, Randolph Mews, is no more than a mile away. This is my first ever stakeout, and after ten minutes waiting I am already bored. There is no sign of Ranger. Is he caught in traffic? Or has he already gone inside? No, I don't recognise any of the nearby vehicles as pool cars. And besides, what reason would he have to speak to Ashleigh without me?

I stare at the woman's house. It is one of those three-storey affairs with a grand, classical air that makes it feel like it is looking down on me. The immaculately groomed hedge in the front garden is a sign of a misspent life. In a first-floor window, I spy movement behind the net curtains. Meaning Ashleigh is home? Good news, since she could equally have been at work.

Though the figure might be a husband or a child instead. Has Ashleigh remarried? Does she have children of her own? I realise I know nothing about the woman's life, or the other lives that will be ruined when she is arrested. Worse, I don't think I care.

Five minutes pass. I turn on the radio and listen to some songs without hearing them.

My windscreen begins to fog up. I shift in my seat.

I cannot face staying in my car any longer, so I get out to stretch my legs. I am more likely to be spotted by Ashleigh this way, but it gives me a chance to check if any parked cars have dented bumpers or cracked windscreens.

No such luck.

I walk as far as the corner with Denholme Road, then turn around and come back. A boy in a hoody slinks past, taking care not to step on any cracks in the pavement. Overhead, a plane roars unseen through the clouds. Reaching Ashleigh's house, I see again the figure in the window, carrying what looks like a pile of clothes. Is Ashleigh putting away the laundry? Or packing for a journey following a warning from Scott?

She pauses at the window and seems to look in my direction. I wish I could make out her face to confirm she is the woman from Cate's memories. But it has to be her, doesn't it? All of the paths of my investigation lead here. Her contact with Scott alone is enough to prove she is the person I am looking for.

The buzz of my phone startles me. It is a text from Ranger:

Got intercepted by Mertin. On my way now.

When he sent it, was he setting out from the station? Or was he already en route and just dashed off the message at a red light? If the former, it could be an age before he gets here. If the latter . . .

I try calling him, but it goes straight to voicemail.

That's it, I have waited long enough. I march to Ashleigh's front door, only to stop with my finger on the bell. I feel as queasy as I used to do before sitting exams. Every instinct tells me to walk away. I came here for answers, yet I cannot shake the feeling I won't like what I am about to hear.

Too bad. No more hiding from the facts. Better the hard truth than the comfortable lie.

I take a breath and press the bell.

# 5

IT TAKES SO LONG FOR Ashleigh to answer, I begin to wonder if she means to ignore me. Then the door opens and I come face-to-face with Cate's would-be killer. Ashleigh is wearing cropped trousers and a black ribbed sweater. She is shorter than I imagined, and her blonde hair has an unexpected note of strawberry to it. But otherwise she is just as I remember from Cate's memories.

She stares at me bleakly. It is clear she isn't surprised to see me. She glances over my shoulder as if expecting to see squad cars with flashing blue lights. When she finds the road empty, some of the tension eases from her expression. She looks at me again. For a second, I think she is going to slam the door in my face. Then her lips quirk in a resigned smile, and she stands aside to let me enter.

The ground floor of her house is an expanse of cream and black. An internal wall or three has been removed to create an open-plan lounge-kitchen-diner, and the sense of space is enhanced by a huge gilt-framed mirror on the wall to my left. The place is cleaner than Cate's hospital ward and equally soulless. There are no splashes of colour, no personal touches. In the lounge, the mantelpiece is devoid of family photos, and there is a pale rectangle on the wall where a portrait once hung—a picture of Ashleigh and Luca, no doubt.

"Can I get you a coffee," Ashleigh asks as she closes the front door.

This encounter is already starting to get an unreal feel to it. Here is the woman who tried to kill Cate and set me up over the burning of the Posthouse. Yet I am supposed to forget that and have a drink with her?

I agree to the coffee anyway; it seems childish not to.

The kitchen has the same drab feel as the lounge. Every surface is immaculate, save for the stainless steel fridge with its incongruous blobs of Blu-tack. I stand in the space between the kitchen island and the dining area. Ashleigh puts the kettle on, and I endure a minute of silence while I wait for the thing to boil. As she adds milk to my cup, I make sure she doesn't slip in anything hazardous like sink cleaner or artificial sweeteners. She offers me the drink, and I set my handbag down on the kitchen island before accepting the cup.

"I wondered when you would show up," Ashleigh says. She has a strange habit of turning her head so she can inspect me with her left eye. Perhaps the vision of the other one is poor.

"If you were that keen to meet me you could have called by any time," I reply. "I'm sure you know where I live."

Ashleigh's attempt at a smile comes out more as a grimace. She is feigning calm, but her act is given the lie by the tightness to her expression. "How did you get this address?"

So Scott hasn't told her everything? Perhaps they are not as close as I thought. "The form from the Posthouse. It had your car's registration number on it."

Ashleigh looks confused.

"When you started the fire, you destroyed the original," I explain. "But Cate already had a copy."

"Fire?" Ashleigh says. "I don't know what you're talking about."

So that's the way it is going to be, is it? With just the two of us here, I don't know what Ashleigh hopes to gain by lying. But perhaps she fears I am not the only person listening to her answers. "I'm not wearing a wire, if that's what you're worried about."

Ashleigh studies me before shrugging. I don't know if she believes me or not.

From upstairs, I hear a creak. For a second I think someone is up there, then I realise it is just the floorboards settling. Ashleigh crosses to a door leading onto the back garden and opens it. A draught steals through. Outside, I hear the whirr of a distant lawnmower, the murmur of traffic from Saltram Crescent.

Ashleigh says, "I wondered if it was Scott who told you where to find me. I thought his conscience would get the better of him eventually, but I guess I underestimated his pettiness." A look flits across her face, but it is gone before I can see it clearly. "You know, when I told him about your affair with Luca, he refused to believe it at first. Created quite a scene, actually. It wasn't that he trusted you—far from it. It was more that his pride wouldn't let him accept the truth. Then I showed him a photo of Luca and he couldn't ignore the resemblance between Ben and his father."

She blows on her coffee, her gaze never leaving mine over the rim of her mug. "Odd, isn't it? When I found out about you and Luca, my instinct was to blame myself for what happened. Maybe I hadn't been attentive enough, or maybe I should have let Luca have that threesome he always hinted at. Scott was different, though. He admitted to having cheated on you, but when it came to your affair with Luca he blamed everyone but himself."

I regard Ashleigh dubiously. Why is she picking on Scott? Is she trying to foster some sort of female solidarity between us? Does she think we'll sing "I Will Survive" together, then embrace and go our separate ways?

Ashleigh's gaze has a discomforting intensity to it. "I always knew Luca had a wandering eye," she says. "When we first got together he was seeing another woman. He said he would end that relationship, but it took him a month to do so. Even afterwards he kept in touch with her because they were such *good friends*." Ashleigh sneers. "When he asked me to marry him, I thought those days were over. I should have known better. But then it's true what they say, isn't it? A woman marries a man expecting him to change, whereas a man marries a woman expecting her to stay the same. And they both end up disappointed."

Ashleigh looks at me as if she wants me to say something, but I haven't come here to talk philosophy.

"I remember after he joined St Joseph's school," she continues. "I invited the other teachers around for a barbeque. Just being friendly, I said. But I made it my business to seek out the pretty women and find out if they were threats. Those that were, I did my best to get to know—less chance of them stabbing me in the back that way." Ashleigh forces a light tone. "But I never counted on you. You must have joined St Joseph's after the party. Imagine how different things might be today if you had arrived sooner. We could even have been friends."

It is a sobering thought. "How did you find out about me and Luca?"

"From the mums outside the school gates. I went to meet Luca one day after work, and I heard two women gossiping about the latest scandal—something about a teacher who had slept with a colleague, then hounded her from school when she ditched him. When I confronted Luca afterwards, he swore you meant nothing to him—like that would make me feel better. Instead it made things worse. If he had loved you, maybe I could have understood it. But to risk our marriage for an affair that meant nothing?"

For a second Ashleigh's mask of composure slips, and I get a glimpse of the predator beneath. Her hatred is so strong I want to step back. Then she recovers her poise. "Did the affair mean anything to you?" she asks, but she does not give me a chance to answer. "Of course it didn't. You were the one who ended it within a week. It makes me curious, though, why you slept with him. Did you wake up one morning and think, 'I know, I'll ruin someone's marriage today'?"

This from the woman who began dating Luca when he was in another relationship. I wonder how much thought Ashleigh gave to Luca's girlfriend at that time. But I know that doesn't excuse what I did. Nothing does. I would tell Ashleigh I am sorry if I believed it would mean anything to her. She would laugh in my face, though, and perhaps she would be right to. This isn't some confession box where I can bare my soul and get my slate wiped clean.

Ashleigh hugs her arms about herself. She is shivering in the draught, but she doesn't close the back door. Maybe she intends to escape through it later. "You weren't Luca's only affair," she says. "There was a family friend in Italy, then a secretary in the school he moved to after St Joseph's. Each time he swore he had learned his lesson, and each time I was stupid enough to believe him. But not to *trust* him, oh no. Which is why I kept an eye on his texts and emails. And do you know what I found in his browsing history one day? A link to your Facebook page. Three years after your affair, he was still keeping tabs on you. I guess he must have lied when he said you meant nothing to him."

My stomach feels sour. "I didn't know he was still watching me. He never tried to get in touch."

Ashleigh shrugs. "When I saw that link, I had to find you. I wasn't sure what I would do when I did. Maybe I wanted to hurt you like you had hurt me. Or maybe I just wanted to find out what was so *special* about you." She sips her coffee. "It wasn't easy to track you down. St Joseph's wouldn't give me your address, and you were sensible enough not to leave clues on your Facebook profile. But you did say who your husband was, and men are never quite so careful about keeping their lives private. They don't have to be, do they? So I went to Scott's Facebook page and guess what I saw?"

The answer is obvious. "A photo of Ben."

Ashleigh nods. "It wasn't the best picture. Ben was wearing a cap that hid half his face, but the resemblance to Luca was clear. I had to be sure, though, and that meant seeing him in person. I found out from Scott's Facebook page where he worked. Then one evening I followed him home from the office." Ashleigh's gaze turns distant. "It was the day you left for the Lake District. I remember sitting outside your house in my car, staring at your closed curtains. I wanted to knock on the door and tell Scott what I knew, but even more than that I wanted to drive home and forget everything. Then you came out holding Ben's hand. He was in a

Winnie the Pooh hat, smiling Luca's smile. All I could think of was how much your affair with Luca had cost me—and how much you had gained from it. Next thing I knew, I was following you to the Lake District."

Ashleigh's voice is all rough edges. I have to remind myself that Cate, and not Ashleigh, is the true victim here. Whatever grudge this woman has against me, there is no excuse for what she did to my daughter. "Did you ever tell Luca about Ben?" I ask.

"No."

"Why not? It was the perfect chance for you to get back at him—to taunt him about the child he wouldn't get to know."

"Revenge was never in my mind."

I bark a laugh. "Of course it was. Why else would you try to kill Cate?"

Ashleigh looks at me mildly. "But I didn't try to kill Cate. As I told Scott, I was at a writer's conference in Edinburgh at the time of the hit-and-run—I'm a freelance journalist, if you didn't know. You can check if you like. God knows, there were enough witnesses." Ashleigh gives a slow smile. "Your precious daughter has been lying to you."

# 6

Tuesday, 31 October
Afternoon

"I DON'T BELIEVE YOU," I say.

"Of course you don't," Ashleigh replies. "But I still have my convention ticket, my receipt from the hotel."

"Which proves only that you paid for those things, not that you were actually there."

"So speak to the other people who were. I'm sure you'll find plenty who can back up my story. And if you don't believe them, why not read my mind? That's what you do, isn't it?"

Meaning Scott has told her about my abilities? If so, I won't be able to trust anything I see in her thoughts. Still, I sneak a look at her memories. She is in a dimly lit conference hall, surrounded by scruffs and fidgeters. At the front, five women sit behind a table on a stage, each with a microphone and a name tag before them. As the one in the middle speaks, the crone on the left yawns and picks her nose.

"That doesn't prove anything either," I tell Ashleigh. "The scene you showed me could have happened at any time. Or you could have made it up entirely."

"Just as Cate made up the memory of me in the car that hit her?"

I don't credit that with a response. I'm not going to let Ashleigh trick me into thinking Cate lied to me. Even if Ashleigh's story of going to Edinburgh checks out, there will be a hole in it somewhere. Maybe she slipped away from the conference and came back to London to attack Cate.

But slipped away with no one noticing? And all the way from Edinburgh? That's a round trip of more than ten hours.

Then maybe she got someone else to drive the car that day.

But no, that isn't possible. In Cate's memory it was definitely Ashleigh behind the wheel.

Ashleigh sets down her coffee cup on the worktop. "Come with me, there's something I want to show you." She leads me into the lounge and to the window fronting onto Saltram Crescent. "Look outside," she says, pulling open the net curtains. "See if you can guess which car is mine."

I am not in the mood for games. "What's your point?"

"Not going to play? Fine. It's the yellow Mini Cooper over there."

"And?"

"And I'm assuming there must have been witnesses to the hit-and-run. What colour did they say the car was?"

I think back to my conversation with the recruitment agent, Paul Jorden. "He didn't see it clearly. It was nighttime."

"But yellow is a colour you can't miss no matter how dark it is. And what about Cate? She must have seen my car if she was able to put me in the driving seat. Was it yellow in her memory?" Ashleigh gives me a second to reply, then adds, "It wasn't, was it? That's because she didn't know what colour my car is. She made it all up."

I struggle to marshal my thoughts. There is a logic to Ashleigh's reasoning that I find hard to dispute. I recall Ranger telling me about a kid who saw the hit-and-run car shortly after the accident. Big and dark, he described it as. Clearly Ashleigh's Mini doesn't fit that description.

And yet, are the details of the car so important? Maybe Cate made a mistake about the vehicle, but I can't believe she was wrong about its driver. In her memory, the image of Ashleigh at the wheel was as clear as it could have been.

"You could have borrowed someone else's car," I tell her. "Or hired one."

"And returned it with a dented bumper?"

"You could have repaired it first."

"I could have done. But where is your evidence? Where is your proof for any of this?" Ashleigh releases the net curtains and they fall back into position. "Scott told me about Cate's accident at the hospital—apparently I am to blame for that as well. Something about a syringe driver. Remind me, when did this happen?"

"Yesterday around six."

"Perfect! Monday night is piano night. I have a watertight alibi—again." Ashleigh looks at me. "You still don't see it, do you? First the hit-and-run, now the syringe driver. I'm supposed to be responsible for both, yet the only proof you have for me being there is your daughter's memories. Did any of the nurses see me in Cate's ward? Did you? I assume you checked the hospital's CCTV."

My mind reels from one revelation to another. Again, Ashleigh's logic is persuasive. I watched hours of CCTV footage from St Christopher's, and I found no conclusive image of her. At the time, I convinced myself she was the woman wearing the cap, but am I guilty of twisting the facts to suit my theory? And whilst her piano-night story for yesterday could be a fabrication, how likely is that? If she made it up, I could disprove it with a few phone calls. What does Ashleigh gain by telling a lie that is so easily refuted?

The alternative, though—that she is speaking the truth—makes no more sense. Cate would not deceive me. Aside from anything else, by pointing the finger at Ashleigh she lets the real hit-and-run driver go free. And why would she blame Ashleigh if the woman wasn't guilty?

"Why would she try to set you up?" I say.

"Ask Cate."

"Are you saying you don't know?"

"I'm saying, if she hasn't seen fit to tell you, I don't see why I should."

That strikes me as an evasion. Ashleigh has no cause to be discreet with Cate's secrets. The only reason for her to keep quiet is because she has something to hide. "Why was Cate so desperate to find you?" I ask. "And why were you so desperate to stay hidden that you set fire to the Posthouse?"

No response.

"Something happened three months ago, didn't it? One minute Cate was getting on with her life, the next she gives up her job to hunt you down. Why?"

Ashleigh glances at the front door. "I think it is time you left."

The hell it is. If Ashleigh doesn't like my line of questioning, that means I am on the right track. I know she won't tell me where that track leads, but with the right prompting she might give away something in her memories. In the meantime, I have to keep her talking. "Do you know the lengths Cate went to trying to find you? Speaking to reporters. Looking at old newspaper clips. She even got a sketch of you made so she could take it to the Lake District and show it around."

Ashleigh says nothing. In her mind, she is still picturing that scene from the writer's conference. Nothing I have said so far has made it waver. Clearly she has fixed on the image in an attempt to stop her thoughts wandering onto something else—something she doesn't want me to witness.

"Cate must have seen you recently," I continue. "Her sketch was as accurate as any I've known. And she wouldn't have remembered your face clearly if she hadn't seen you for five years. Did she spot your picture on Facebook? Or in a newspaper, maybe?"

"Get out," Ashleigh says, but what is she going to do if I refuse? Call the police?

For a second the image of the conference hall in her mind wavers, and I get a glimpse of a railway station. There is a crowd around Ashleigh and another one on the opposite platform. But that is all I see before the picture is replaced by the five women on stage again. Ashleigh is guarding her thoughts well. How long can she keep it up?

"Why did Cate try to track you down after she saw you?" I ask. "Because she recognised you from the Lake District? No, there has to be more to it than that."

Could it have been because she saw Ashleigh with Scott? That would have drawn her curiosity, and I know from Scott that Ashleigh first approached him around that time. But is it enough to explain the file of papers Cate collected about the woman? I don't think so. Cate could have just asked Scott who Ashleigh was. And why would Ashleigh be reluctant to tell me about that now?

An idea comes to me suddenly, and it feels as if someone has grabbed a handful of my guts. There is a way to fit all the missing puzzle pieces into place, but the picture it forms is . . . impossible.

I look around Ashleigh's lounge and see with fresh eyes the empty mantelpiece and the pale rectangle on the wall. I had thought the missing photos were of Ashleigh and Luca. But they separated many years ago. Any pictures of the two of them would have long since been taken down. Those gaps make me think the photos were removed recently—because Ashleigh knew I was coming, most likely. And the Blu-tack on the fridge? Maybe there was once something there too that she didn't want me to see. The same thing that Cate saw three months ago, perhaps?

Because instead of seeing Ashleigh with Scott, maybe Cate saw the woman with someone else. Someone who shouldn't have been there.

As I search Ashleigh's eyes for confirmation, her gaze shifts to something behind me and a look of alarm crosses her face. I hear a footfall. Then a small voice says, "Is it okay if I come down now, Mummy?"

I spin around. Before me stands a boy wearing a Batman tee-shirt and a solemn expression. He must be eight now, but there is no mistaking him.

It is Ben.

# 7

Tuesday, 31 October
Afternoon

I STARE AT MY SON. The chubbiness of his toddler days has gone, and he is now all arms and legs. Five years ago, his fringe seemed to get in his eyes no matter how often it was cut. Now his hair has been trimmed short and is as tidy as everything else in this house. I recognise my own features in the shape of his eyes and jaw. As a baby he looked like Luca's child, but the years have transformed him into mine.

And yet it cannot be Ben. In Cate's memories, I saw him fall into the stream. I saw him swept away.

*You lost sight of him behind the bridge*, a voice inside me says. *You didn't see him drown.*

But others did. There was that couple—Uwais Fairall and Danielle Cooper—who were walking by the lake. In their witness statements they said Fairall swam out into Derwentwater to try and save Ben.

*Then they lied. Or they were confused about what they saw. Ben's body was never found.*

Only because the floodwaters carried him far into the lake. And because DI Hewitt was slow to organise police divers. Ben was only three. He couldn't have survived the water. Everyone said so, even the coroner.

*But "everyone" had no reason to think Ashleigh might have kidnapped him. Ashleigh, who followed you all the way from London. Ashleigh, who had cause to resent Ben's birth after your affair with Luca.*

I remember the statement she gave to DC Knox—the one where she claimed she was by the lake when Ben drowned. I thought she had only said that to hide the fact she was in the woods, but she must have actually gone to Derwentwater so she could give false evidence. It was a clever move, too. From that moment, the police were looking for a body rather than a missing child. And Knox had no reason to think Ashleigh was lying. He didn't know who she was. Even I wouldn't have recognised her if I'd seen her at that time.

I feel as if a weight is pressing against my chest. My son is alive! I want to run to him and hug him, but my limbs are like mud. He called Ashleigh "Mummy". When he glances my way now, there is no recognition in his gaze. He does not know me—nor I him. I have missed the last five years of his life. With Cate, those years were the happiest of my life. It is the time when the toddler fades and the person they will become starts to emerge. The time when a parent is their child's whole world, and they are yours.

Ashley has taken that from me. The thought of this woman playing mother to my son triggers a rush of blood so hot I want to scream in her face.

"Go to your room and shut the door," Ashleigh tells Ben.

"But Mummy—"

"Go!"

I raise my hand to halt him, then let it fall. I don't want to let him out of my sight, but if I grab him and make a run for the door, Ashleigh will try to stop me. Most likely Ben will too. I am a stranger to him. And I am not going to abduct my own son. In any event, there are things I still need to ask Ashleigh, and her answers are not for his ears.

So I let him go.

He trudges upstairs.

Ashleigh returns to the kitchen, and I follow her. She closes the back door. I suspect she only opened it earlier to cover any noise Ben made upstairs, but the need for that has now passed. Ashleigh stands with her back to me, looking out into the garden. In her mind, I glimpse an image of her pushing Ben on an old swing while they sing "Row Your Boat". The memory should be mine. But she has stolen that too.

"I imagine you have questions," she says.

I do not respond. I want to speak—to give her a piece of my mind—but the words trip on my tongue.

Ashleigh is silent for a while. "You already know that I followed you to the Lake District that day," she says finally. "By the time we got there, I regretted going after you. But it was too late to drive home again, so I stayed the night in the Posthouse. I planned to drive back to London the next morning, yet I ended up taking so many sleeping pills that I slept through until lunch. Then, when I woke up, I wanted to see Ben one more time. So after I checked out of the guest house, I went back to your cottage and waited for him to appear."

She turns to face me. "I saw Ben fall in the water. Cate tried to catch up to him, but there was no path on her side of the stream. When she ran back to get you, I went after Ben. I found him just beyond the bridge. The stream takes a turn there, and Ben was floating face down by the outer bend. By the time I dragged him to the bank, he had stopped breathing. It must have only been for a few seconds, though, because when I rolled him onto his stomach he started coughing."

I witness the scene in Ashleigh's memories. To her left is the bridge, while in front is the bend in the stream where a jumble of sticks and leaves has collected. Ashleigh gathers Ben up in her arms. He is choking and crying and calling all at once. Calling for me.

"My car was parked on a nearby road," Ashleigh goes on. "I carried Ben to it and wrapped him in a blanket. He was in shock. I told him I was going to find you. Maybe some part of me meant it too, but I don't think so." She shrugs. "My mind kept turning over. I knew everyone would think Ben was dead. So what was there to stop me from taking him? Cate had seen me at the stream, but she didn't know who I was. And I hadn't met anyone else while I carried Ben to the car. I had this mad idea of taking him to Luca and pretending he was ours. Luca would see himself in Ben's features just as I had. Then he would come back to me, and we would have the family I always wanted." Her left eye focuses on me. "The family you took from me."

From upstairs comes the sound of a cupboard door slamming. Ben begins stomping around his room in an apparent effort to get attention. I want to go to him, but Ashleigh's voice holds me.

"So when Ben finally calmed down, I took his hat and coat and went to Derwentwater. My plan was to leave his clothes in the shallows, but I got lucky. There was a couple walking by the lake, close to where the stream enters it. When they weren't looking, I threw Ben's hat and coat as far as I could into the water. Then I started screaming and shouting about a boy drowning."

Ashleigh's mouth turns up in the faintest of smiles, yet somehow that makes her face look harder. "The man was so desperate to be a hero. He swam out to where Ben's coat was floating, even dived under the surface to look for him. Of course, he returned empty-handed. But afterwards I kept telling him and his girlfriend about how I'd seen Ben in the water. Eventually they convinced themselves they had seen him too." Ashleigh's smile disappears; maybe it was never there at all. "The rest you probably know. When you turned up at the lake looking for Ben, I made sure to keep my distance. I went back to the car for a while to stay with Ben, then returned in time to give a statement to the police. They made things easy for me by losing their file. If they had discovered I gave them false details, they might have come looking for me to ask why. But they didn't. No one did."

She looks at me, but I say nothing. My mind is only starting to function again. Ashleigh takes my silence as a cue to continue. "I know I shouldn't have stolen him," she says. "But I never planned it that way when I followed you to Keswick. I never wanted any of this."

There is no way I am letting that go. "Bullshit," I say. "When you checked in at the Posthouse, you gave a false name and address. You must already have been planning to do something, else you wouldn't have given the wrong details. What were you planning to do, Ashleigh?"

"I don't know! All I could think about at the time was you and Luca. I wanted to get back at you, but I didn't know how. When Ben fell in the stream, I just reacted." Her look is pleading. "You have to understand. This was only a few days after I learned about him for the first time. I wasn't thinking straight. Later, when I came to my senses, I knew I had made a mistake. That's why I didn't tell Luca about Ben as I had planned. I wanted to bring Ben back to you. But I knew if I did, the police would come looking for me. And I still hadn't forgiven you for Luca." She tries to stare me down. "But this isn't about you and me any more. This is about what is best for Ben."

"And what is that?" I ask. As if I don't already know what she is going to say.

Ashleigh does not answer straight away. I can see her struggling for words. "The years after the accident were hard on Ben," she says at last. "You don't know what he went through. For months he had nightmares . . ." She breaks off. "If I had come home with a child, my neighbours would have noticed, so I had to leave my old life behind. My house, my job, my friends—gone overnight. I moved from place to place, never staying long enough for people to ask questions. And we lived that way until Ben forgot about you and the accident." She is sounding increasingly desperate. "Don't you see? We are settled here. He is happy."

"Happy," I repeat dully. How dare she use that word of a boy she has stolen from his family? Of a boy who is living a lie?

"He remembers nothing of his old life," Ashleigh says. "As far as he is concerned, I am his mother. You can't take that away from him." Her voice cracks with emotion. "Please. He is only eight.

Maybe when he gets older, he will be ready for the truth. But not now. Until then, you could see him occasionally. Get to know him again."

I cannot believe what I am hearing. The woman is offering to let me spend time with my own son? Like this is some fucking custody battle. What will she suggest next? That I pay maintenance towards Ben's upbringing?

And yet, what happens if I turn her in? Ashleigh will go to jail for snatching Ben, and he will lose the only family he knows. Will the fact that I am his real mother soften the blow for him? Of course not. He doesn't remember me. Worse, I will be the person who separated him from Ashleigh. I will ruin his life. How long will it take him to recover from that? He might never forgive me. For Ben, it would be better if I had not come here.

But I cannot just walk away. I doubt anyone could. Does that make me selfish? Would leaving him with Ashleigh be the "right" thing to do? Is there such a thing as a correct choice here?

I wonder if Ashleigh would be so noble if our roles were reversed. She talks about putting Ben first, but she wasn't thinking of him when she stole him five years ago. And how convenient that what is "best" for him now happens also to be what is best for her.

She must have guessed my thoughts, for a shadow falls across her face. "I saved Ben," she says. "If I hadn't found him in that stream, he would be dead."

"And I am grateful," I reply. Truly, I am. But she is a few currants short of a fruitcake if she thinks that gives her the right to kidnap Ben.

"You owe me," she says. "Twice over, actually, considering what happened between you and Luca." She takes a step towards me. "You took something from me, so I took something from you. That is only fair."

There is nothing I can say to that, so I do not respond. How messed up must Ashleigh be that any of this makes sense to her?

She advances another step. The contrite, humble act is wearing thin, I notice. "It was your fault he almost drowned," she says.

"You let him play by that stream with only Cate to watch over him. But then failing your children is what you are best at, isn't it? Scott told me what kind of mother you are. After Ben's accident, you were so busy feeling sorry for yourself, you left Cate to deal with her guilt alone. Now, she didn't even trust you enough to tell you Ben was alive." Ashleigh twists the knife deeper. "Falling in that stream was the best thing that ever happened to Ben. You don't deserve to be his mother."

Her words hit hard, yet which of her accusations have I not levelled at myself before? As Scott pointed out, when I first read Cate's mind last week, I put my desire for vengeance over her well-being. Then I ignored the risks again when I did the same to find out how Cate knew Mystery Woman.

But I have learned my lesson. No one knows my flaws better than I do. I will make it up to Cate in future. It is all I can do.

And I will not take lectures on parenthood from a woman who steals children.

"I've heard enough," I say. "I'm leaving, and I am taking Ben with me."

Ashleigh's expression crumbles. Her look is one of such misery that for a second I can't help feeling pity for her.

Then she pulls a knife from a knife block on the worktop and jumps at me.

# 8

Tuesday, 31 October
Afternoon

THERE IS NO TIME TO turn and run. Ashleigh lashes out with her knife, and I stagger back into the dining area. Three more steps, and the dining table presses into the small of my back. I have heard people say that at moments like this, time slows down. Maybe that is true, but not in a good way. For when Ashleigh aims another swing at me, my body feels like it is working on a half-second time lag. I try to block her arm, but her knife cuts a line of fire across my bicep.

I shove Ashleigh back and scramble out of range.

Blood runs down my arm, soaking my shirt crimson. Ashleigh comes after me, her knife held out in front. I look around for a weapon of my own, but the only thing I can use is a ceramic vase on the table. I grab it and hurl it at Ashleigh.

She ducks, and the vase sails over her head. Threads of spilled water whip through the air. The vase flies into the lounge and lands on a sofa before depositing its flowers on the floor.

Ashleigh advances.

Fighting down panic, I retreat behind the dining table. I was a fool to let things come to this. What did I think Ashleigh would do when I threatened to take Ben away? When you back an animal into a corner, it shows its claws. But the self-recrimination will have to wait until later. For now, I need a plan.

I could shout for help, yet what are the odds of someone outside hearing me? I could risk a dash for the back door, but if I flee the house I will leave Ben alone with this woman. And I am not going to do that. Better to run upstairs and barricade myself in a room with my son. If I push a bed or a wardrobe across his door, Ashleigh won't be able to break through to us.

The trouble is, I am presently on the wrong side of the table to go for the stairs. And as I start to circle towards them, Ashleigh halts and blocks my way. Has she read my intent? The knife in her hand has a hypnotic draw; I cannot take my eyes off it.

"It's over," I tell her. I'm not stupid enough to think she will believe me, but I have to try something to distract her.

Ashleigh does not reply.

"Put the knife down," I say. "You still have a chance to walk away from this."

Still no answer. It seems the time for talking is past.

Across the table, Ashleigh tenses. I think she is going to hurl herself at me, but instead she puts her hands under the table and *lifts*. The tablecloth slides to the floor. Then the table itself tips and falls onto its side before bouncing and shuddering to a stop.

The barrier between us is a lot smaller all of a sudden.

I swallow. My injured arm now has a chill to it, as if warmth is seeping out through the cut. I half lift one of the dining chairs, thinking to use it to keep Ashleigh at bay, but the damn thing weighs more than I do.

"Think of Ben," I say, a quaver in my voice. "If you do this, you will never see him again."

Ashleigh shakes her head. "He is my son now. No one is going to take him away from me."

With the table on its side, we are standing only a metre apart. I feint to run to my right, but Ashleigh steps across to block me again. She jabs the knife at me to force me back. Then she starts clambering over the table, throwing her left leg across first. For an awkward second she straddles the wood.

This is my chance. With Ashleigh hampered, I rush for the stairs.

But Ashleigh must have anticipated the move. Withdrawing her left leg, she kicks a chair into my path. It catches my hip as it falls, and the impact half spins me round. For an instant I am running sideways, my legs overtaking the rest of my body. Then I sprawl to the floor.

I can sense as much as hear Ashleigh behind me.

Flipping onto my back, I see her drop to her knees beside me. Her knife stabs for my chest. With both my hands, I grab her wrist on the downswing.

The knife's tip stops a short distance from my body.

Ashleigh bares her teeth, air snorting in her nose. The muscles in her forearms stand out. Blood has run down from my arm to my hand, making my grip on her wrist slick. I buck and twist, but Ashleigh's full weight is bearing down on me, and I do not have the strength to throw her off. Sweat stings my eyes. Inch by relentless inch, the knife moves closer. Ashleigh's face hovers above mine, her eyes fever bright.

The knife presses into me. Pain rips through my chest. I scream as the blade burrows into my flesh before scraping against one of my ribs.

Then another pair of hands closes around Ashleigh's wrists and drags her off.

# 9

Tuesday, 31 October
Afternoon

MY BREATH SAWS IN MY throat. When I try to get up, my vision swims. Across my chest, my blouse is wet with blood. Am I dying? No, the knife didn't go past my ribs. There is no way such a shallow wound could prove fatal. I am . . . almost certain of it.

I hear a man's grunt. Ranger's, I know instinctively. He must have come in via the back door. Through my streaming eyes, he and Ashleigh appear as wavering shadows, like reflections on water. They wrestle for the knife, tottering and rocking as if they are standing on the deck of a pitching ship.

I try to rise again. The mistake I made the first time was to attempt to move all at once. Instead, I start by lifting my head, then a hand, then an arm. My chest burns so hot it feels like someone has lit a fire there. Blackness hovers at the edge of my vision, but I will not succumb to unconsciousness and leave Ranger to deal with Ashleigh alone. So I stagger upright and cling to the arm of the sofa while I wait for the room to decide which way is up.

On the sofa I notice the vase I threw at Ashleigh. I grab it and turn.

My sight blurs once more, but it clears in time for me to see Ranger and Ashleigh lurch into a wall. They dislodge a framed Dali print that crashes to the floor. Ranger has one hand around Ashleigh's wrist, the other around her neck. Ashleigh brings her knee up and catches him a blow amidships. Blood drips from the end of her knife—my blood, I realise.

I stumble towards them. With my wits scrambled I am as likely to hit my partner as Ashleigh, but I reckon Ranger's skull is thick enough to take a blow.

I wait for Ashleigh to turn her back on me. Then I swing the vase with all my strength, almost swinging myself off my feet in the process.

It connects with Ashleigh's head and shatters into a dozen pieces. Bullseye.

Ashleigh drops to the floor like wet sand, dragging Ranger down with her. He lands on top of her, and the air leaves his lungs with a great *whoosh*. For a few seconds he lies across her in a strangely intimate embrace. Then he rolls off her and onto his back, fragments of the vase crunching beneath him.

My legs give way, and I sit down with a bump. The floor is spinning so much it feels like I am going to fall off it. When I smashed the vase on Ashleigh's head, I managed to slice open my left palm. I close my hand and watch blood ooze between my fingers. A wave of nausea sweeps over me. I'm sure there must be some part of my body that doesn't hurt, but I can't think of anywhere in particular.

I look at Ashleigh. She has finished up on her side. There is a graze on her cheek where Ranger must have scratched her, and blood leaks from her scalp where the vase struck her, staining her blonde hair crimson. I guess I should call for an ambulance, but my phone is in my bag on the kitchen island.

From upstairs comes a creak. I hear a door open, then Ben's steps on the landing.

"Mummy?" he calls.

"Don't come down!" I shout. Ben must not see me or Ashleigh like this. "Ranger," I hiss. "Keep him up there."

But Ranger does not respond.

That is when I spot the knife sticking out of my partner's chest. I feel the colour drain from my cheeks. He lies staring up at the ceiling, his face pinched with pain, his breaths coming quickly.

And each one shallower than the last.

# PART SEVEN

# Sacrifice

# 1

Wednesday, 1 November
Morning

CATE STIRS IN HER SLEEP. The air in her room is heavy with scent. My parents have turned this place into an exhibit for the Chelsea Flower Show, but the bunches by Cate's bed are already wilting. Outside, a storm is brewing. Rain lashes the window. The lights in the room have been turned on, yet shadows gather in the corners.

My eyelids feel as heavy as tombstones. I slept for less than an hour last night. I couldn't shake the images of Ranger lying in a pool of blood, or Ben clutching a Spider-Man toy as he was led away by a WPC. He was crying for his mother. It took all my strength not to go to him.

As I watch Cate doze, Ashleigh's words from yesterday come back to me. "Your precious daughter has been lying to you." I haven't yet checked Ashleigh's alibis for the hit-and-run and the syringe driver. Perhaps I am afraid of what I will find. For whilst the woman had every reason to lie to me, I find myself believing her story. Cate has misled me before, after all. Like that time we had dinner together, when she dressed up as if she were still working at Simpsons, then talked about the imaginary jobs she was doing.

And yet why would she lie to me about Ashleigh trying to kill her? I have an idea, but I need to hear the truth from her.

I reach out to pick up a fallen petal from her pillow.

Cate's eyes flicker open.

My daughter is one of those fortunate people who is alert from the moment they stir. Whereas I seem to wake up fully only five minutes before it is time to go to bed again. A minute passes in silence. This is the first chance I have had to talk to Cate since my confrontation with Ashleigh. I came to see her yesterday after my stab wound was tended to, but she was sleeping. So when I left again to deal with the fallout of the events at Ashleigh's house, it fell to my parents to tell Cate about Ben. Already she seems brighter for the news. Neyland says her prognosis is improving by the hour. She can now hold a conversation, and her control of her body is returning.

"Hi," she says in a slurred voice—a consequence of the drugs she is on, no doubt.

"How are you feeling?" I ask.

"Sore."

"Legs, head or ribs?"

"Yes," she replies.

I smile.

"Neyland asked me if I wanted her to increase my levels of morphine," Cate says. "But a side effect of the painkillers is drowsiness. And I have slept enough already."

It is good to know one of us has.

Cate shifts position. When I adjust her pillows and help her sit up, I feel the pull of the stitches from my chest wound. The thing still hurts like . . . well, like being stabbed with a knife is supposed to hurt, I guess.

"How is Ben?" Cate asks.

"He's with social services while they do a DNA check. I'm seeing him this afternoon."

"What was he like when you met him?"

"Tall," is all I can think to say. I wish I had been with him long enough to form a better impression. I recall hearing somewhere that a child's personality is set by the time they reach six. What if Ashleigh has shaped him in her image? What damage has she done that I cannot undo? My only consolation is that she seemed to genuinely care for him. "He didn't remember me," I tell Cate.

"He will," Cate says, reaching for my hand.

There she goes again, supporting me when it should be the other way round. "As soon as you get better, we will go and see him together. We've got a lot of catching up to do." When Cate does not respond, I add, "You saw him, didn't you? A few months ago with Ashleigh."

Cate releases my hand and nods. "I was in Liverpool Street station. They were on the opposite platform. I saw Ashleigh first. I don't think I would have recognised her—except that she spotted me too, and this look of panic came over her face. I've never seen anything like it. She was terrified. I hadn't noticed she was with anyone until she tried to hide a boy behind her. I only got a glimpse of his face. Then a train pulled up between us, and I didn't see them again."

"Did you know it was Ben?"

"No. In fact I convinced myself it wasn't. When I told my therapist about him, she said it was common for grieving people to notice loved ones in a crowd. But I couldn't forget how Ashleigh reacted to seeing me. And why did she try to hide the boy? The more I thought about it, the more I wondered if it was Ben. It was the only thing that made sense—even though it made no sense at all." Cate pauses to catch her breath. "I had to find Ashleigh. Every day for a week, I went back to Liverpool Street station to see if she showed up again. But she didn't. Then I remembered you talking about a sketch artist in one of your cases. So I decided to get my own sketch done and take it to Keswick."

"Is that when you left Simpsons?"

"No, that came before. I'd tried to take some holiday so I could look for Ben, but my boss wouldn't let me. There was always some deal going on. I used what time I had at weekends. But the more I learned about Ashleigh, the more I wanted to find out. And work kept getting in the way."

Cate looks paler than she did before we began talking. I should give her a chance to recover, but first I need to know the answer to my next question. "Why didn't you tell me any of this?" I ask.

Cate looks away. "I wanted to—and not just because I thought you should know. My attempts to find Ashleigh were going nowhere. I'd spoken to Knox and McGrath, even got a copy of Ashleigh's form from the Posthouse. But then I found out the address on it was false. I had reached a dead end. My only hope was that your police contacts could help me track her down." She pulls her blanket up higher over her body. "I was going to tell you everything at our dinner. When I brought the conversation around to Ben, though, you made it clear you didn't want to talk about him. After that, I couldn't risk telling you. What if I was wrong about the boy being Ben? Or what if I was right, but we never found him? I didn't think you could cope with having your hopes raised and dashed."

I don't think I could have either. "What about the hit-and-run? Was Ashleigh telling the truth when she said you made it up about her being the driver?"

"Yes," Cate says without hesitation. "I had no choice. After the accident, I thought I was going to die. The nurses here were careful what they said around me, but I heard enough to know I was in bad shape. If I wasn't going to make it, I needed a way to put you onto Ashleigh's trail so you could carry on from where I left off."

"But why show me Ashleigh in the car? Why not show me her and Ben in Liverpool Street station?"

"Because you wouldn't have taken me seriously. You would have assumed I was just dreaming or delirious. Everyone thought Ben was dead. I had to give you another reason to look for Ashleigh. Making her the hit-and-run driver seemed the best way."

"Did you see who the real driver was?"

"No."

"And the time you showed me Ashleigh in this room? Did you make that up too?"

Cate nods. "After you read my memory of Ben falling in the stream, you never mentioned whether you were looking for

Ashleigh. I couldn't be sure if you were searching for her or if you had dismissed my memories as fantasies. So I showed you Ashleigh here in case you needed a nudge."

"So the morphine overdose was just an accident?"

"I guess."

Outside, the darkness is deepening. Cate's skin looks as pale as porcelain; I can see the blue veins flowing under it.

"Who is Ashleigh?" she asks me after a while. "Why did she take Ben?"

I consider how to answer that before deciding to hold nothing back. No more evasions and half-truths. When we lie to those close to us, we tell a bigger lie to ourselves when we pretend we are doing it for their sake, not ours. So I fill her in about my affair with Luca. I tell her that Ben is Luca's son—and thus Cate's half-brother only. I even tell her about Scott's lurid history, and about the argument the two of us had yesterday.

Cate shows no reaction to my revelations. After what she has gone through, I would be surprised if any news could move her. Or perhaps she already suspected much of what I have told her, particularly as regards the tension between me and Scott. Children always know more than their parents give them credit for.

"Where is Dad now?" Cate asks me.

"I haven't seen him since yesterday." And I wouldn't care if I never saw him again. But Ben is going to need him, and so will Cate. So I take a breath and say, "I don't think he knew that Ben was alive. He might have hidden that from me, but not from you. And he never believed Ashleigh was responsible for your hit-and-run or the syringe driver. He thought I was making it up."

Cate remains impassive. For all that I am sitting next to her, I feel a distance between us as if we were on opposite sides of the hospital. I worry I have lost a part of her to her coma. Even if she makes a full recovery, her experiences aren't something you survive without being changed.

"Making things up is all I've done since I got here," she says at last. "When I was unconscious, I used to dream. I remember one of them. We were in this room, and you had Ben with you. He looked the same as he did five years ago, but his voice was all gurgling like his lungs were full of water. He said he forgave me for my part in his accident—for texting when I should have been watching him."

I shoot her a look. If she wants to play the self-blame game, she should know she is up against a master. "I see your texting, and I raise you an affair and a broken marriage."

Cate's face softens, but that is all the response I get. I would do anything to see her smile.

"When I was awake and alone," she says, "I invented this whole new world. Ben was alive, but he was older than me. You and Dad were still together. We lived in our house in West Hampstead, and there was no such thing as flooded streams. Sometimes when I stirred, I would forget which life was real and which was false."

I rub my hand across my eyes. "I'm sorry."

"For what?"

"For not making a reality for you that was better than the fantasy."

Cate gives me a rueful look. "Everyone needs to dream."

"Well, that's all going to change," I say. "This is a new start for us. There will be no more not calling you. No more secrets and silences. We can make our three-monthly night out a weekly thing. You could even move in with me. I can give you the room over-looking the garden and we can share gin and tonic-making duties."

I look at her expectantly, and she stares back at me. Her face remains studiously blank, but I can tell she is horrified.

Then I lean forwards and say, "Got you."

And finally I earn my smile.

Cate's energy must be failing because her eyelids start to droop. The other things we need to talk about can wait until tomorrow. I offer to read to her, and she accepts.

Opening her Agatha Christie book, I launch into my best Miss Marple impression. As I turn the pages, I let my mind drift, think-ing about my impending meeting with Ben, and about everything that has happened these past few days. The hit-and-run. The fight with Ashleigh. Now that Cate is on the mend and Ben is alive, I should feel a sense of elation. But others have paid too high a price for my gains.

Eventually Cate's eyes close, and her breathing settles.

I shut the book and set it down. It is time for me to go. I have one more appointment to fulfil before I see Ben, and I do not want to be late. As I make for the door, my mind is racing, still processing the things I learned from Cate. Through the internal window, I see my father patrolling the corridor in case Scott or Jake show up . . .

A light goes off in my head, and I stop.

Because I know now who was driving the car that hit Cate.

# 2

RANGER'S ROOM IS ALONG THE corridor from my daughter's. With the amount of time I am spending at St Christopher's these days, I will need to take out a second mortgage on my flat to pay for parking.

Ranger looks like Cate's ghostly twin, yet he seems uncommonly chirpy for a man so recently out of surgery. In addition to being stabbed in the stomach, he sustained a cut to his neck which is covered by a bandage. The sight of it provokes a sympathetic twinge from my own wound. I know how easily it could have been me in that bed instead of him.

Ranger's room is a mirror image of Cate's in size and specification. On a table beside his bed is a copy of the *Daily Express* newspaper. There is also the obligatory basket of fruit, a selection of "Get Well" cards, and a book that is thick enough to deflect small arms fire. *Crime and Punishment* by Dostoevsky, it reads on the spine.

"How cultured of you," I say, gesturing to the book.

When Ranger speaks, his voice is a croak. "It was a present from DCI Mertin. The book is boring as hell, but at least it's kept me busy. I've been working on the spine all morning to make it look like I've read it."

I take a seat beside the bed. "How are you doing?"

"As well as can be expected. The surgeon says I'm lucky that Ashleigh's knife missed everything important. Though I can't say I'm feeling lucky just now."

"I'm surprised you needed surgery at all. A little knife like that."

Ranger is indignant. "What? That thing was practically a sword. Six inches long at least."

"That's what all the men say."

Ranger chuckles, then clutches his stomach. "Please," he says. "It hurts when I laugh."

Behind me, footsteps sound in the corridor before stopping at Ranger's doorway. I turn to see a woman in her sixties watching me. She has ash-blonde hair and is carrying a walking stick. Ranger's mother, perhaps? Ranger doesn't introduce us, merely holds up a hand to the newcomer in a give-me-a-minute signal. The woman retreats.

"I never got a chance to thank you before," I say to Ranger. "For saving me from Ashleigh, I mean. You arrived at the perfect time."

"The perfect time would have been before she stabbed you. You shouldn't have gone in without me."

"I waited as long as I could. I saw Ashleigh packing inside and thought she was going to make a run for it." And my suspicions were confirmed yesterday when two half-full suitcases were found in Ashleigh's bedroom. Evidently, she was planning to flee with Ben as I had feared. A desperate and hopeless move, but the only one she had left.

"How did you know her from before?" Ranger asks.

I pause, considering. I have no more wish to reveal my past to Ranger now than I did before, but the truth is going to come out in the review that follows this affair. So I tell Ranger everything I told Cate. And I pretend not to notice when his expression grows grave as I speak about the breakdown of my marriage. I finish by explaining how Ben came downstairs as I was talking to Ashleigh, and how she pulled the knife on me when I threatened to take him.

"Wow," Ranger says. "A thing like that could really make rushing in to confront a madwoman alone seem like a bad idea."

He has a point. But then bad ideas are a speciality of mine.

I glance at his book. "When Mertin came around, did he ask what you were doing at Ashleigh's?"

"No."

"Good. That gives me a chance to convince you to tell him the truth. About how I tricked you into finding Ashleigh, then lured you to her house by claiming she was connected to the Thornton case." Both Ranger and I are suspended pending an investigation by professional standards. I can't allow Ranger to be punished for helping me. The consequences of my search for Ben must fall on my head alone. If that means I get kicked off the force, so be it.

Ranger thinks about my suggestion before shaking his head. "I'd rather come clean," he says. "Mertin would see through the lie, and I don't want that sort of thing hanging over me. Better to take it on the chin."

"The chin might not be an option. Mertin will aim his blows below the belt."

"Even so."

I stare at him for a moment but don't press the point. Just because Ranger wants to throw himself under a bus doesn't mean I have to stand by and watch it happen. I know Mertin has it in for me, so it shouldn't be hard to persuade him that Ranger is trying to protect me. In a way, that's what he was doing when he insisted on being present when I met Ashleigh.

Ranger says, "Have you been in touch with Knox to tell him what happened?"

"Yes. Knox wants to charge Ashleigh with arson for setting fire to the Posthouse. But he'll have to wait until we've finished with her for kidnapping Ben and trying to kill the two of us."

"You're forgetting the hit-and-run on Cate."

I hold his gaze. "No, I'm not. It seems that Scott may have been right after all. When I read Cate's mind and saw Ashleigh in the car, I was seeing a dream, not a memory. Somehow I managed to confuse the two."

"You're saying Ashleigh had nothing to do with the accident?"

"Correct."

"And the incident with Cate's syringe driver?"

"The same."

Ranger gives me a long look. I don't like deceiving him, but he has already said he intends to tell Mertin the truth, and I can't risk him revealing Cate's secrets. I'm not sure what trouble she could get in for trying to frame Ashleigh, but whatever that trouble is, I will not let her face it—even if it means more trouble for me. Because Mertin is bound to use my "misreading" of Cate's thoughts as ammunition to attack my competence. If I cannot be relied upon to distinguish real memories from false, he will say, how can I be relied upon in future investigations?

"If it's any consolation," I tell Ranger, "I know who *was* driving the car that hit Cate."

"Who?"

"Lily. Thornton's daughter."

Ranger stares at me.

"Think about it," I say. "We know Lily left the housewarming party at 9.45 on Monday. Cate was hit a few minutes afterwards. And Fletcher Street lies on a route Lily could have taken to get home."

"But Lily wasn't driving that night. Thornton says he picked her up."

"He says that, yes, but we only have his word for it. No one at the party saw him collect her. Who's to say she didn't borrow his car and drive herself to Camberwell? Her friend Olivia didn't mention it, but maybe that's because she didn't know. Lily was hardly going to advertise the fact she was drinking and driving. Someone at the party could have reported her."

Ranger strokes his sideburns. "Have you spoken to Cate about this? Did she identify Lily as the person who hit her?"

"No. But if Lily was the driver, it explains a lot of things. Like why she fled the country the morning after the accident. And why

I saw a memory of Thornton pushing his car into a lake—he was disposing of the evidence." I give that a moment to sink in, then continue: "After the hit-and-run, Lily knew she was in trouble. She was already serving a ban for drink-driving, now she thought she had killed Cate. If she got caught, she would have been looking at a ten-year sentence. Thornton couldn't let that happen. So he helped her run away, then did his best to muddy the waters of our investigation by ditching his car and phoning in an anonymous tip that Lily was dead. He must have known we would work out the truth eventually, but by then Lily would be in Brazil. And since she's got dual nationality, who knows if we'll ever get her back."

"So Lily gets away with the hit-and-run, while Thornton goes to jail for perverting the course of justice and a string of other offences?"

I nod. "He sacrificed himself for his daughter." After the events of the past week, I understand his motivation too. If I had been in his position, I might have done the same. He is protecting Lily, just as I am protecting Cate by covering up the fact she tried to frame Ashleigh.

Ranger picks at the bandage on his neck. Specks of blood have seeped through the gauze. "I don't suppose you can prove any of this?" he asks.

"No. The only way we could do that would be to find Thornton's car."

"Which we might never do. Mertin has closed the case, remember? And even if the car turns up, there's no guarantee we'll be able to use it to make a case against Lily. Any evidence tying the Audi to the hit-and-run will probably be tainted by now. Plus you'd still have to put Lily behind the wheel. Knowing Thornton, he will claim he was the one driving when Cate got hit."

"And Lily lets him take the fall again?"

Ranger shrugs. "Why not? Parents have to be good for something, don't they?"

I look at the open door, wondering if Ranger's words were heard by his mother along the corridor.

"So what will you do next?" he asks me.

"I thought I'd go and speak to Thornton, see what he has to say for himself. I'm sure Mertin wouldn't mind me paying him a visit."

I hadn't thought it was possible for Ranger to go any paler than he already is, but apparently I was wrong. He stares at me, wide-eyed, trying to decide if I am serious or not.

"I should go," I say, rising. "But I'll call by later if that's okay?"

"That would be good."

"It might be a while, though," I add. "I'm not sure how long social services will give me with Ben."

"I'll try not to go anywhere in the meantime. Oh, and don't forget, it's your turn to smuggle in the drinks this time. I don't know how alcohol will mix with my painkillers, but I can certainly have fun finding out."

"Sounds great."

After my meeting with Ben later, I suspect I will need a stiff drink as much as Ranger does.

# 3

THE WALLS OF THE ASSESSMENT room are decorated with transfers of smiling Disney characters, yet the place is still as cheerful as concrete. I sit on the floor beside Ben at a play table. The staff have done their best to kit out the room, but every pencil has a broken tip, every toy a lost piece. In the corner to my right is a video camera, and beneath it is a nappy changing mat. The lone window has frosted glass to ensure the children here can't look out at the world they are missing.

The sooner I take Ben home, the better.

My son is dressed in jeans and a checked shirt, and his hair stands on end as if he has just been roused from his sleep. Since I arrived, he has barely looked at me. I pick up a Lego brick. In the past half hour I have built an entire castle in the hope of tempting Ben to join in. But he hasn't. I wonder what he is thinking. The one time I tuned into his mind earlier, he was daydreaming about playing the piano with Ashleigh. The memory cut me deeper than the woman's knife did. Yet I am determined not to let my sadness show.

I did the right thing taking Ben from Ashleigh, I tell myself.

As if thinking it makes it so.

I add a Lego brick to my castle. There must be some way I can coax Ben out of his shell. I want to talk to him, but I know that children have their own language, and I am ill-practised at speaking it. I quiz him on his favourite dinosaurs and superheroes, but he does not answer. My question about the latest Star Wars film draws the same nonresponse. If I knew what his interests were, I might have a better idea of what to say. But I only know what he liked five years ago, not what he likes now.

How much does he remember about his life before Ashleigh? My own first childhood recollections are from the time when I was three. Among other things, I recall falling out of a cherry tree at the bottom of my family's garden; of redecorating our lounge walls with crayons; of using a chair to reach the highest cupboard in the kitchen, then gobbling down an entire packet of custard creams. My dad was particularly impressed by that last one. He used to say I would go places. Not good places, perhaps, but places nonetheless. I guess time has proved him right.

But if I can remember my life at that age, surely Ben can too.

I begin talking. I tell him stories about Cate from before he was born. Like the time she and I went camping with Scott in the New Forest only for our tent to get blown away. And the time we built a snowman bigger than Cate in the front yard of our Finsbury Park house.

Then I turn the clock forward. I tell Ben about Easter egg hunting at my parents' home; about catching butterflies in the gardens at Nunnington Hall; about burying Scott in the sand at Holywell Bay Beach and giving him a seaweed hairstyle. On each occasion, Ben was present, yet I do not mention him. I want to awaken his own memories, not imprint him with mine.

Finally I talk about his third birthday at Legoland. I describe looking at the model of the London Eye in Miniland, and panning for gold at the Pirate Goldwash. At the mention of pirates, Ben stirs and blinks. He looks at me as if seeing me for the first time. There is no more recognition in his eyes now than there was a minute ago. Yet when I peek at his memories, I see him riding Scott's shoulders and watching as the Pirate Falls log flume crashes down in a deluge of spray. The picture is painted in shades of grey as if all the joy has leached out of it, and beside him Cate and I are mere shadows. But at least there is no sign of Ashleigh.

I smile at Ben, and he responds with a hesitant smile of his own. It is a start.

Printed in the USA
CPSIA information can be obtained
at www.ICGtesting.com
LVHW040758060923
757193LV00005B/20